W9-BXW-742

Welcome back to *Eclipse Bay* . . .

"An entertaining mix of . . . sex and mystery."
—*Publishers Weekly*

"It's Krentz at her best." —*Detroit Free Press*

Dear Reader,

Welcome back to Eclipse Bay where the long-simmering Harte-Madison feud is once again about to erupt into some pretty spectacular fireworks. Lillian Harte has been doing quite well with her matchmaking service but disaster has just struck in the form of her latest client. Of course, anyone in town could have warned her about the risks of trying to find a perfect match for Gabe Madison.

Tongues are wagging and no one in either the Harte or the Madison clan can resist the temptation to meddle in this explosive affair. But then, everyone knows that when it comes to love, Hartes and Madisons always do things the hard way!

I want to take this opportunity to thank those of you who wrote or e-mailed me to tell me that you enjoyed the first book of this trilogy. To readers who are joining us in Eclipse Bay for the first time, don't worry, each story stands on its own. This is a *very* small town. You won't get lost.

Yours,

Jayne

This one is for Don and Joan:
May you live happily ever after!

# DAWN IN ECLIPSE BAY

*Jayne Ann Krentz*

JOVE BOOKS, NEW YORK

DAWN IN ECLIPSE BAY

A Jove Book / published by arrangement with
the author

PRINTING HISTORY
Jove edition / May 2001

All rights reserved.
Copyright © 2001 by Jayne Ann Krentz.
This book, or parts thereof, may not be reproduced in any form
without permission.
For information address: The Berkley Publishing Group,
a division of Penguin Putnam Inc.,
375 Hudson Street, New York, New York 10014.

The Penguin Putnam Inc. World Wide Web site address is
http://www.penguinputnam.com

ISBN: 0-515-13092-3

A JOVE BOOK®
Jove Books are published by The Berkley Publishing Group,
a division of Penguin Putnam Inc.,
375 Hudson Street, New York, New York 10014.
JOVE and the "J" design
are trademarks belonging to Penguin Putnam Inc.

PRINTED IN THE UNITED STATES OF AMERICA

10  9  8  7  6  5  4  3  2  1

# chapter 1

"Fire me?" Gabe Madison came to a halt in the center of the carpet. Disbelief warred with outrage on his hard face. "You can't fire me. I'm a client. You don't fire clients."

"I do." Lillian Harte sat very stiffly behind her sleek, Euro-style desk, her hands clasped firmly atop the polished glass surface. She struggled to hold on to what was left of her temper. "I've been downsizing for the past few months."

"Downsizing is for getting rid of employees, not customers. What's the matter with you? You're supposed to be running a matchmaking business here." Gabe swept out a hand to indicate the expensively furnished office and the skyline of the city of Portland, Oregon, beyond. "You need clients. You want clients. You don't fire them."

"Some clients are more trouble than they're worth."

He narrowed dangerously green eyes. "And I'm one of them, is that it?"

"I'm afraid so." She unclasped her hands and leaned back in her chair. "Look, I'm sorry about this. Really."

"Oh, yeah, I can see that." His smile was cold.

"This was a mistake, Gabe. I told you that when you talked me into letting you sign on with Private Arrangements. I explained that it probably wouldn't work out well. But you refused to take no for an answer."

Which was hardly a major shock, she thought. It was a good bet that Gabe had not overcome his wild Madison family legacy to build Madison Commercial, a very successful venture capital firm, by taking no for an answer. Only a Harte, such as herself, could fully appreciate the magnitude of his accomplishment. Only a Harte knew just how far Gabe had had to go in order to live down three generations of spectacularly failed potential to rebuild an empire.

Her father had frequently speculated that Gabe had been successful because he had mastered the art of self-discipline, a rare accomplishment for a Madison. But in the few weeks that he had been a Private Arrangements client she had begun to suspect that Gabe had done more than merely learn how to control the notoriously hot blood that ran in his veins. He had subdued it with such ruthlessness that she suspected he had also crushed a lot of perfectly normal emotions along with it. As far as she could tell, he did not allow himself any strong feelings. She was convinced that he had paid a far higher price for his personal triumphs than anyone had realized.

Gabe smiled with relative ease, but he didn't laugh out loud. He didn't seem to know how to have fun. She had seen him annoyed, as he was now, but she had never seen him lose his temper. Her feminine intuition told her that he was very definitely attracted to women, but she was pretty sure that he did not permit himself to cross the line that separated physical satisfaction from mind-spinning passion. She was willing to bet that Gabe Madison had never allowed himself to take the risk of falling in love.

And he had expected her to find him a wife? Not a chance.

"It wasn't a mistake on my part," Gabe said. "I knew exactly what I was doing and what I wanted when I signed on with you. You're the one who made the mistakes. Five of them, so far."

"The fact that all five of the dates that I arranged for you went bad, should tell both of us something," she said, trying for a soothing note.

"It tells me something, all right. It tells me that you screwed up five times."

She had known that this would be a difficult conversation but she had not expected him to be quite so rigid about the matter. After all, it was obvious that the project had not been a success. One would have thought that he would have been content with merely demanding that his money be refunded.

His icy determination not to be dismissed from her client roster was starting to make her a little uneasy. Belatedly it occurred to her that Gabe was accustomed to fighting for what he wanted. She should have known that he would not abandon a goal without a battle.

She propped her elbows on the desk and balanced a capped pen between her forefingers, buying herself a little time to compose her arguments. Nothing was ever simple between a Madison and a Harte, she reminded herself. The younger members of the two families liked to pretend that the old feud that had erupted between their grandfathers and destroyed a thriving business empire all those years ago didn't affect them. But they were wrong. The fallout had echoed down through three generations. Gabe was living proof that the past had the power to haunt.

"I feel I have lived up to my part of the arrangement," she said. "I have sent you out on five dates in the past three weeks."

"Big deal. Five dates. I paid for six."

"You have complained about all five dates. In my opinion a sixth date would be a total waste of everyone's time."

"Those five bad dates were your fault." His jaw tightened. "Or maybe the fault of your computer program. Doesn't matter. The point is, they weren't good matches."

"Really?" She gave him a small, brightly polished smile. "I can't imagine how they could have been anything but perfect matches. According to my computer analysis the women I paired you with met over eighty-five percent of your requirements."

"Only eighty-five percent? Well, there's your problem." He grinned humorlessly. "The real issue here is that you and your computer aren't doing a very good job. You haven't found me any one hundred percent matches."

"Get real, Gabe." She put the pen down very precisely using both fingers. "There is no such thing as a one hundred percent perfect match. I use a computer program, not a magic wand."

"So, go for ninety-five." He spread his hands. "I'm flexible."

"Flexible?" She stared at him, completely nonplussed for two or three seconds, and then she swallowed a laugh. "No offense, but you're about as flexible as one of those steel beams they use in high-rise construction projects."

And just as tough, she thought. His hallmark uniform—expensive steel-gray suits, charcoal-gray shirts, silver-and-onyx cuff links, and striped silver-and-black ties—had taken on near-legendary status in the Northwest business community, which tended toward a more relaxed look. But the classy attire was poor camouflage for an iron will that had been forged in a strong fire.

The evidence of that will was plain to see. At least, it was obvious to her. It was there in the way he moved with the unconscious grace of a natural hunter. It was clear in the way he held himself and in the cool, remote, watchful expression in his eyes. Always on the alert, even when he appeared to be relaxed. There was a centered quality to him that was so strong it formed an invisible aura around him. This was a man who did nothing on impulse. A man in control.

What worried her the most, she admitted silently, was that she found him both compelling and fascinating.

In one sense she had known Gabe all of her life. He hailed from Eclipse Bay on the coast of Oregon where her family had always maintained a summer and vacation home. Growing up she had encountered him from time to time in the small town—but he was a Madison. Everyone knew that Madison males were trouble. Nice girls might indulge a few fantasies, but they didn't date Madisons. That, coupled with their complicated family history and the fact that he was five years older than she, had formed a huge barrier. The stone wall had not been breached until the wedding of her sister, Hannah, to his brother, Rafe, a few months ago. The event had shocked and delighted the entire town, leading to much speculation about whether or not the infamous Harte-Madison feud had finally ended. The question was still unanswered in most quarters.

Meeting Gabe at the reception had left her unsettled and unaccountably restless. She had told herself she would get over it. But when he had walked into her office a few weeks later she had realized that, on some level, she had been waiting for him. She could not explain her anticipation but it had come as a cold shock to learn that he was there on business. His only goal had been to sign up as a client.

Still, she had allowed herself a few interesting daydreams.

Then, of course, he had filled out the lengthy questionnaire she used to feed client data into her program and she had realized just how hopeless it all was. *No arty types.* It was, she reflected, one of the few places on the form where she was pretty certain he had been completely candid in his responses.

"It's not my fault you picked five bad matches in a row," he said.

"I picked five excellent matches." She raised one hand, fingers bunched into a loose fist. "They were all college-educated." She extended one finger. "They were all within the age span that you specified." She extended a second finger. "They all had successful careers and were financially independent." Another finger. "They were all comfortable with the idea of helping you entertain your business clients." A fourth finger went up. "And, as you stipulated, not one of them could even remotely be described as the *arty* type."

"All five made less than subtle inquiries about my portfolio."

"Why shouldn't they have shown an interest in it? You certainly showed great interest in *their* financial status. You made a huge deal about it, in fact. You wanted someone who was clearly financially well-situated."

"Only because I don't want to be married for my money." He turned and started to prowl the room. "Another thing, all five acted offended when I brought up the subject of a prenuptial contract."

"You should have known better than to bring up a subject like that on a first date, for heaven's sake."

He ignored that. "All five talked about extended vacations in the south of France and second homes on Maui. I don't take monthlong vacations."

"Do you take *any* vacations?"

"I've got a company to run, damn it."

"Uh-huh." No vacations. A real fun guy. But she refrained from voicing that observation aloud.

"And another thing." He turned back around to face her. "All five of those women looked very high-maintenance to me."

"And you're not high-maintenance?"

He appeared genuinely startled that she would even suggest such a possibility. His expression darkened. "Of course not. I just told you, I'm a very flexible man."

She sat forward abruptly. "Pay attention here, Gabe. According to the feedback I got from the five women I sent you out with, you showed distinct signs of being bored and impatient within half an hour after each date began."

He shrugged. "That was approximately how long it took each time before I realized that you had picked another bad match."

"Did you have to start sneaking glances at your watch before the entrées arrived?"

"I wasn't *sneaking* glances. So I checked my watch occasionally. So what? Time is money."

"There was also a general consensus among all five women that you do not have a romantic bone in your body."

"Those dates weren't about romance." He sliced one hand through the air in a quick, thoroughly disgusted arc. "They were business meetings as far as I was concerned."

"Business meetings," she replied, keeping her tone very neutral. "Oddly enough, the women I matched you with did not view the dates in quite the same light."

"I'm looking for a wife, damn it. Not a girlfriend."

"I see." She cleared her throat delicately. "All five of the women reported that when they did manage to get a conversation going with you, it went nowhere because you are clearly paranoid about being married for your money."

"You'd be paranoid, too, if every person you dated wanted to know how much you had invested in high-tech stocks and how much in bonds and real estate." He broke off, looking thoughtful. "Maybe I should have adopted an alias for the dates."

"Oh, sure. Lying about your identity is a great way to start a long-term relationship. And for your information, I have had more than one date with men who took what I considered an unpleasant interest in my finances. I'm a Harte, remember?"

"Oh, yeah. Right. Harte Investments."

"Exactly. Anyone who knows me well understands that my brother and sister and I will each inherit a large chunk of my family's company. In addition, I haven't done badly with Private Arrangements."

He surveyed the well-appointed office. "I've heard that your client list is very high-end. And you sure do charge high-end fees for your services."

She gave him a cool smile. "In short, my balance sheets look very appetizing to a certain type of man. But I don't allow that fact to color my view of the entire male population. I'm not totally paranoid that every guy who asks me out is hoping to marry into money."

"Nice for you," he muttered. "But a little naïve, don't you think?"

She could feel her teeth starting to clench together. "I am not naïve."

He shrugged and went to stand at the window that looked out across the rain-swept city toward the Willamette River. She followed his gaze and saw that lights were coming on all over town. The late winter day was ending swiftly. Here in the Northwest there was a price to be paid for the long, long days of summer. That fee came in the form of very short days at this time of year.

"Okay, maybe I am a little paranoid about being married because of Madison Commercial," Gabe said quietly. "I've had a couple of close calls."

"Give me a break. Are you telling me that the reason you've never married is because you're afraid that every woman you meet is after your money?" She did not bother to keep the skepticism out of her voice. "I find that a little tough to swallow. You haven't always been wealthy and successful. Far from it. I know exactly where you came from, remember?"

He contemplated the mist that shrouded the darkening city. "During the time when I didn't have any money I was too busy with Madison Commercial to get seriously involved with anyone."

"Now that I do believe."

There was a short silence.

"It isn't just caution that kept me from getting married."

"No?"

"I wasn't in any hurry to follow the Madison tradition."

She watched him narrowly. "Which tradition, exactly, would that be?"

"Messy relationships and divorce run in my family. We're not real good at marriage."

She straightened in her chair. "Sorry, you can't use that

excuse anymore. Your brother put an end to that famous Madison tradition when he married my sister. Rafe and Hannah's marriage is going to work out brilliantly."

"You sound very sure of that."

"I *am* sure of it."

He glanced at her over his shoulder, intent curiosity gleaming in his eyes. "Why? You didn't run them through your computer program to see if they were a good match. How can you be so certain that their marriage will work?"

"You can feel it when you're with them," she said quietly. "There's a bond. I don't think either of them will ever look at anyone else as long as they have each other."

"You can *feel* it, huh?"

"Call it female intuition."

"Intuition is a funny word coming from a woman who uses a computer to match people. Wouldn't have thought you would be real big on intuition."

She stiffened. "Every woman likes to think she has good intuition." This was getting into dangerous territory. "Don't you believe their marriage will work?"

"Oh, yeah," he said with stunning casualness. "It'll work."

The absolute conviction in his words took her back for a second or two. "I beg your pardon? You just accused me of relying on intuition. What makes you so sure their marriage will hold up?"

"It sure as hell isn't my intuition."

"What is it?"

"Simple logic. For starters, it's obvious that Hannah is Rafe's passion. You know what they say about us Madisons."

"Nothing gets between a Madison and his passion," she recited evenly.

"Right. In addition, your family has a reputation for

being good at marriage. I've never heard of a Harte getting a divorce. I figure that makes for a winning combination for Rafe and Hannah."

"I see." Time to change the topic. "Well, we seem to be in agreement on that point. Why are we arguing about it?"

Gabe turned away from the window and resumed prowling the room. "We're not arguing. I just wondered how you could be so sure of your conclusions when you hadn't run Rafe and Hannah through your computer, that's all."

She glanced uneasily at the laptop on her desk. She was not about to explain that in the past few months she had been forced to admit to herself that her computer program was not the sole secret of her success as a matchmaker. But the truth was too disturbing to discuss with anyone else, let alone a Madison. She was having a hard enough time dealing with it herself.

The realization that she was relying on her intuition and a hefty dose of common sense combined with the computer's analysis to get successful matches was fraught with disturbing implications. She was, after all, assuming a huge responsibility with each client. She guided and assisted them in making one of the most important decisions of their lives. The possibility of making a mistake weighed more heavily on her with each passing day. Although nothing awful had happened yet, lately she'd had the uneasy sensation that she was on extremely thin ice.

The time to get out was now, before disaster struck.

She was ready to switch careers, anyway. While her rapidly accumulating qualms about the risks of the matchmaking field were not the main reason she had decided to close down her business, they definitely constituted an added incentive to shut her doors. Fast.

She was not looking forward to announcing her intentions to her family. She knew only too well that the news would not be greeted with wild enthusiasm in the Harte clan. But she had made her plans. The only thing standing between her and her new profession was Gabe Madison. He was the last client left on her active list.

Unfortunately, getting rid of him was proving more difficult than she had anticipated.

Gabe came to a halt in front of her desk, shoved aside one edge of his sleekly cut jacket and hooked his thumb in his belt.

"Let's get to the bottom line here," he said. "You want to ditch me because I'm a Madison and you're a Harte."

She raised her eyes to the ceiling, seeking patience and forbearance. When she got no help from that direction, she took a deep breath instead.

"That's got nothing to do with this," she said. "I don't give a darn about the family feud. Even if I did, I could hardly use it as a reason to drop you from my list now that your brother and my sister are married."

"Just because Rafe and Hannah got together doesn't mean that you've changed your opinion about the rest of us Madisons."

"Oh, for heaven's sake, Gabe, it was our grandfathers who started the feud. I couldn't care less about that old nonsense."

"Yeah?" He gave her a razor-sharp smile. "You mean that you really believe that I'm capable of making a long-term commitment?"

The sarcasm was too much. She had been through a lot since the day Gabe had shown up here in her office, demanding to sign on as a client. The way he had demolished her private fantasies was the least of it.

"I think you're perfectly capable of a long-term commitment," she said. "But it looks to me like you've already made it."

"What the hell are you talking about? I'm not in a relationship."

"Yes, you are. You've got a very serious, very committed, one hundred percent exclusive relationship with Madison Commercial."

"Madison Commercial is my company," he said. "Of course I'm committed to it. That's got nothing to do with getting married."

"That company is your passion, Gabe. You've devoted your entire life to building that business."

"So what?"

"You're a Madison," she said, thoroughly exasperated now. "As you just pointed out, nothing comes between a Madison and his passion."

"Damn, this *is* about me being a Madison." He jerked his thumb out of his belt and planted his hands flat on her desk. "You *are* biased against me because our families have a history."

"It's not our family history that is the problem here." She could feel her temper rising. She had a nasty suspicion that her face was flushed. Probably an unpleasant shade of red. "*You're* the problem."

"Are you telling me that just because I'm running a successful corporation, I can't commit to a wife?"

That gave her pause.

"I wouldn't go that far," she said carefully. "But I do think that you're going to have to refocus if you want to make a relationship work."

"Define refocus."

She sighed. "You're going about this all wrong, Gabe."

"I'm trying to use a logical, rational, scientifically based technique to find a wife. I would have thought you, of all people, would appreciate that approach."

"Why? Because I'm a Harte and you Madisons think all Hartes have ice water in their veins?"

"You do own and operate a computerized matchmaking firm, don't you? Some people would say your line of work requires a pretty cold-blooded approach to marriage."

Damn. She would not allow Gabriel Madison to make her feel awkward right here in her own office. She was a Harte, after all. Hartes did not put up with this sort of behavior from Madisons.

"There's a difference between going about the process of finding a mate in an intelligent, logical manner and going about it in a cold-blooded fashion," she said evenly.

"And I'm being cold-blooded, is that it?"

"Look, you're the one who filled out the questionnaire that I fed into my computer program, not me."

There was a beat or two of silence. He watched her with a shuttered look.

"What was wrong with the way I filled it out?" he asked a little too softly.

She tapped the printouts in front of her. "According to these results, you want a robot for a wife."

"That's crazy." He straightened and shoved his fingers through his dark hair. "If that's the conclusion your idiotic program came up with, you'd damn well better see about getting some new software."

"I don't think the program is at fault here."

"A robot, huh?" He nodded once. "Maybe that's what went wrong on those five dates you arranged for me. Maybe you sent me out with five robots. Come to think of it, they were all a little too thin and there was something very computerlike about the way they tried to grill me on the subject of my portfolio."

"You got exactly what you said you wanted, according to the questionnaire," she said very sweetly. "There was no strong emotion in any of your responses except when it came to the importance of not being matched with what you call *arty* types and your insistence on a prenuptial agreement."

"What's the problem with the lack of strong emotions?"

"For one thing, it makes it extremely difficult to find a match for you."

"I would have thought taking emotion out of the equation would have made it easier to match me, not harder."

"Don't get me wrong," she said. "I'm a big believer in approaching marriage logically. I've built this business on that premise. But you've gone to extremes. You're hunting for a wife as if you were interviewing a potential employee for an executive slot at Madison Commercial. It won't work."

"Why not?" His eyes were emerald hard. His voice fell to an even softer pitch. "Because I'm a Madison and Madisons can't do anything without getting emotional?"

"That does it." She powered down the laptop. "It has nothing to do with the fact that you're a Madison. You can't expect me to find you a proper match when you insist on concealing your true feelings on certain matters."

"Concealing my true feelings?"

"Yes." She closed the lid of the laptop, reached down, opened a drawer and removed her shoulder bag.

"Just a minute. Are you accusing me of having deliberately shaded a few of my answers on that questionnaire?"

"No." She straightened and slung the strap of the bag over her shoulder. "I don't think you *shaded* a few of your responses. I think you lied through your teeth about everything except prenuptial agreements and arty types."

"Why the hell would I lie on that stupid questionnaire?"

"How should I know? You'd need to discuss that with a trained therapist. I can give you the name of one, if you want to pursue the matter. He's right here in this building. Three floors down. Dr. J. Anderson Flint."

Gabe's expression hardened. "His name certainly popped up in a hurry in the course of this conversation."

"Probably because he's on my mind at the moment." She glanced at the roman numerals etched on the jade green face of her watch. "I'm on my way to his office."

"You're seeing a therapist?"

"In a manner of speaking." She went to the small closet behind the desk, opened it and removed the hooded, ankle-length rain cloak inside. "Anderson is doing research for a book. He wants to interview me."

"Why?"

"Because he specializes in treating people who have problems in their uh, physical relationships with their partners."

"In other words, he's a sex therapist?"

She could feel herself turning red again. "I believe sex therapy constitutes the major portion of his practice, yes."

"And he wants to interview you. Well, now, that would certainly raise a few eyebrows back in Eclipse Bay."

"Try to get your mind out of the gutter." She scooped the laptop off her desk and stuffed it into a waterproof case. "I've got a very high success rate here at Private Arrangements. Anderson feels my computer program is the key. He is looking for ways to incorporate the principles of that program into a useful guide for couples seeking committed relationships."

"You sure can't prove your very high success rate by me."

"No." She picked up the case containing the laptop and

walked around the corner of her desk. "I admit you are a glaring failure. Most of my clients, however, are satisfied with the results they get here at Private Arrangements."

*And I intend to quit while they all feel that way,* she thought, heading for the door.

Gabe grabbed his black trench coat off the coatrack. "Your matchmaking program sucks in my opinion."

"You've made your feelings on the subject quite clear." She opened the door. "And that is why I'm releasing you from your contract with Private Arrangements."

"You're not releasing me, you're firing me."

"Whatever." She flipped the bank of wall switches, plunging the office into stygian gloom.

"What the hell? Hold on, damn it." Gabe hoisted the monogrammed leather briefcase sitting on the floor near the coatrack. "You can't just walk out on me like this."

"I'm not walking out, I'm closing my office." She stepped into the hall and jangled her keys in a pointed fashion. "I just told you, I'm on my way to see Dr. Flint."

He shrugged into his trench coat, leaving it unbuttoned. "You're certainly in a rush to keep the appointment. A sex therapist. I still can't believe it."

"I don't have an appointment. I'm just going to drop by his office. I need to tell him something important. Not that it's any of your business. Furthermore, I don't like the sarcastic tone of your voice. I'll have you know that Anderson is a thorough-going professional."

"Is that so? A professional sex therapist." Gabe moved out into the hall. "Guess I should show some respect. They do say it's the oldest profession. No, wait, maybe I've got that mixed up with another line of work."

She would not dignify that with a response, she thought. She locked the office door with a quick twist of her hand

and dropped the keys into her shoulder bag. Whirling around, she strode toward the elevators.

Gabe fell into step beside her. "Don't forget, you owe me another date."

"I beg your pardon?"

"I only got five dates, remember? The contract guarantees six matches."

"Don't sweat it. I'll refund one-sixth of the fee you paid me."

"I don't want my money back, I want my sixth date."

"Better take the money." She came to a halt in front of the bank of elevators and stabbed the call button. "It's all you're going to get."

He flattened one hand on the wall beside her head, leaned in very close and lowered his voice to a low, dangerous pitch that made tiny chills chase down her spine.

"Trust me," Gabe said very deliberately. "You don't want a lawsuit over this."

She spun around to face him and found him standing much too close.

"Are you trying to intimidate me?" she asked.

"Just making an observation."

She gave him a frigid smile. "I can see the headlines now. *President of Madison Commercial Threatens Lawsuit over Cancelled Date.* Talk about looking ridiculous."

"You owe me that date."

"Back off, Gabe. We both know you're not going to sue me. You'd look like a fool in the press and that's the last thing you'd want. Just think of what the publicity would do to the image of your company."

Gabe said nothing—just looked at her the way Roman gladiators had no doubt studied each other before an event in the arena. Behind her the elevator doors opened with a soft sighing hiss. She turned quickly and got into the cab.

Gabe got in behind her.

She punched the floor number she wanted and then, without much hope, she also selected the lobby button. Maybe Gabe would take the hint and remain in the elevator when she got off on Anderson's floor.

She stood tensely near the control panel, watching the doors close. She was very aware of Gabe there at her shoulder, dominating the small space, using up all the oxygen so that she could hardly breathe.

"Admit it," she said when she could no longer stand the silence. "You lied on that questionnaire."

"The questionnaire has nothing to do with this. You owe me a date."

"You didn't enter the truth when you made your responses. You put down what you thought the truth should be."

He quirked one brow. "There's a difference?"

"Night and day in most cases."

The elevator doors opened. She walked quickly out into the hall.

Gabe glided out after her. So much for hoping he would stay on board and descend to the lobby.

"What do you think you're doing?" she said. "I told you, I'm on my way to talk to Dr. Flint."

"I'll wait until you're finished."

"You can't do that."

"Why not? Doesn't he have a waiting room?"

"I don't believe this."

"I'm not leaving until you guarantee me a sixth match."

"We'll talk about it some other time. Give me a call tomorrow."

"We'll talk about it today."

"I refuse to let you push me around like this."

"I haven't touched you," Gabe said.

She would not lower herself to his level, she thought. She was a mature, sophisticated woman. More to the point, she was a Harte. Hartes did not engage in public scenes. That was more of a Madison thing.

The only option to yelling at Gabe was to pretend he was not right here, shadowing her down the hall. It was not easy.

Obviously she had pushed her luck with Private Arrangements, she thought morosely. She had waited a little too long to go out of business. If only she had stopped accepting clients the day *before* Gabe had walked into her office.

She reached the door marked *Dr. J. Anderson Flint*, opened it and walked into the waiting room. Gabe flowed in behind her, Dracula in a very expensive black trench coat.

The first clue that the situation had the potential to deteriorate further came when she noticed that Anderson's secretary, Mrs. Collins, was not behind her desk. She realized that she had been counting on the woman's presence to ensure that Gabe behaved himself.

She glanced quickly around the serene, vaguely beige room, hoping to spot the secretary somewhere in the shadows. There was no one in sight.

The muffled strains of some loud, hard-core, sixties-era rock music reverberated through the wooden panels of the closed door that separated Anderson's inner office from the waiting room.

Her sense of foreboding increased for some unaccountable reason.

"It looks like Anderson's secretary has gone home early today," she said. "He's probably working on his notes."

"Sounds like rock music."

"Anderson enjoys classic rock."

"You know him pretty well, huh?"

"We met last month in the coffee shop downstairs." She knocked lightly on the inner door. "We have a lot in common. Similar professional interests."

"Is that right?" Gabe said. "You know, I don't think he can hear you above the music. He's really got it cranked up in there."

The music was loud and getting louder and more intense by the second.

She twisted the knob and opened the door.

And stopped short at the sight of J. Anderson Flint stretched out on his office sofa. He was naked except for a pair of very small, very red bikini briefs that did nothing to conceal his erection. His hands were bound at the wrists above his head. A blindfold was secured around his eyes.

A solidly built woman dressed in a skintight leather catsuit, long black leather gloves, and a pair of five-inch stiletto heels stood over him. She had one leg balanced on the back of the sofa, the other braced on the coffee table. Her back was to the door but Lillian could see that she held a small velvet whip in her right hand and a steel-studded dog collar in her left.

Neither of the room's occupants heard the door open because the music was building to its crashing finale.

Lillian tried to move and could not. It was as if she had been frozen in place by some futuristic ray gun.

"Similar professional interests, you say?" Gabe murmured into her left ear.

His undisguised amusement freed her from the effects of the invisible force field that held her immobile. With a gasp, she managed to turn around. He blocked her path, his attention focused on the scene taking place on the sofa. He smiled.

"Excuse me," she croaked. She put both hands on his chest and shoved hard to get him out of the way.

Gabe obligingly moved, stepping aside and simultaneously reaching around her to pull the door shut on the lurid scene.

The music thundered to its rousing climax.

Lillian fled through the tasteful waiting room out into the hallway. She did not look back.

Gabe caught up with her at the elevator.

An eerie silence gripped the corridor for the count of five.

"Dr. Flint obviously believes in a hands-on approach to sex therapy," Gabe remarked. "I wonder just how he plans to incorporate your computer program into his treatment plans."

This could not be happening, she thought. It was some kind of bizarre hallucination, the sort of thing that could turn a person into a full-blown conspiracy theorist. Maybe some secret government agency was conducting experiments with chemicals in the drinking water.

Or maybe she was losing it. She'd been under a lot of stress lately, what with making the decision to close down Private Arrangements and change careers. Having Gabe as a client hadn't helped matters, either.

No doubt about it, stress combined with secret government drinking water experiments could account for what she had just seen in Anderson's office.

"I think you need a drink," Gabe said.

# chapter 2

Outside on the sidewalk the weird afterglow of the rainy twilight combined with the streetlamps to infuse the city with a surreal atmosphere. It was as if he and Lillian were moving through a dream sequence, Gabe thought. It was easy to believe that they were the only real, solid beings in a world composed of eerie lights and shadows.

In the strange, vaporlike mist, Lillian's flowing, iridescent rain cloak glittered like a cape woven of otherworldly gemstones. He wanted to reach out and pull her close against his side; feel the heat of her body; inhale her scent.

It was getting worse, he thought. This gut-deep awareness had hit him hard when he had first experienced it at Rafe's wedding. He had told himself it would fade quickly. Just a passing sexual attraction. Or maybe a little fevered imagination brought on by the monklike existence he had been living ever since he had turned his attention to the business of finding himself a wife.

The decision to go celibate after the end of the affair

with Jennifer several months ago had seemed like a good idea at the time. He had not wanted something as superficial as lust to screw up his thinking processes while he concentrated on such an important matter. To avoid complications, he had deliberately opted to put his sex life on a temporarily inactive status.

Within about six seconds of seeing Lillian after all those years of living in separate universes, he had been inspired to revisit that particular executive decision, however.

Thankfully, he'd had enough common sense still functioning at that point to convince himself that an affair with her was probably not a brilliant idea. She was a Harte, after all. Things between Hartes and Madisons were always complicated. He had come up with a compromise solution. Instead of asking her out on a date, he had signed up as a client of Private Arrangements. He had spent an inordinate amount of time convincing himself that using a professional matchmaking firm was actually a terrific plan. What better, more efficient way to find a wife?

But things had rapidly gone from dicey to disastrous. He had endured five seemingly endless evenings with five very attractive, very successful women. He had spent each of the five dates tormenting himself with visions of how much more interesting things would have been if Lillian had been the woman seated across the candlelit table.

The uncanny part was that he had never been aware of her as anything other than a Harte kid while he had been growing up in Eclipse Bay. But then, in all fairness, the only thing that had held his attention in those days was his dream of rebuilding the financial empire that had been shattered by the Harte-Madison feud.

The fact that the Hartes had resurrected themselves after the bankruptcy and gone on to prosper while his family had floundered and pretty much self-destructed had added fuel to the fire that had consumed him.

He had left Eclipse Bay the day after he graduated from high school, headed off to college and the big city to pursue his vision. He had not seen Lillian at all during the years of empire-building. He had not even thought about her.

But ever since the wedding he had been unable to think about anything else.

If this was lust, it was anything but superficial. If it was something more, he was in trouble because Lillian was not what he had pictured when he set out to look for a wife. For the first time since he had decided to get married he wondered if he should put the search for a wife on hold for a while. Just until he got this murky situation with Lillian cleared up and out of the way. He needed to be able to concentrate and she was making that impossible.

He realized they had halted at a crosswalk.

"Where are we going?" he asked.

"I don't know where you're going, but I'm walking home." Her voice was slightly muffled by the hood of her cloak.

"What do you say we stop somewhere and get you that drink I suggested? I have to tell you that after watching your colleague work with a patient, I could use one, myself."

"Don't start with me on that subject, Madison."

He smiled and reached out to take her arm. "Come on, I'll buy."

He steered her toward the small café in the middle of the block.

She peered fixedly through the glass panes into the cozily lit interior.

"You know what?" she said. "I think you're right. A glass of wine sounds like an excellent idea."

She pulled free of his hand and went toward the door with quick, crisp steps. She did not look around to see if he was following.

He made it to the door a half a step ahead of her and got it open. She did not thank him, just swept past him into the café.

The place was just starting to fill up with the after-work crowd. A cheerful gas fire cast an inviting glow. The chalkboard listed several brands of beer from local microbreweries and half a dozen premium wines by the glass. Another hand-lettered menu on the wall featured a variety of oyster appetizers and happy-hour specials.

He knew this place. It was only a few streets over from the office tower that housed the headquarters of Madison Commercial. He stopped in here occasionally on his way home to his empty apartment.

"Come here a lot?" he asked as they settled into a wooden booth.

"No." She picked up the miniature wine menu and studied it intently. "Why?"

"Portland is a small town in a lot of ways. It's a wonder our paths haven't crossed before," he said, trying for a neutral topic of conversation.

She frowned at the little menu. "I haven't lived here much in recent years."

"Where have you been since college?"

"You really want to know?"

"Sure." He was suddenly more curious than he wanted to let on.

She shrugged and put down the menu. Before she

could answer his question, however, the waiter arrived to take their orders. She chose a glass of chardonnay. He asked for a beer.

When the waiter left, there was a short silence. He thought he might have to remind Lillian of the question. Somewhat to his surprise, however, she started to talk.

"After I graduated from college I worked in Seattle for a while," she said. "Then I moved to Hawaii. Spent a year there. After that I went to California and then back to Seattle. I didn't return to Oregon until I decided to open Private Arrangements."

"Were you running matchmaking businesses in all those different places?"

She eyed him with a wary expression. "Why do you want to know?"

"Been a while. Just catching up."

"You and I don't have any catching up to do. We hardly even know each other."

That was almost funny, he thought.

"I'm a Harte and you're a Madison," he said. "My brother is now married to your sister. Trust me, we know each other."

The waiter returned with their drinks and disappeared once more. Lillian picked up her chardonnay, took a sip and set the glass down very precisely on the little napkin. He got the feeling she was debating how much to tell him about herself.

"The official Harte family version of events is that I've spent the last few years trying to find myself," she said.

"What's the unofficial version?"

"That I'm a little flaky."

Definitely not wife material, he thought. Probably not good affair material either. He did not date flakes. He didn't do business with flakes, either. If he had known Private Arrangements was run by a flake, he would never have signed on as a client.

Then again, who was he kidding?

Damn. This was not a good idea. If he had any sense he would run, not walk, to the nearest exit. Some lingering vestige of self-preservation made him glance toward the door.

What the hell, he thought, turning back to Lillian. Plenty of time to escape later.

"Didn't realize any of you Hartes had to find yourselves," he said after a while. "Figured you were all born knowing where you wanted to go in life and how you would get there."

"You're thinking of everyone else in the family." She wrinkled her nose. "I'm the exception."

"Yeah? How exceptional are you?"

She studied the wine in her glass. "Let's just say I haven't found my niche yet."

"From all accounts you've been extremely successful with Private Arrangements."

"Oh, sure." She raised one shoulder in dismissal. "If you're talking business success."

He went blank.

"There's another kind?" he asked.

Irritation gleamed in her eyes. "Of course there's another kind."

He leaned back in the booth. "This isn't about finding yourself and inner peace through work, is it?"

"You've got a problem with the concept of work as a source of happiness and personal fulfillment?"

"I've got a problem with people who think work is supposed to be entertainment. Work is work." He paused.

"Probably why they call it work instead of, say, fun. A lot of folks don't seem to get that."

"You ought to know," she said.

"What's that supposed to mean?"

"You've been working night and day since you were a boy to build Madison Commercial." She smiled wryly. "Folks back in Eclipse Bay always said that you were a different kind of Madison."

"Different?"

"One who might actually make a success of himself. You certainly proved them right, didn't you?"

How the hell had the conversation turned back on him like this?

"All I proved," he said carefully, "is that you can get someplace if you want to go there badly enough."

"And you wanted to get where you are now very, very badly, didn't you?"

He did not know what to make of her in this mood, so he took another swallow of beer to give himself time to come up with a strategy.

"Tell me, Gabe, what do you do for fun?"

"Fun?" The question put him off stride again. He was still working on strategy.

"As far as I can tell, all you do is work. If work isn't fun for you, where do you go and what do you do when you're looking for a good time?"

He frowned. "You make it sound like I never get out of the office."

"Do you?"

"I'm here, aren't I? This sure as hell isn't my office."

"You're right. This isn't your office. So, tell me, are you having fun yet?"

"I didn't come here to have fun. We're here because you received a severe shock back there in Dr. J. Anderson Flint's office. I figured you needed a glass of wine for medicinal purposes."

"The only reason you're still hanging around is because you're trying to figure out how to get your sixth date. Forget it. Never happen."

"We'll see."

"Pay attention, Madison." She leaned forward and narrowed her eyes. "It will never happen because Private Arrangements is closed."

"So? We'll talk about my sixth date when you reopen on Monday."

"I meant closed for good. Today was the last day of business. As of five o'clock this afternoon, my firm ceased operations. Get it?"

She was serious, he thought. "You can't just shut down a moneymaking enterprise like that."

"Watch me."

"What about your clients?"

"You are the last one." She raised her glass in a mocking little toast. "Here's to you. Good luck finding yourself a robot."

"A wife."

"Whatever." She took a sip of the wine.

"Why the hell would you want to go out of business? You're a huge success."

"Financially, yes." She sat back. "That isn't enough."

"Damn. You really are into this work-has-got-to-be-a-transcendent-experience thing, aren't you?"

"Yep." She propped one elbow on the table and rested her chin in her hand. "Let's get back to you and fun."

"Thought you just got through implying that the two don't belong in the same sentence."

"Well, let's talk about your relationship with Madison Commercial, then."

"Relationship? Are you suggesting that the company is my mistress or something?"

"That's certainly what it looks like to me."

He was getting irritated. "Is that your *professional* opinion?"

"I'm a matchmaker, remember? I know a good match when I see one. Tell me, what, exactly, do you get out of Madison Commercial?"

He was wary now. "What do I *get* out of it?"

She gave him a bright-eyed, innocently inquiring look. "Do you think your relationship with the company is a substitute for sex?"

She was a Harte, he reminded himself. Damned if he would let her goad him.

"Got news for you. In case you don't know, Ms. Matchmaker, there is no substitute for sex. What I get out of Madison Commercial is a lot of money."

"And power," she added a little too helpfully. "But, then, the two usually go together, don't they?"

"Power?" he repeated neutrally.

"Sure. You have a lot of clout here in Portland. You mingle with the movers and shakers. You're on the boards of some of the major charitable organizations. You know the players in business and politics. People listen to you. That's called power."

He thought about it and then shrugged. "I do get stuck with a lot of board meetings."

"Don't try to pretend you don't know what I'm talking about. I can't believe you would have worked so hard to make Madison Commercial such an important and influential company if you weren't getting something very personal out of it. Something besides money."

"You know," he said, "this kind of conversation isn't my forte."

"Really? I would never have guessed."

"My turn," he said. "Just what were you doing in all those different places you were living in for the past few years?"

"You want my whole résumé?"

"Just hit the high spots."

She put the tips of her thumbs and forefingers together, forming a triangle around the base of her glass, and looked down into her wine.

"Well, let's see," she said. "After I graduated from college, I worked in a museum for a few years."

"Why did you quit?"

"The public never seemed to be compelled by the same art that fascinates me and the whole point of a successful museum is to attract the attention of the public. I wasn't very creative with the exhibitions and displays."

"Because you were not real interested in the subjects you were supposed to make attractive to the public."

"Probably. After that I worked in various art galleries. I had no problem figuring out what would sell, but I wasn't personally attracted to the art that most of the clients wanted to buy."

"Hard to stay in business when you don't want to give your customers what they want to buy."

Her mouth curved ruefully. "Oddly enough, that's what the gallery owners said."

"What came next?"

She turned the base of the wineglass slowly between her fingers. "I switched to a career in interior design. It was okay for a while but then I started getting into arguments with my clients. They didn't always like what I thought they ought to have in their homes and offices."

"Nothing worse than a client with his own personal opinion, I always say."

"Very true. I decided to get out of that field, too, but before I did, I introduced one of my clients, a software designer, to a friend of mine. I thought they made a good match and I was right. After the wedding, my software client got enthusiastic about the whole idea of designing a matchmaking program. It sounded interesting, so I agreed to work with her on it. We consulted with some experts. I designed the questionnaire. She did the technical part. When it was finished, I bought her out."

"That's how you got into the matchmaking business? You just sort of fell into it?"

"Chilling, isn't it?"

He exhaled slowly. "Well, yeah, as a matter of fact, it is."

"You're not the only one who has pointed that out recently. I never set out to get into the business, you understand. After my ex-client finished the program, I tested it. More or less as a lark, I tried it on some acquaintances and got lucky a couple of times. People went out on dates, had a good time. An engagement or two was announced. All of a sudden, I was in the matchmaking business."

"Damn." He rubbed his jaw. "Are you sure that's legal?"

"Got news for you, Madison, anyone can set up in business as a matchmaker."

"Sort of like the sex therapy business, huh?"

"Don't." She leveled a warning finger at him. "Mention that subject again."

"Hard to resist."

"Try." She gave him an evil smile. "Now that you know the gruesome truth, that you placed your entire future in the hands of an amateur, maybe you'd like to rethink your insistence on that sixth date you say I owe you."

"No way." He picked up his beer, tilted it to his mouth, and took a long swallow. Then he put the bottle down again. "I paid for it. I want it."

She made a face. "Anyone ever told you that you've got a real stubborn streak?"

"It's a Madison thing." He studied her across the table. "What are you going to do next? After I get my sixth date and you shut down Private Arrangements, that is?"

"Gee, I don't know. Maybe I'll apply for an executive position at Madison Commercial."

"Don't bother. Something tells me you wouldn't last long there, either."

"You're probably right," she said. "I'm what you'd call a self-motivated type. I don't like working for other people. I prefer to make the decisions and set the agenda. It would be inevitable that sooner or later I would start telling you how to run your company."

"At which point I would have to can you."

"Of course." She waved a dismissive hand. "Another career path down the tubes."

"How important is Flint to you?"

"I told you not to mention his name to me again." But there was no heat in her words this time.

He decided to take a chance and push a little harder.

"If the two of you had something serious going on, I can see where the sight of all the leather might have been a little traumatic."

"Anderson and I don't have anything serious going on," she said very steadily. "Not in the way you mean. I won't say I didn't enjoy his company on a few occasions but I knew from the start that he wasn't interested in me personally."

"Just your program."

"Yes.

"Are you going to help him out with his book?"

"No," she said.

"Was it the scene in his office that made you change your mind?"

"No." She went to work on the little paper napkin that had accompanied the glass of wine, folding and creasing it in an abstract pattern. "I changed my mind several days ago. That's what I was going to tell Anderson this afternoon when I went downstairs to see him."

"Why back out of the project?"

"I've got my mind on other things right now."

He had been through too many negotiations, played too many games of strategy and brinksmanship not to know when an opponent was being evasive. But he had also had enough experience to know when to push and when to let things ride.

"As long as we're here," he said. "We might as well have dinner."

She looked up from her origami project. "Dinner?"

"We both have to eat. Unless you've got other plans?"

"No," she said slowly. "I don't have any other plans."

He walked her back to a handsome brick building and saw her to her front door on the top floor. When she turned in the doorway to say good-night, he looked past her through a small foyer into the living room of her apartment. He could see warm yellow walls, white moldings near the ceiling and a lot of vividly patterned velvet pillows heaped on a brilliant purple sofa. The curved arm of a scarlet wingback chair was visible near the window. The edge of a green, yellow, and purple patterned rug peeked out from beneath an abstract glass coffee table.

The strange combination of colors and designs should have looked garish but for some reason it all went together perfectly. That was a disturbing sign but it was not what really worried him.

What bothered him the most were the glimpses he caught of the paintings hanging on the yellow walls. There were a number of them. Not framed reproductions or posters. Lillian bought originals, apparently. A real bad sign. She obviously cared enough about art to have formed her own opinions.

From where he stood in the doorway, he could not get a good look at any of the pictures but he got an impression of strong light and dark, edgy shadows. He thought back to the conversation in the café, the part where she had detailed her job history working mostly in museums and art galleries.

A sense of deep gloom settled on him. He could no longer deny the evidence of his own eyes. Lillian was into art big-time.

"Thank you for the drink and for dinner," she said politely.

He pulled his attention back from the ominous scene inside her apartment. Realized that she was watching him closely, maybe reading his mind.

"Sure," he said. "My pleasure."

She gripped the door with one hand, preparing to close it. A speculative expression crossed her face. "You know, when you think about it—"

"Forget it," he said.

"Forget what?"

"You aren't going to get away with calling that dinner we just had my sixth date. I'm not letting Private Arrangements off the hook that easily."

Her mouth tightened. "You have been a difficult client from day one, Madison."

"People say stuff like that to me all the time. I try not to take it personally."

# chapter 3

Lillian watched Octavia Brightwell's expressive face while she examined the painting. Rapt attention radiated from the gallery owner.

Octavia stood in the center of the studio, her red hair aglow in the strong light cast by the ceiling fixtures. Her slender frame was taut with concentration; she seemed lost somewhere inside the picture propped in front of her.

Or maybe she hated the painting and didn't know how to deliver the bad news, Lillian thought.

She berated herself for the negative thinking. She considered herself to be a positive, glass-half-full kind of person under most circumstances, but when it came to her art she knew she was vulnerable.

Octavia was the first and, thus far, the only person from the art world who had seen her work. Until recently, she had allowed only the members of her family and a very few close friends to view the paintings.

She had always drawn and painted. She could not remember a time when she had not kept a sketchbook close

at hand. She had been fascinated with watercolors and
acrylics and pastels since childhood. She picked up her
brushes as easily as other people picked up a knife and
fork. Her family considered her painting as nothing more
than a hobby but she knew the truth. It was as necessary
to her as food and water and fresh air.

She had been born into a family of financial wizards
and entrepreneurs. It was not that art was not respected
in the Harte clan. Some of the members of her family
actively collected it. But they treated it as they would any
other investment. Hartes did not establish careers as artists.
She'd dreamed her dreams of becoming an artist but she'd
kept them to herself.

Until now.

The time had come to turn her dreams into reality. She
could feel it. She was ready. Something inside her had
changed. She sensed new dimensions in her work, new
layers that had not been there in the past.

She was sure of her decision to try her hand at painting full time, but she did not know if her work had a
market. She had enough Harte business instincts to understand that in the real world, art was a commodity like
any other. If there was no consumer demand for her work,
there was no possibility of making her living as an artist.

The route to financial success as an artist required the
support and savvy marketing of a respected dealer. The
decision to show her paintings to Octavia Brightwell first
had been based entirely on intuition.

Octavia owned and operated an influential gallery,
Bright Visions, here in Portland. She had also opened a
branch in Eclipse Bay.

"Well?" Lillian prompted when she could no longer
stand the suspense. "What do you think?"

"What do I think?" Octavia appeared to have trouble

dragging her gaze away from the painting. "I think it's absolutely extraordinary, just like the others in your *Between Midnight and Dawn* series."

Something inside Lillian relaxed a little. "Good. Great. Thanks."

Octavia turned back to the painting. "I'm pulling out all the stops for your upcoming show. I want maximum impact."

"I don't know how to thank you, Octavia."

"Don't bother. We're both in this thing together. I have a feeling that it isn't just your career that will take off when I hang your work in my gallery. Mine is going to get a real shot in the arm as well."

Lillian laughed. "Sounds good to me. I'll leave you to do your job. I'm off to Eclipse Bay on Wednesday."

"You're really going to do it? You're going to close down Private Arrangements?"

"Yes, but keep it to yourself for a while." Lillian folded her arms and studied the paintings that lined the studio wall. "I'm still working on figuring out how to break it to the family gently."

"I suppose it will come as a shock."

"Well, it won't be quite as much of a blow as it was when Nick announced that he was leaving Harte Investments to write mysteries full time. After all, my grandfather had counted on him taking over the company when my father retires. But no one is going to be real thrilled when I announce that I intend to paint full time. Hartes don't become artists. They're businesspeople."

Half an hour later, the laptop under her arm, the hood of her rain cloak pulled low over her face, Lillian walked quickly through the misty rain toward the building that housed the offices of Private Arrangements. Her thoughts were on the conversation with Octavia. She did not see the big man until he stepped right into her path.

"You're Lillian Harte, aren't you?" he said fiercely.

The anger in his voice made her mouth go dry. She came to a halt in the middle of the busy sidewalk, fervently grateful for the fact that she was surrounded by a large number of people.

The man looming in front of her appeared to be in his mid-forties, big, heavily built with blunt features and thinning, short-cropped hair. She could not see his eyes. They were concealed behind a pair of dark sunglasses. Not real useful on a cloudy, rainy day, she reflected, but they certainly added a note of menacing drama.

"Do I know you?" she asked cautiously.

"No." His heavy jaw jerked. "But I know you, lady. You're the matchmaker, aren't you?"

She clutched the laptop very tightly. "How do you know that?"

His mouth twisted. "I've been watching you for the past couple of days."

A blast of stark fear left her palms damp. "You *followed* me? You had no right to do that. I'll report you to the police."

"I didn't do anything illegal." He looked disgusted. "I just wanted to be sure."

"Sure of what?"

"Sure you were the woman who runs that matchmaking outfit, Private Arrangements."

"Why do you care who I am?"

He moved in closer. "You're the one who took Heather away from me. You hooked her up with someone else, didn't you? I called her a couple of days ago. Thought I'd give her another chance, y'know? That's when she told me that she planned to marry this guy you set her up with. She thinks she's in love. I think you messed with her mind."

Ice touched Lillian's spine. "Are you talking about Heather Summers?"

"Heather was with me before you tricked her into thinking I was no good for her. She left me because of you."

It took everything Lillian had to stand her ground. "Who are you?"

"My name's Witley." He took another step toward her, his face clenching with anger. "Campbell Witley. Heather and I were together before you came along. You ruined everything."

She glanced quickly around again, reassuring herself that she was not alone here on the sidewalk. Then she looked very steadily at Campbell Witley.

"Please, calm down, Mr. Witley. I did match a woman named Heather but when she filled out the forms I gave her she stated that she was not currently seeing anyone. I always insist that my clients be single and unattached when they sign up with my firm."

"I don't care what Heather said on your damned forms." He tapped his wide chest with a stubby thumb. "She was with *me*."

Lillian remembered Heather very well. She was a shy, nonconfrontational type who would have found it extremely difficult to deal with an aggressive man like Witley.

She also recalled that Heather had been a different woman after her first date with Ted Baker. Baker was the quiet, studious sort, very much a gentleman. He and Heather had attended the opera together. It had been love at first sight.

"Out of curiosity," Lillian said, "do you enjoy the opera, Mr. Witley?"

"What business is it of yours?"

"Heather loves the opera. I just wondered if you shared her interests."

Witley's mouth creased into a thin line. "Are you saying I didn't have anything in common with her just because I wouldn't go to the damned opera? That's bullshit. Heather and I had a lot in common. We went to ball games. I took her camping. We went white-water rafting. We did lots of stuff together."

"Those were all things that you enjoyed. But it doesn't sound as if you did many things that she liked to do."

"How do you know what she liked?"

"She was very specific on the questionnaire I had her fill out. She is really quite passionate about the opera, you know. And she likes to attend film festivals."

"I took Heather to the movies. We saw *Battle Zone* twice."

This was hopeless, Lillian thought. Campbell Witley would probably never understand, much less care, that he and Heather had had no common interests.

"I'm sorry about your personal problems, Mr. Witley, but I assure you, I had nothing to do with the breakup of your relationship," she said.

"The hell you didn't. If it hadn't been for you, Heather would be with me now."

"When did she end your relationship?"

Witley scowled furiously. "The night we went to see *Battle Zone* the second time. When I took her home that evening, she said she didn't want to date me again. Why?"

"You say that she broke up with you after you took her to back-to-back screenings of *Battle Zone*. As I recall, that film came out early last fall. I remember the ads were everywhere."

"So what?"

"Heather didn't register with Private Arrangements until December. I matched her in January."

"Who cares when she registered with your damned agency?"

"I'm trying to explain that my firm had nothing to do with the end of your relationship with Heather," Lillian said patiently. "She didn't come to me until after the two of you had stopped seeing each other."

"Don't try to weasel out of this. She'd have come back to me by now if you hadn't fixed her up with someone else."

"I don't think so," Lillian said as gently as possible. "It doesn't sound like the two of you were a good match. You need an outdoorsy type. Someone who likes to camp and hike. Someone who isn't afraid to argue with you."

"That just shows how much you know. One of the things I really liked about Heather was that she never argued with me."

"Guess there wouldn't have been much point."

His face worked. "What's that supposed to mean?"

"I get the feeling you didn't listen to her very well, Mr. Witley."

"That's a damned lie. I listened to her."

"Can you honestly say that Heather never once indicated that she preferred attending the opera to camping?"

Witley grimaced. "She may have mentioned the opera crap a couple of times but I told her to forget it. That highbrow stuff is boring. No beat to it, y'know?"

"In other words Heather did everything you wanted to do but you didn't do any of the things she liked. You don't see that as a problem in a relationship?"

"I told you, Heather and I had a great relationship." Witley's voice got louder. "And you wrecked it. What gives you the right to play games with other people's lives, Lillian Harte? You can't get away with treating folks like lab rats."

She held the laptop in front of her as if it were a shield. "I don't treat them that way."

"Using a damned computer to figure out who people should date and marry? You don't think that isn't treating them like rats in a maze? Hell, you're like some mad scientist in a movie or something. Like you know what's best for everyone else."

"Mr. Witley, I can't discuss this with you. Not while you're in this mood."

She made to step around him but he blocked her path.

"You can't mess up my life like this and then just blow me off," he said. "You took Heather away from me. You had no right to do that. You got that? No right, damn it."

"Excuse me, I've got to go now," Lillian said.

She whirled abruptly to the left and plunged through the glass doors of the large department store that occupied most of the block. There would be security staff inside if she needed help, she thought.

But Campbell Witley did not follow her into the store. She paused in front of a cosmetics counter and glanced over her shoulder to see if he was still on the sidewalk outside.

There was no sign of him.

She stared down through the polished glass at a display of elegantly packaged face creams. Her pulse was beating too rapidly. Her stomach was doing weird things.

*What gives you the right to play games with other people's lives, Lillian Harte? You can't get away with treating folks like lab rats.*

She could not blame this queasy, slightly panicky feeling entirely on the scene with Campbell Witley, as unpleasant as it had been. She had been getting little foretastes of this nasty sensation for several weeks. It was one of the reasons why she knew she had to shut down Private Arrangements.

"Can I help you?" a solicitous voice asked from the other side of the counter.

Lillian looked up and saw immediately that the saleswoman was not offering to summon medical assistance. She was looking to make a sale.

"Uh, no." Lillian pulled herself together with an effort. "No thanks. Just browsing."

The clerk's smile slipped a little the way clerks' smiles always did when you used the magic words.

"Let me know if I can be of service," she said and moved off toward another potential customer.

"Yes. Thanks. I'll do that."

Lillian turned away. She wove a path through the remaining cosmetic counters, angled across accessories and shoes and exited the store through the doors on the cross street.

Outside on the sidewalk she glanced uneasily in both directions. Campbell Witley was gone.

But he had followed her home the other night. He knew where she lived.

This was scary stuff.

She took a steadying breath and walked purposefully toward her office building. She had definitely made the right decision when she had made up her mind to close down Private Arrangements.

A short while later she stepped off the elevator. Halfway down the hall she saw a familiar figure waiting for her in front of the door marked Private Arrangements. J. Anderson Flint.

She was immediately hit with a full-color flashback to the scene in Anderson's office on Friday afternoon. Every

lurid detail was there, including the red bikini briefs. One
of the drawbacks to having an artist's eye, she thought.
You sometimes remembered things that you would just
as soon forget.

It was all she could do to resist the urge to leap back
into the elevator before the doors closed.

She made herself continue moving forward. There were
things that had to be done before she left town. She could
not avoid Anderson. Running away was not going to solve
anything. Sooner or later she had to deal with the man.

Anderson did not notice her immediately. He was too
busy checking the time on his very elegant black and gold
wristwatch.

"Good morning, Anderson."

He turned slightly at the sound of her voice and smiled.
It struck her, not for the first time, that he could have
played the part of the wise, understanding, all-knowing
therapist in a soap opera. He certainly had the cheekbones
and the jaw for television. He also had the eyes. They
were very, very blue and filled with what looked like in-
sight. He was in his late thirties but he projected an image
of wisdom and maturity far beyond his years. His thick,
precision-cut, prematurely silver hair and the precision-
trimmed goatee added to the impression.

Anderson was dressed more conventionally this morning than he had been the last time she had seen him. He
wore a gray chunky-weave turtleneck sweater, dark tailored trousers, and loafers. He had explained to her once
over coffee that a formal business suit and tie made pa-
tients tense and uncomfortable. She tried not to think
about whether he had on the red bikini briefs.

"Lillian." He looked relieved to see her. "I was getting a little worried. It's nearly eleven o'clock. I called
your office several times this morning. When there was

no response I thought I'd come up here and see what was going on."

"Good morning, Anderson." She jammed the keys in the lock and opened the door with a single twist of her hand. "I didn't have any appointments today so I used the time to take care of some personal business."

"Of course."

She flipped on the lights and went toward her desk. "Was there something you wanted?"

Anderson followed her into the office. "I thought we might have dinner tonight."

"Thanks, but I'm afraid that won't be possible." She gave him an apologetic smile and put the laptop down on her desk. "I'm going to be busy all day and I have a lot to do tonight."

"You just said you didn't have any appointments."

"I'm getting ready to leave town for a while."

"You never said anything about planning a trip."

"I'm not going on vacation. I'm changing careers."

"Changing—?" he asked with concern. "What's going on here? You're not making any sense, Lillian. You seem tense. Is something wrong?"

"Nothing's wrong, Anderson. I'm going to stay at my family's place in Eclipse Bay for a while, that's all."

"How long will you be gone?"

"A month."

He stared at her. She doubted that he could have looked any more dumbfounded if she had just told him that she intended to join a cloistered order of nuns.

"I see." He pulled himself together with a visible effort. "I hadn't realized. Can you take that much time off from Private Arrangements?"

"I can take all the time I want, Anderson. Private Arrangements went out of business Friday afternoon."

His jaw dropped a second time.

"I don't understand," he said, looking genuinely baffled. "What do you mean?"

"You heard me. I've closed my doors."

"But that's impossible," he sputtered. "You can't just walk away from Private Arrangements."

"Why not?"

"For one thing, you've got too much invested in it." He swept out his hand to indicate their surroundings. "Your office. Your program. Your client list."

"My lease is up next month. I made back my investment in the program several times over a long time ago. And I've whittled my client list down to one." She waved one hand. "I admit I'm having a small problem getting rid of him, but I'm sure that situation will soon be resolved."

"What about our book project?"

"That's another thing, Anderson. I'm sorry, but I've decided not to get involved in helping you with your book."

He went very still. "Something is wrong here. This isn't like you. Your behavior is very abnormal. It's obvious that you've got some issues."

She propped herself on the edge of the desk and looked at him. "Anderson, a very unpleasant thing happened to me this morning. A man named Campbell Witley stopped me on the street. He used to date one of my clients. You know what? Mr. Witley was really, really mad at me because I'd helped his girlfriend find someone else to date."

"What does this Witley have to do with your decision to shut down your business?"

"He pointed out in no uncertain terms that I had no right to use my computer program to meddle in other people's lives."

"That's ridiculous."

"As it happens, I tend to agree with him."

Anderson stared at her, clearly appalled.

"What do you mean?" he asked sharply. "Why do you say that?"

She eyed the closed laptop and wondered how to explain things to him. He probably wouldn't believe her if she told him that the program only worked in conjunction with her intuition and a dose of common sense. She hadn't wanted to believe it, herself.

She needed a more technical-sounding excuse with which to fob him off.

"The program is flawed," she said finally. In a way, that wasn't really far from the truth, she thought.

"*Flawed*. Are you certain?"

"Yes."

"I don't understand. You've been so successful. You've attracted so many high-end clients."

"Dumb luck, I'm afraid." She shrugged. "Keep in mind that I don't have any long-term statistics yet because I haven't been in business long enough to obtain them. It's possible that over time my matches won't prove any more successful than the ones people make on their own in the usual ways."

Anderson gave her a long, considering look. "I think I see the problem here."

"The problem," she said very deliberately, "is that Campbell Witley has a point. I don't have the right to fiddle with other people's lives. Besides, it's too stressful."

"Stressful?"

"Lately I've begun to wonder—what would happen if I screw up badly someday and put the wrong people together? Oh, sure, I do a comprehensive background check on all of my clients to make certain they don't have a criminal record or any history of serious mental disorders. But what if I miss something? Don't you see? There's a very real potential for disaster."

Anderson nodded soberly. "I agree."

"You do?"

"Yes." He shoved his hands into his pockets and rocked a little in his tasseled loafers. "To be perfectly frank, I had been meaning to broach the subject, myself."

"You were?"

"Yes. But I wanted to get to know you a little better before I raised such a delicate question. After all, Private Arrangements is your business."

There was something distinctly patronizing about his smile, she decided.

"What delicate question?" she asked carefully.

He looked at the laptop. "As you know, I have been deeply intrigued by your program for some time now, but I must admit that the fact that you have been using it without professional guidance has worried me more than somewhat."

She waited a beat. "Professional guidance?"

"Let's be honest here, Lillian. You don't have a background in psychology. You have no training or experience in clinical therapy or counseling techniques. It says a great deal for your program that you've been as successful as you have thus far. But I agree that in using it for real-life matchmaking, you assumed an enormous responsibility and a degree of risk. Obviously such a sophisticated program should be used only by a professional."

"I see. A professional. Like you."

"Actually, yes. If you're serious about getting out of the business, I would like to make you an offer for the program and the related files that you've developed in the course of your work."

That stopped her momentarily. She hadn't bargained on this. The last thing she wanted to do was sell the program to Anderson. If he used it, he would soon discover that it didn't work very well on its own. No telling how many mistakes he might make before he realized that it was not magic.

"No," she said. "I told you, it's flawed."

"You mean there are bugs in the program?"

"Not technical bugs," she said, trying to keep things vague. "It just doesn't work very well."

He chuckled. "I'm sure that I have the professional background necessary to fix any small problems that might come up. I'll make you a fair offer. We can work out mutually satisfactory terms. Perhaps a licensing agreement?"

"The Private Arrangements program is not for sale."

"Lillian, be reasonable."

"I'm sorry, but I've made my decision."

He frowned. "Obviously that confrontation with Witley was traumatic. Your state of generalized anxiety is extremely high. But I think that when you have a chance to calm down you'll see that you're overreacting."

She straightened away from the desk, walked to the door and yanked it open. "If you don't mind, I have a lot of things to do here today, Anderson. I want to leave town the day after tomorrow. That means I don't have time for this conversation."

He hesitated and then apparently decided that further argument would get him nowhere. "Very well. We'll discuss this later."

*Don't hold your breath,* she thought. But she managed what she hoped was a civil smile.

He hesitated and then took the hint and walked out into the hall. He paused.

"Lillian, perhaps—"

"Goodbye, Anderson." She shut the door very firmly in his face.

It felt good.

Probably overreacting, but what the heck. She had a right to overreact. Between Gabe, Witley, and Anderson, she'd had a very difficult week.

She went back to the desk, picked up the phone and called a familiar number.

Nella Townsend answered on the second ring.

"Townsend Investigations."

"Nella, its me."

"Hi, Lil. What can I do for you? Got a new client you want me to check out?"

"Not exactly. I want you to get some background on a man named Campbell Witley."

"Not a client?"

"No. Ex-boyfriend of one."

There was a short, distinct pause on the other end of the line.

"A problem?" Nella asked.

"I don't know. That's what I want you to find out for me."

"Okay, what have you got?"

"Not much. All I know is that until sometime last fall he was seeing Heather Summers, a client, on a regular basis. You did a check on her when she signed up with Private Arrangements."

"Got it. This shouldn't take long. He'll probably pop up in her file. I should have a preliminary report ready for you by the end of the day."

"Great. I'll pick it up on my way home. Thanks, Nella. I really appreciate this."

"No problem. Got any plans for tonight?"

"I'll be packing."

"Packing takes energy. You need to eat. Why don't you have dinner with Charles and me?"

"I'll bring the wine."

At five-thirty that afternoon, Lillian sank into a deeply cushioned chair in the living room of Nella's apartment and kicked off her shoes.

"I'm exhausted. It took an entire day to pack up that office. I thought I'd be finished by two o'clock. How can a person accumulate so much stuff in an office?"

"One of the great mysteries of life."

Nella picked up the blue folder lying on the table and carried it across the room. She wore jeans and a deep yellow blouse with a spread collar. The gold necklace at her throat gleamed against her dark brown skin. She wore her black hair cut close to her head in a style that showed off her excellent bone structure.

She took the chair that faced Lillian's, curled one leg under her and opened the folder.

"I thought you told me all of your files were stored on the hard drive of your computer," she said.

"The client files are on the computer along with the program, but that still leaves a lot of paper. Receipts, correspondence, notes to the janitorial staff, messages from the company that leased me the space, you name it. I had to go through every single item and make a decision about whether to keep it or toss it." Lillian exhaled deeply. "But it's done and Private Arrangements is no longer in business."

"Congratulations," Nella said. "Feel good?"

"Yes, but I'll feel even better after you assure me that Campbell Witley is not a serial killer."

"He looks squeaky clean to me." Nella glanced at some of her notes. "Witley was in the military at one time, as you guessed. He received an honorable discharge. After leaving the service he took over his father's construction business and has been very successful. He was married for six years. Divorced. No children. No record of arrests, no outstanding warrants, no history of violence or abuse."

"Just what I wanted to hear," Lillian said.

"I also managed to get hold of his ex-wife. She said Witley was the domineering type and inclined to get a little loud at times, but she sounded shocked at the suggestion that he might turn violent. She said he was, and I quote, 'harmless.' "

"Excellent."

Nella closed the file and looked seriously at Lillian. "None of this means that he might not be dangerous under certain circumstances, you understand."

"I know. But I suppose you could say that about any man."

"True." Nella pursed her lips. "This was a fairly superficial check. I didn't have time to go deep. Want me to continue looking in the morning?"

"No, I don't think it's necessary. If his ex-wife vouched for him, I'm satisfied. Thanks, Nella. I really appreciate it. I'll sleep better tonight."

The sound of a key in the lock interrupted her.

Nella uncoiled from the chair. "That'll be Charles. Time to pour the wine."

Lillian twisted in the chair to give Nella's husband a welcoming wave. Charles came through the door, a long paper sack with a loaf of bread peeking out of the top in one arm, a briefcase in his hand.

He was a slender black man with serious dark eyes framed by gold-rimmed glasses and the air of an academic. He kissed his wife and released the bread to her custody. She disappeared into the kitchen.

Charles turned his slow smile on Lillian while he removed his jacket. "I hear we're celebrating the closure of Private Arrangements tonight."

"Yep. I finally took the big step. I am now officially a full-time painter. Or officially unemployed, depending on your point of view."

He nodded gravely. "This is going to put a dent in Nella's business, but I've told you all along, that matchmaking business of yours was nothing but a lawsuit waiting to happen."

Nella walked out of the kitchen with a tray of wine and cheese. She wrinkled her nose. "You're a lawyer, Charles. To you, just walking down the street is a lawsuit waiting to happen."

"Dangerous places, streets." Charles took one of the wineglasses off the tray and lifted it in a toast. "Here's to art."

# chapter 4

"I love what you've done with the guest rooms," Lillian said. "Very spacious and airy." She opened the French doors of the corner suite and stepped out onto the balcony. "Fabulous views, too. "

Her sister, Hannah, glanced around the suite with satisfaction and then followed Lillian outside into the chilly evening.

"It wasn't cheap getting plumbing into all of the rooms," she said. "And installing balcony doors in each one was a major project but I think it will be worth it. Considering what we plan to charge for an overnight stay here at Dreamscape, Rafe and I have to be able to provide our guests with privacy and a sense of luxury."

Lillian wrapped one hand around the railing. "You and Rafe are going to do it, aren't you? You're going to make this inn and restaurant idea work."

Hannah looked amused. "You had doubts?"

"No, not really. You're both so committed to making a success of this venture that I knew you couldn't fail."

"We owe it all to Great-Aunt Isabel." Hannah smiled. "Although I must admit that when I first learned that she had left a half-interest in Dreamscape to Rafe in her will, I didn't feel quite so grateful."

Lillian looked out across the bay. Night was closing in rapidly. The wind was picking up, bringing with it the unmistakable scent of rain off the sea. Another storm was approaching. She had always loved this time of year here on the rugged Oregon coast. The stark contrasts of the season appealed to the artist in her. The dark, blustery storms drove away the summer tourists, leaving the town to the locals.

The shops on the pier and the handful of small, casual eateries geared down for the long, quiet months. In summer the establishments were crowded with vacationers from Portland and Seattle. But when you went out to dinner in winter, you usually knew the folks sitting at the next table. If you didn't recognize them, they were probably students at nearby Chamberlain College or visitors attending a seminar at the Eclipse Bay Policy Studies Institute. The think tank and the school were both located on the hillside overlooking the tiny town.

When they blew ashore, the wind-driven rains of winter churned the waters of the bay, created boiling cauldrons in the coves and lashed the weather-beaten cottages on the cliffs. The squalls were often separated by periods of bright, chilly sunlight and crisp, intensely clear air. There was an energy in winter that was very different from the moody, atmospheric, fog-bound summers, she thought.

The evening was still clear. From her perch on the balcony she could see straight across the curving expanse of the semi-circular bay to where a cluster of lights marked the location of the small town and the marina. Another string of lights identified the pier.

The sweeping arc of Bayview Drive followed the edge of the rocky beach. The road started just outside of town near Hidden Cove, which marked the northern tip of the bay. It linked the tiny community to the beach houses and cottages scattered loosely about on the bluffs. It continued past her parents' summer place and beyond Dreamscape, to terminate at Sundown Point, the bay's southern boundary.

It was a familiar landscape, Lillian reflected, one she had known all of her life. She had not spent a lot of time here in recent years, but that did not affect the strong sense of connection that had swept through her earlier this afternoon when she drove into town.

For three generations Hartes had been a part of this community. Their roots went deep here; as deep as those of the Madison men.

She hugged herself against the brisk night air. "Aunt Isabel knew all along that you and Rafe were meant for each other."

"If that's true, she was certainly the only one who knew it." Hannah shook her head. "Personally, I think it's far more likely that she just hoped to goodness we were meant for each other. It was her dream to resolve the feud. She saw Rafe and me as Romeo and Juliet with the right ending. She left us Dreamscape in an effort to make her fantasy of reconnecting the Hartes and the Madisons come true."

"Either way, it worked out for you and Rafe."

"Maybe she had a touch of your gift for matchmaking," Hannah said lightly. "Could be it runs in the family."

"I don't think so."

"Okay, Lil, what's going on here? Don't get me wrong, I'm delighted to see you. I think it's great that you've decided to take some time off from work. But this is your sister, Hannah, remember? I know you haven't given me the whole story."

There was no point trying to evade the questions, Lillian thought. Hannah knew her too well. They had always been close even though they were different in so many ways. Hannah was nearly two years younger but she had always been the more levelheaded and goal-oriented of the two. Hannah was the one who had always known where she was going; at least that had been the general opinion in the Harte family until she had stunned everyone by announcing that she intended to marry Rafe Madison and turn Dreamscape into an inn.

True to form, however, even that uncharacteristically wild decision had turned out to be a sound one. It was obvious that Rafe and Hannah were happy together and that they would make a success of the inn.

"I closed Private Arrangements," Lillian said.

Hannah looked bemused. "For a few days? A couple of weeks? A month?"

"For good."

Hannah took a long moment to absorb and process that announcement.

Then she gave a low, soft, tuneless whistle.

"Oh, my," she said.

"I know."

"Just when Mom and Dad were getting used to the idea of you being a professional matchmaker."

"I'm not sure they would ever have come around completely, anyway." Lillian sighed. "They still have a hard time telling their friends what I do for a living. In their minds my matchmaking enterprise was always a little suspect. Not nearly as respectable as that wedding consultant agency you owned before you decided to go into the inn business."

"Okay, I'll agree that Mom and Dad thought the whole thing was a little flaky, but you were *successful*. They couldn't deny that. You have an impressive list of clients. All those new, wealthy software folks love the idea of computerized matchmaking. You were turning a serious profit and that counts for a lot in this family."

"If Mom and Dad think matchmaking is flaky, I can't wait to hear what they'll say about my next career move."

"Well?" Hannah tilted her head slightly. "Don't keep me in suspense."

"It's a long story."

"I want to hear every word of it." Hannah paused when a set of headlights turned into the drive that led toward Dreamscape. "But I'm afraid the tale will have to wait. Here comes dinner."

The low growl of a powerful, finely tuned engine rumbled in the gathering night. Lillian watched the sleek Porsche prowl down the drive.

The vehicle came to a halt near the inn's main entrance. The engine went silent. The door on the driver's side opened. Hannah's husband, Rafe, got out, moving with the easy masculine grace that characterized all the Madison males.

A dapper salt-and-pepper Schnauzer jumped out of the open car door after him. The dog paused and looked up toward the balcony.

"Hello, Winston," Lillian called down. "You're as handsome as ever."

Winston bounced a little in refined appreciation of what he obviously considered no more than his due. Then he trotted briskly up the steps and disappeared under the overhanging roof.

Rafe retrieved two grocery sacks from the interior of the car.

"About time you guys got home," Hannah said to him. "We were starting to wonder if the two of you had stopped off at the Total Eclipse for a beer and a fast game of pool."

Rafe nudged the door of the Porsche closed and looked up. He gave Hannah and Lillian the patented Madison smile, all rakish charm and a promise of trouble to come.

"Sorry we're a little late," he said. "Ran into an old pal who just happened to show up in town late this afternoon. I invited him for dinner. Hope you don't mind."

"Who is he?" Hannah asked curiously.

"Just some guy I know."

Rafe turned to look back toward the far end of the drive. Lillian followed his gaze and saw a second set of headlights coming toward the inn.

A dark-green Jaguar glided down the drive and stopped next to the Porsche.

A sudden premonition sizzled through Lillian. She gripped the railing very tightly and leaned forward to get a better look.

"No," she muttered. "Surely he wouldn't—"

Hannah glanced at her in surprise. "What's wrong?"

Before Lillian could answer the Jag's door opened. Gabe climbed out. His gaze went straight to the balcony.

"Hello, Lillian," he said much too easily. "I see you got invited to dinner, too. Isn't this an amazing coincidence?"

"There are no coincidences," Lillian said darkly.

"I've heard that."

She was intensely aware of Rafe and Hannah watching the little scene. They both looked amused and intrigued. "What are you doing here? And don't try to tell me that you just decided to take a mini-vacation this weekend."

"One thing you should know about me." Gabe walked around the front of the Jag, making for the front steps. "I never do anything on a whim. You're probably thinking of Rafe, here. He's been known to get a little wild and crazy at times."

"Hey, don't look at me," Rafe said quickly. "I'm a married man now. I've settled down. I only get wild and crazy with Hannah." He gazed up at the balcony. "Isn't that right, honey?"

"If you know what's good for you, it is," Hannah said. There was warmth and laughter in the words.

Gabe stopped at the foot of the steps and looked at Lillian. "You didn't really believe that I was going to let you skip out on me, did you?"

She dug her fingers into the rail. "I offered to repay your money."

"I don't want a refund. I want what I paid for."

"I don't believe this," Lillian said.

Rafe paused, one booted foot on the bottom step, and gave his brother an inquiring look. "What's this all about? Sounds interesting."

"She owes me a date," Gabe explained. "I paid for six. I only got five."

"That is not true," Lillian said loudly.

"It is true," Gabe assured Rafe and Hannah. "I've got a signed contract to prove it."

Aware of Rafe's and Hannah's thinly veiled amusement, Lillian felt called upon to defend herself. "He lied on the questionnaire."

"You're just saying that to cover up the fact that you

did such a lousy job of matching me. Bottom line here is that I've got another date coming."

"Lots of luck," she shot back. "Nobody gets any more dates from Private Arrangements. The company is out of business. You'll have to get your last date somewhere else."

Gabe started up the steps. "Nobody takes my money and leaves town without delivering the goods."

"For crying out loud." Lillian leaned a little farther out over the rail. "This is ridiculous. You can't possibly be serious about one lousy date."

"When it comes to business, I'm always serious." He disappeared into the house.

"That's my brother for you," Rafe said, mockingly apologetic. "Could have written the book on how not to get screwed in a business deal. He fixates, you know?"

Before Lillian could tell him what she thought about Gabe's business style, Rafe, too, vanished beneath the overhang.

"Well," Hannah said thoughtfully. "This is an interesting turn of events."

"This isn't interesting, it's seriously aberrant behavior." Lillian continued to look uneasily over the railing into the now-empty drive. "You think maybe Gabe's gone a little nuts or something in the years since he left Eclipse Bay? Maybe the stress of building his business empire has been too much for him."

"I don't think it's the empire building that's making him act weird," Hannah said. "I think it's the fact that he's a Madison."

"I was afraid you were going to say that."

"Something tells me there's more to this story than your failure to live up to your end of a business contract."

"Believe it or not, things started out fairly normally when Gabe signed up with Private Arrangements. I had stopped taking new clients but he seemed serious and determined. I figured okay, he's not exactly an old *friend* of the family, but he certainly qualifies as a longtime acquaintance, and we *are* sort of connected because of you and Rafe and all. I thought, what the heck? I still had the names of several nice women in my files."

"What went wrong?"

"What can I say?" Lillian held out both hands, palms up. "Gabe became the client from hell."

"We've got no choice but to move out for at least three weeks," Hannah said an hour later. She passed a large ceramic bowl across the table to Lillian. "The Willis brothers have sent us straight into remodel hell. It was bad enough when they were doing the plumbing."

"They kept shutting off the water without warning and we had to cope with a stack of bathroom fixtures in the front hall for ages," Rafe said. "I started having nightmares featuring endless mazes of gleaming porcelain commodes."

"We keep assuring each other that we're lucky to have the full attention of the Willis brothers," Hannah said. "There's a new wing being built up at the institute and we were worried for a while that the folks up there would lure Torrance and Walter away. Fortunately they called in outside contractors."

"We made it through the endless commodes phase," Rafe concluded, "but there's no way we can live here while they refinish the wood floors and paint the rooms."

"I can see the problem." Lillian gripped the bowl in one hand and served herself a large helping of Rafe's dill-and-yogurt-laced cucumber salad. "The dust and fumes would be bad for Winston."

"Wouldn't do us much good, either," Rafe said dryly. "Besides, we need a vacation before we open for business. We're going down to California to tour some wineries in the Napa Valley. It will be a good opportunity to finalize my selections for the wine list that we'll be using in the restaurant."

"Another astounding coincidence." Gabe dipped the edge of a wedge of sourdough bread into the fragrant curried potato stew on his plate. "I've decided to take some time off, myself."

Rafe raised a brow. "Good idea. About time you grabbed a few days off. It's been a while since you got out of your office."

"So they tell me," Gabe said noncommittally.

Lillian stilled. "You're going to be here in Eclipse Bay for three or four days? That's all?"

Rafe chuckled. "Don't worry, Lillian, he won't loiter long in the vicinity, if that's what's worrying you. He can stay at Mitchell's place for a couple of days, at least until Mitchell gets back from Hawaii. But after that he'll be on borrowed time. I can safely predict that after forty-eight hours the two of them will be at each other's throat."

"Really? Just two days?"

"Sure. Take it from me. Mitchell will start in with his usual lectures, telling Gabe how he's become too obsessed with M.C. Gabe will tell him where to get off. Next thing you know, Gabe will be packing his bags."

Lillian allowed herself to relax. Rafe had a point. Everyone knew that the three Madison men were notoriously stubborn and hardheaded. The trait no doubt made it next to impossible for any two or more of them to share a house for an extended period of time.

"You're right." Gabe raised one shoulder in easy acquiescence to Rafe's prediction. "A day or two of sharing a house with Mitchell would be about all I could take."

Rafe winked at Lillian. "Told you so."

"Lately he's been getting worse with the lectures, if you can believe it," Gabe continued. He shook his head sadly. "In hindsight, giving him a computer was a major mistake."

"Are you kidding?" Rafe chuckled. "He loves that thing. Took to it like a duck to water."

"He's got an aptitude for it, all right," Gabe said. "But he's not using it the way I thought he would."

Lillian paused, her fork in midair. "How did you expect him to use it?"

"For good, wholesome, educational purposes. I figured he'd wile away many happy hours checking out senior porn sites. Instead, he's gotten into the habit of e-mailing me every day."

Rafe grinned. "Bet I can guess the content of those e-mail notes."

"They cover a variety of topics but they all come down to his opinion of how I'm running my business and my personal life."

Lillian cleared her throat. "I take it he doesn't approve of how you're handling either one?"

The strong emotion in Gabe's voice startled her. Whatever was going on between Gabe and his grandfather was more than just annoying to Gabe. It was generating some real pain.

"No," he said quietly. "He doesn't approve."

"I'm sorry if you were planning to stay with us," Hannah said gently. "As you can see, things are a mess. No one can be in here while the floors are being redone."

"I know." Gabe added some of Rafe's homemade tomato chutney to his curry.

Rafe watched him expectantly. "So, how long, exactly, do you think you'll stay with Mitchell?"

"I won't be staying with him at all." Gabe waited a beat. "I rented the old Buckley place."

"For how long?" Lillian asked warily.

"A month."

There was a moment of acute shock.

"You're actually going to take off an entire month?" Hannah asked in disbelief.

"I'll have to make a couple of trips back to town for some events that I couldn't scrub from my calendar," Gabe said. "I'm scheduled to deliver the introduction at a banquet to honor one of my former college professors, for instance. But otherwise I don't see any reason why I can't handle anything that might come up at Madison Commercial from here. I brought my computer and my fax machine and there's always the phone."

"I don't believe it," Lillian said flatly. "Something weird is going on here."

"She's right," Rafe said. "This is weird. I don't care how good you are at telecommuting. You'll have withdrawal symptoms, probably get the shakes or something if you try to stay away from your office for a whole month."

Gabe said nothing, just kept eating curry.

"Damn." Rafe looked intrigued now. "You're serious about this, aren't you?"

A sardonic look gleamed in Gabe's eyes. "You've known me all of your life. Ever known me when I wasn't serious?"

"No, can't say that I have."

An ominous sensation drifted through Lillian. She studied Gabe more closely. Something dangerous moved beneath the cool, controlled surface he presented to the world.

"This isn't about getting your sixth date out of Private Arrangements, is it?" she asked. "You were just teasing me with that nonsense. You're here because you really do want to get away for a while."

Gabe shrugged again but he did not argue the point.

Hannah turned to Gabe. "Is everything okay at Madison Commercial?" she asked hesitantly.

Lillian was startled by her question. She understood Hannah's concern. Anyone who knew anything about Gabe, even indirectly, was aware of how much the company meant to him. Impending trouble at Madison Commercial would certainly account for odd behavior on his part.

But she was very sure that if there were a problem with his business he would be living at his office twenty-four hours a day, seven days a week while he worked to fix it. He would not take a month off and head for the coast in the face of impending disaster.

"Things are fine at M.C." Gabe ate more curry.

"But?" Rafe prompted.

Gabe swallowed, put down his fork and leaned back in his chair.

"But, nothing," he said. "I need a little time to concentrate on something else, that's all. I hate to admit it, but Mitchell might have a point. Maybe I have been a little too focused on business for the past few years."

"Burnout," Lillian said quietly.

They all looked at her. Gabe and Rafe had the baffled, blank expressions that were common to the male of the species when psychological explanations for behavior were offered. But Hannah nodded in immediate agreement.

"Yes, of course," she said. "Makes sense. Lil's right. Sounds like burnout."

"Sounds like psychobabble to me," Gabe said. "What's this about burnout?"

"Think about it," Lillian said patiently. "You've expended an enormous amount of physical and mental energy on Madison Commercial for years. It's no secret that you've driven yourself very hard to make your company successful. That kind of intense focus over a long period of time takes its toll."

"How would you know?" he asked. The words were spoken in deceptively silky tones. "From what you've told me about your checkered job history, you haven't stuck with anything long enough to burn out on it."

The blatant rudeness crackled in the solarium like sheet lightning. To Hannah and Rafe, the sharp retort must have appeared to come out of nowhere.

Afraid that Rafe was going to say something to his brother that was probably better left unsaid, Lillian moved to defuse the situation.

"You're right about my job history," she said to Gabe. "Guess some of us are just born to be free spirits. Funny, isn't it?"

"What's funny about it?" Gabe asked.

"Most people would have assumed that you would have been the one who wound up with the spotty employment record."

"Because I'm a Madison?"

"Yes." She gave him a steely smile. "Whereas I am a stable, steady, long-range planning Harte." She turned to the others. "I suggested to Gabe that he might want to hire me into an executive position at Madison Commercial, but he declined on the basis of my erratic résumé."

Gabe rested an arm along the back of his chair. He did not take his eyes off Lillian. "That wasn't the reason I said I wouldn't hire you."

"What was the reason?" Hannah asked curiously.

"She pointed out that within a very short time she would probably be trying to tell me how to run my company. I said if that happened, I'd have to fire her. We both agreed there was no point even starting down that road, given the foregone conclusion."

"As you can see," Lillian said, "the decision not to hire me at M.C. was mutual. The last thing I need is another short-term position on my résumé."

The tension that had cloaked the dining room lightened, as she had hoped. Hannah took her cue and shifted deftly to the new topic.

"But you are looking for a new job, I take it, now that you've closed Private Arrangements?" she asked.

"Well, no," Lillian said.

"You're going to apply for unemployment? That'd be a first for a Harte," Gabe mused.

"I'm not going on unemployment."

Rafe raised one brow. "Accepting a position with Harte Investments?"

"Never in a million years. It's not just that I can't work for my father. The main problem is that I'm not the corporate type."

Gabe sat forward and folded his arms on the table. "Okay, I'll bite. What are you going to do next?"

"Paint."

"You've always painted," Hannah replied.

"I'm going to do it full time now. I'm turning pro."

All three of them contemplated her as if she had just

announced that she intended to go to work in a carnival sideshow.

Hannah groaned. "Please don't tell me that you've closed Private Arrangements so that you can devote yourself to art."

"I've closed Private Arrangements so that I can devote myself to art."

"Mom and Dad are going to have a fit." Hannah flopped back in her chair. "To say nothing of Granddad."

"I know," Lillian said.

Rafe reached for the coffeepot. "Got any reason to think you can make a living painting?"

"I'll find out soon enough whether it will work. Octavia Brightwell is going to put on a show of my work in her Portland gallery in a few weeks."

Rafe smiled wryly. "I'd give you the standard advice about not quitting your day job. But I guess it's too late."

"Much too late," she agreed.

Gabe stood at the rail of the inn's broad front porch and watched the taillights of Lillian's car disappear down the drive. Rafe leaned against a nearby post. Winston was stretched out at the top of the steps, his paws dangling over the edge, ears and nose angled to take in the sounds and scents of the night. Hannah had disappeared back into the warmth of the kitchen.

"If you're going to be here in Eclipse Bay for a whole month, maybe I'd better fill you in on some of the local news," Rafe said after a while.

"Save your breath. I'm not real interested in gossip."

"This concerns Marilyn Thornley."

Gabe took a moment to rummage around in his memory for some images of the woman he had dated for a time in those first years after college. She had been Marilyn Caldwell in those days, the daughter of one of the wealthiest men in the region. The Caldwells' home was in Portland but, like the Hartes, they had always kept a second home in Eclipse Bay. They also had a third in Palm Springs.

Marilyn had excellent instincts when it came to selecting winners. Gabe knew that while she had viewed him as having long-term potential, Trevor Thornley had looked like more of a sure thing. She had taken a long, hard look at the two men and chosen to cast her lot with Thornley.

There had been no hard feelings on his part, Gabe reflected. He certainly couldn't fault her decision. It had been a sensible, businesslike move. Trevor had been on the fast track in the political world. It was obvious even back then that he had the charisma, the glibness and the looks required to grab and hold the media's and the public's attention. It was clear that, barring some major disaster, he would go far, maybe all the way to Washington, D.C. All he required was money. Lots of it. Marilyn's family had supplied the missing commodity. Everyone had agreed that it made sense to invest in a son-in-law who was on his way to becoming a major political powerhouse.

There had been an unexpected bonus for Thornley in the arrangement. Marilyn had proven to be a brilliant campaign strategist. With the help of the politically astute staff of the Eclipse Bay Policy Studies Institute, she had orchestrated every step of Trevor's career. Under her guidance, he had moved up steadily through the political ranks. Last fall, he had announced that he was making a bid for the U.S. Senate.

To everyone's surprise, he had pulled out of the race shortly before Thanksgiving. The only explanation Gabe had seen in the papers was the ubiquitous *personal reasons.*

"What about Marilyn?" Gabe asked.

"Haven't you heard? She and Thornley have filed for divorce. She moved into her folks' summer place here in town last month. She's got an office at the institute."

"A staff position?"

Rafe shook his head. "She's getting set to launch her own career in politics."

"Huh. Doesn't surprise me. She was born for politics."

"Yeah. Just one problem."

"What's that?" Gabe asked.

"Word is she burned through a big pile of her family's money financing Thornley's career. Apparently her folks have declined to invest any more cash in politics for a while. Rumor has it they won't be backing her. At least not until she's proven that she can win."

"In other words, she needs money."

"Yeah. Lots and lots of it," Rafe said knowingly. "I mention this because it occurs to me that you have what she wants. Expect you'll be hearing from her as soon as she learns that you're back in town."

"Thanks for the heads-up. But don't worry about it. One thing I can spot real quick is a woman who's after my money."

Rafe looked out over the dark bay. "The two of you were once an item."

"That was a long time ago."

"Sure." Rafe shoved his hands into his front pockets. "Consider yourself forewarned."

"Okay."

There was another pause. Gabe could feel his brother shifting mental gears.

"You really rented the old Buckley place for an entire month?" Rafe asked after a while.

"Yes."

"Got to admit, it does seem a little uncharacteristic for you to do something like that. You think maybe Lillian is right? You burned out or something?"

"Madisons don't do burnout. You ever heard of a Madison burning out?"

Rafe thought about that. "No. Heard of one or two exploding. Couple have imploded. Of course you've got your occasional cases of spontaneous combustion in the family. But never heard of any burnout."

"Right."

"What's with you and Lillian, anyway?"

"What makes you think there's anything between us?"

"I'll be the first to admit that I'm not the most sensitive, intuitive, perceptive guy around."

"Course not. You're a Madison."

"But even I could see that every time you looked at Lillian tonight you had the same expression you get when you've got a major deal going down at Madison Commercial."

"Like you said, you're not real sensitive, intuitive, or perceptive."

"I'm not real stupid, either," Rafe reminded him. "I've never seen that particular look when you were with any other woman."

"Lillian's not a business deal."

"Hold on to that thought, because I've got a hunch that if you treat her like you would an M.C. investment you're gonna have some serious problems."

Gabe looked at Winston. "My brother, the advice columnist."

Winston cocked his head and looked intelligent. It was an expression he did very well.

Rafe contemplated the empty drive. "Always figured you'd go off the rails someday."

"Being a Madison and all."

"Probably inevitable. Question of genetic destiny or something. You know, I'm a little sorry Hannah and Winston and I are leaving town tomorrow. Would have been interesting to see it."

"What?"

"The train wreck."

# chapter 5

The storm came and went during the night. The morning dawned bright and mild for the time of year. The temperature was somewhere in the high fifties.

Gabe came to a halt at the top of the small bluff and looked down into Dead Hand Cove. The tide was out, exposing the five finger-shaped rocks that had given the cove its name. There were a number of dark holes and voids in the base of the cliffs. They marked a series of small caverns and caves that nature had punched into the rock.

He saw Lillian perched on one of the carelessly strewn boulders near the water's edge. The winter sun gleamed on her dark hair. The keen edge of expectation that shafted through him heightened all his senses. He felt the now-familiar tightness in his lower body.

She wore a pair of snug black leggings that emphasized the neat curve of her calves and trim ankles. The neckline of an orange-gold sweater was visible above the collar of a scarlet jacket. Her hair was coiled into a knot at the back of her head.

She was bent intently over an open sketchbook propped on her knees.

Last night at Rafe and Hannah's he had learned the terrible truth. She wasn't just an arty type. She was a for real artist.

He watched the deft, economical movements of her hand as she worked on the drawing. There was a supple, controlled grace in the way she wielded the pencil that fascinated him. A sorceress at work on a magical spell.

A gull screeched overhead, breaking the trance that held him still at the top of the short cliff.

He pulled the collar of his black-and-tan jacket up around his ears and went down the pebbled path, moving quickly, perversely eager to get closer to his own doom. Probably a Madison thing, he thought.

She became aware of his presence when he reached the rocky patch of ground that formed the tiny sliver of beach. Lillian looked up quickly, turning her head to watch him. She seemed to go very still there on the rock. Sorceress caught in the act. He could sense the cool caution in her.

Maybe she was right to be wary of him. He sure as hell didn't understand what was happening here, either. He forced himself to move more slowly as he neared her perch, trying for the laid-back, easygoing, nonthreatening look.

"How long were you standing up there spying on me?" she asked.

"You sure know how to make a man feel welcome."

"I thought I was alone. You startled me."

"Sorry. I usually work out in the mornings. There's no

gym in the vicinity so I thought I'd take a long walk, instead."

"You just decided to walk in this direction?"

He smiled. "Is it me or do you always wake up in this charming mood?"

She hesitated and then returned his smile. "My turn to apologize. I shouldn't have snapped at you. I've been feeling a little edgy lately."

"What a coincidence. So have I."

"I'm not surprised." She looked wise and all-knowing. "Probably the burnout."

"You've got me all analyzed and diagnosed, don't you?" He lowered himself onto a nearby rock. "Are you on edge because I'm here in Eclipse Bay?"

"No," she said.

"Liar."

She shot him an irritated look. "It's the truth. I'm on edge for a lot of reasons that have nothing to do with you."

"Such as?"

"You want a list?"

"Let's hear it."

Her mouth firmed. "Well, let's see. There's the fact that I'm not currently employed because I just closed my business."

"Your own fault."

"Thank you for reminding me. I'm also nervous about how well my show at the gallery will be received."

He couldn't think of anything to say to that so he let it go.

"Also, I had a couple of rather unpleasant scenes before I left Portland. I've been worrying about them. Wondering if I handled them properly."

"What kind of scenes?"

She looked out toward the five finger rocks. "Anderson came to see me. He did not take it well when I told him I didn't want to work on his book."

"I'll bet he didn't. Did you mention that you had seen him in his red underwear?"

"Of course not."

"Just as well. I wouldn't worry too much about that scene, if I were you. What was the other one?"

"A man named Campbell Witley stopped me on the street to tell me that I had no business messing around in other people's lives."

Something in the tone of her voice made him look at her more closely. "This Witley guy scared you?"

She hesitated. "Maybe. A little."

"Who is he?"

"The disgruntled ex-boyfriend of one of my clients. He didn't like the fact that I had matched her with someone else, even though it's obvious that Witley and Heather were not meant for each other."

He searched her face. "Did he threaten you?"

"No."

"I'll have him checked out." He reached for the cell phone in the pocket of his jacket. "Madison Commercial keeps an investigation agency on retainer."

"Thanks, but that's not necessary. I had Townsend Investigations run a quick background check. Witley has no history of violence or abuse."

"You're sure?"

"Yes. It's okay, really. Nella Townsend knows what she's doing. The guy was just mad. I think what bothered me the most is that he had a point."

"Bullshit."

"He accused me of messing around with people's lives and that's exactly what I did. As a professional matchmaker I assumed a massive responsibility. What if I had made a terrible mistake? I could have seriously impacted someone's future negatively."

"Stop beating yourself up over this. You were a consultant. People paid you for advice. You gave it. They made their own decisions. A simple business transaction. You have absolutely no reason to feel guilty."

She was silent for a moment, considering his words. Then her voice brightened.

"You do have a way of boiling things down to the bare essence, Madison."

"One of the things I'm good at." He leaned a little to get a look at the drawing on her lap. "Can I see what you're working on there?"

She handed the sketchpad to him without comment.

He examined the drawing for a while and discovered that the longer he studied it, the more he wanted to look at it.

It was a picture of Dead Hand Cove but it was the cove as he had never really seen it, at least not consciously. There was a riveting intensity about Lillian's rendering of this small chunk of nature—a dark promise of potent, primordial power. It called to something deep within him—made him aware that he was forever linked on the cellular level to these wild forces of life.

Damn. All that in a simple sketch. It was worse than he had thought. She was good. Very, very good.

"One thing's for sure," he said finally. "You were wasting your time in the matchmaking business. You're an artist, all right. This is your calling."

"Doesn't mean my work will sell," she said.

"No." He handed the sketchpad back to her. "It also doesn't change the fact that this is what you were born to do. Can I ask you a question?"

"What is it?"

"Could you stop doing your art?"

"Stop? You mean, just call it quits?"

"Say someone came along and said he'd give you a million bucks if you agreed to never draw or paint again. Could you take the money and keep your promise?"

"No." She looked down at the sketch. "Sooner or later, I'd have to go back to it. It's a compulsion, not a choice."

"That's what I figured." He exhaled deeply. "So you'll keep doing it, even if you have to get another day job."

"Yes."

"You're an artist."

"Yes," she said again. "I guess so."

She sounded a little startled. Thoughtful. As if he had surprised her.

He listened to the seawater tumble in the cove. The tide was returning. Soon only the tips of the fingers would be visible.

"Madison Commercial must have been like that for you all these years," Lillian said slowly. "A compulsion. Something you had to do."

"Maybe."

"Why?"

"Who knows?" He picked up a small stone and sent it spinning out into the foaming water. "Maybe I just wanted to prove that a Madison could do what you Hartes seemed to do so well."

"What's that?"

"Not screw up."

She looked toward the point where the stone had disappeared into the water. "Are you telling me that everything you've accomplished, all your success, happened just because you felt a sense of competition with my family?"

He shrugged. "That was part of it. At least at first. I grew up knowing that you Hartes were smart enough not to make the mistakes we Madisons have always been so good at. Your businesses prosper. Your families are solid. Hell, your parents were actually married. What a concept."

She did not respond to that. There was no need. They both knew each other's family histories as well as they knew their own. His father, Sinclair, had been a sculptor with a passion for his art and his model, Natalie. Gabe and Rafe had been the result of that union.

The relationship between his parents had lived up to the expectations of everyone familiar with the Madison clan. The long-running affair had been fiery and tempestuous. Sinclair had never seen any reason to burden himself with the petty strings of marriage. Gabe was pretty sure his parents had loved each other in their own stormy fashion, but family life had not been what anyone could call stable, let alone normal.

He and Rafe had each learned to cope in their own ways with their erratic, eccentric, larger-than-life father and their beautiful, temperamental mother. Rafe had chosen to pretend to himself and everyone else that he did not give a damn about his own future. "Live for the moment" had been his motto, at least until he'd come within a hair's breadth of getting himself arrested for murder.

Gabe knew that he, on the other hand, had probably gone to the other extreme. Control and a sense of order had been his bulwarks against the shifting tides of fortune and emotion that had roiled his childhood. In putting together Madison Commercial he had done everything he could to carve his own future out of granite.

"What's the rest?" Lillian asked.

"The rest?"

"I don't believe you could have accomplished so much just because you were inspired by a sense of competition with my family."

He shook off the brooding sensation that had settled around him like an old, well-worn coat. "I'm not the introspective type."

"Oh, yes that's right. How could I forget? You made that fact very clear on the questionnaire that you filled out for Private Arrangements."

"Probably."

"As I recall," she continued, "on the portion of the form reserved for 'Other Comments,' you wrote that you considered yourself pragmatic and realistic by nature. You instructed me not to waste your valuable time with any elitist academics or fuzzy-brained New Age thinkers."

"Uh-huh."

Lillian closed the sketchpad with a snap. "You also noted that you did not want to be matched with what you called *arty types.*"

*Well, hell.*

"Correct me if I'm wrong," Lillian said, "but I got the impression that the 'other comments' section of the questionnaire was one of the few places on the form where you were actually more or less truthful in your responses. Or did you shade those answers, too?"

Definitely time to change the subject.

"You got anything to eat back in your cottage?" he asked.

She blinked and refocused. "You're hungry?"

"Starving. I woke up this morning and realized I didn't have any coffee in the house. Nothing to eat, either. Forgot to stop at a grocery store last night."

"You expect me to feed you breakfast?"

"Why not? Be the neighborly thing to do. If I had coffee and toast and maybe some peanut butter, I'd invite you to my place."

"Peanut butter?"

"Be amazed at what you can do with peanut butter."

"I see. Well, sorry to disappoint you, but I didn't pick up anything yesterday, either. I'm planning to drive into town in a few minutes to get something from that bakery Rafe raved about last night."

"Incandescent Body?" He got to his feet. "Good idea. My brother knows food."

She was not sure why she had allowed herself to get talked into accompanying Gabe into town. Something to do with the odd mood she was in, no doubt. But when she walked through the doors of the bakery a short time later, the heavenly fragrance of freshly baked bread quickly resolved any doubts about her decision. She suddenly realized that she was ravenous.

No one knew much about the group of New Age types who had moved into town a year ago and opened Incandescent Body near the pier. They dressed in long, colorful robes, wore a lot of jewelry that appeared to have been inspired by ancient Egyptian and Roman artifacts, and seemed a little too serene to be real. They called themselves Heralds of Future History.

The initial reaction of the town folk had been one of acute disgust and, in some quarters, outright alarm, according to Rafe and Hannah. The town council had expressed deep concerns about the possibility that Eclipse Bay had a genuine wacko cult in its midst. The *Eclipse Bay Journal* had run an editorial that had advised the authorities to keep a close watch on the new crowd.

But in a town in which the only bakery had been closed for nearly three years, the Heralds of Future History soon proved to possess one major redeeming feature. They baked like angels.

It was going on ten o'clock when Lillian and Gabe arrived. A number of people were sprinkled around the handful of tables. The customers were primarily a mix of local residents, a couple of rare winter tourists, and some young people in denim and khaki who looked like students from Chamberlain College.

The heads of the locals swiveled immediately toward the door when Lillian walked in with Gabe on her heels. Lillian could guess their thoughts. Hannah and Rafe's marriage a few months ago had thrilled and fascinated the entire town. And now here was another Harte woman with a Madison male. Would wonders never cease?

"Maybe this wasn't such a good idea," she whispered to Gabe.

"Don't be ridiculous." He came to a halt at the counter and studied the artfully arranged breakfast pastries behind the glass. "The only other place open at this hour is the Total Eclipse. You don't want to eat breakfast there, trust me."

"Good point. Any restaurant that uses the motto 'Where the sun don't shine' probably isn't a terrific breakfast spot."

"Right. Besides, those corn bread muffins look incredible. I'm going to have two. What do you want?"

"People are staring at us."

"Yeah?" He glanced around curiously, nodded civilly at the people he recognized and then turned back to the croissant display. "So what? You're a Harte. I'm a Madison. Put the two together in this town and you're bound to get a few stares."

"It doesn't bother you?"

"Nope."

"Of course, a few stares don't bother you," she muttered. "You're a Madison."

"You got that right."

He approached the middle-aged woman dressed in a long, pale robe standing behind the counter. She wore a white scarf over her graying hair and a pristine white apron. A crescent-shaped amulet hung from a chain around her neck.

"May the light of future history be with you," she said politely.

"Thanks," Gabe said. "Same to you. I'll have a couple of those corn bread muffins and a cup of coffee, please." He looked over his shoulder. "Decided what you want, Lillian?"

She hurried forward. "A croissant, please. And green tea."

"For here or to go?" the woman asked.

"For here," Gabe said.

"Say, I recognize those voices," boomed a whiskey-and-cigar voice from the other side of a curtained doorway.

Lillian suppressed a small groan and summoned up a smile for the husky, robust woman dressed in military fatigues and boots who appeared in the opening. Arizona Snow had long since passed the age that officially placed her in the senior citizen category but she had enough energy for a far younger person. She also had a cause.

"Well, now, I call this perfect timing," Arizona Snow said with evident satisfaction.

"Morning, A.Z." Gabe said. "How's the conspiracy business these days?"

"Those bastards up at the institute laid low for a while after your brother and Hannah managed to put a spoke in their wheel, but things are heating up again." Arizona beamed at Lillian. "Good to see you back in town."

"Nice to see you, too," Lillian said. She waved a hand to indicate the bakery. "What are you doing here?"

"Regular weekly briefing with the Heralds." Arizona lowered her voice to what she no doubt thought was a confidential level. "Instituted the routine a couple of months ago after I got to know 'em better and discovered that they're not naïve dupes of the agency like most everyone else around these parts. They understand what's happenin'."

"Glad someone does," Gabe said.

Arizona leaned a little farther out the doorway, swept the outer room with a quick glance and then motioned to Lillian and Gabe. "Come on back. I'll bring you up to date, too."

"Uh, that's okay, Arizona," Lillian said hastily. "We're a little busy this morning. Aren't we, Gabe?"

"Don't know about you." Gabe put some money down on the counter. "But I'm in no rush."

"You're *not*?" In her wildest flights of imagination she would never have envisioned him willingly going down the rabbit hole into the alternate universe that was Arizona Snow's world.

He glanced at her, brows raised. "What?" he asked amused.

"Don't you, uh, have some telecommuting to do?" she asked weakly.

"It'll keep."

Arizona gave Lillian a knowing look, squinting slightly. "Hannah and Rafe weren't real interested in what was going on up at the institute, either, until it was damn near too late."

Lillian knew when she was beaten. She tried and failed

to come up with an excuse but nothing came to mind. The bottom line was that the Hartes and the Madisons owed Arizona Snow. She was more than a little eccentric but a few months ago it had been her meticulously kept logbooks that had provided the clues Rafe and Hannah had needed to identify a murderer.

"I suppose we can stay for a few minutes," Lillian said.

"Forewarned is forearmed." Arizona held the curtain aside.

"Can't argue with that," Gabe said. He picked up his muffins and coffee and went around the counter.

Lillian reluctantly collected her croissant and tea and trailed after him.

Arizona let the curtain fall behind them. Lillian stopped at the sight of the three men and two women grouped around a large, floured worktable. All were dressed in Herald-style attire, complete with robes and ancient-looking jewelry. Their ages were varied. The youngest was a man whose long hair was neatly bound up in a white sanitary cap. Lillian thought he was probably in his mid-twenties. The oldest was a woman with silver hair and a matronly figure. A tall man with a shaved head and a stately air appeared to be the authority figure in the group.

The Heralds regarded Lillian and Gabe with serenely polite expressions.

Arizona took up a position at the head of the table and fixed everyone in turn with a steely look.

"Gabe, Lillian, meet Photon, Rainbow, Daybreak, Dawn, and Beacon." She gave the Heralds a pointed look. "Gabe and Lillian are friends of mine. Take it from me, you can trust 'em. Fact is, in this town, you can trust anyone with the last name of Harte or Madison."

Lillian nodded, determined to be polite. "Good morning."

Gabe inclined his head in an easy greeting. He set his mug down on a nearby table and took a bite of one of the muffins on his plate.

"Great corn bread," he said.

Photon, the man with the shaved head who seemed to be in charge, said, "Thank you. We do our best to introduce the light of future history into all our products. But we're only human. Sometimes our negative thoughts get into the dough in spite of our best efforts."

"Light's your secret ingredient, huh?" Gabe picked up the remaining portion of the muffin. "Works for me." He took another bite.

Arizona picked up a large rolling pin and rapped it smartly on the table to get everyone's attention.

"Enough with the chitchat," she said. "Got a briefing to get through here. Not like we have time to waste. The future of this town, not to mention the whole country, is hanging in the balance."

Everyone obediently moved a little closer to the table.

Arizona cleared her throat loudly.

"Now, then, as I was sayin' before I heard Lillian and Gabe out front, I've put the evidence together and it's become real clear why they're building the new wing at the institute. Official word, of course, is that it's supposed to be additional office and conference space." She broke off to give everyone at the table a meaningful look. "But I think everyone here knows that's just another one of their lies."

Lillian studied the map spread out on the table. It showed the hillside above town where the Eclipse Bay Policy Studies Institute was located. A handful of photos that looked as if they had been snapped with a long-range lens were scattered around the edges. They were pictures of what was obviously a construction zone at the institute. She could make out a truck and something that looked like electrical equipment.

Gabe leaned over the photos. "Good long-range recon shots, A.Z."

"Thanks." A.Z. allowed herself a proud smile. "Took 'em with my new surveillance camera. A genuine VPX 5000. Latest model. Replaces the old 4000 series. Telephoto lens, sniper grip shutter release trigger. Half a dozen filters for day and night photo work. And a real nice leather carrying case."

"I hate to sound like just another naïve, innocent dupe," Lillian said, "but what makes you think they aren't adding office and conference space?"

"Number of factors." Arizona motioned toward the map with the rolling pin. "First, increased volume of traffic in this sector during the past six months."

"Are we talking out-of-town traffic?" Gabe asked.

"We are, for sure," Arizona said.

"Huh." Gabe took another bite of the muffin. "That's suspicious, all right."

"For heaven's sake," said Lillian. "Everyone knows the institute has been growing rapidly for some time now. They give seminars, receptions, and political theory retreats on a regular basis. In addition, they provided the springboard for Trevor Thornley's campaign. It's only natural that there would be a lot of traffic."

Arizona squinted. "Cover, is what it is. All that political think-tank stuff and those seminars and such make good camouflage for concealing what's really goin' on up there. Furthermore, the traffic volume didn't fall off for long after Thornley pulled out of the campaign. No sir.

There was a brief lull, but by the end of November, there were more vehicles than ever going in and out of there."

"Sounds serious, all right," Gabe concurred. "What other factors besides increased traffic point to a clandestine operation?"

"Oh, geez," Lillian muttered. No one paid any attention.

"Most of the construction work on the new wing is being done by contractors who aren't from around here," Arizona said ominously.

"Heard something about that." Gabe examined another photo. "My brother said the Willis brothers didn't get a chunk of the construction action."

"No, they didn't and that tells us a lot, doesn't it?" Arizona said.

"Uh, what, exactly, does it tell us?" Lillian asked cautiously.

"That they didn't want no one from around here getting a close look at what's going on up there," Arizona announced. "That's what it tells us."

"Probably knew the Willis brothers couldn't be bribed to keep their mouths shut if they saw something suspicious," Gabe said. "Everyone knows how Walter and Torrance talk."

Lillian had an urge to stomp hard on the toe of his large running shoe. She managed, with an effort, to resist.

"Stands to reason they would bring in outside contractors when you think about it," she said quickly. "Hannah and Rafe have been keeping the Willis brothers busy for months turning Dreamscape into an inn. They wouldn't have had time to work on the new wing."

They all ignored her. So much for being the voice of reason, she thought.

"Volume of overnight and regular freight deliveries has picked up recently, too," Arizona droned on. "I staked out the loading dock for a couple of days. Took a whole series of shots with the VPX 5000. Amazing how much equipment and material is being moved into that place."

"High-tech stuff?" Gabe asked.

"You bet. Tons of it."

Gabe looked up from the photos. "What about heavy-duty heating, ventilation, and air-conditioning equipment?"

Lillian glared at him. He paid no attention. He was really getting into this, she realized with a shock. Enjoying himself.

Arizona gave him an approving look. "They started unloading HVAC crates last week. Got 'em on film."

Gabe shook his head. "Not good."

The Heralds murmured among themselves, obviously agreeing with that conclusion.

"What do you mean, it's not a good sign?" Lillian knew her voice was rising but there was nothing she could do about it. She was getting desperate. "Any large, modern business structure needs a lot of computers and commercial-grade heating and air-conditioning equipment."

This time she was totally ignored.

"I'd estimate their security level as Class Three at the moment," Arizona said. "Fences have gone up around the construction perimeter."

"Perfectly normal," Lillian said. "The last thing the institute would want is a lawsuit filed by someone who happened to trip and fall over a pile of pipes."

"Guards on the premises?" Gabe asked.

"Yep. Disguised as low-profile security, though," Arizona said. "Didn't see any weapons. Probably knew that would attract too much attention in a small town like this where there's not much of a crime problem. Expect they'll wait until after the big move before they go to Class Two status and arm the guards."

Lillian clutched her untouched croissant. "What are you talking about? What big move?"

"We all know what's happening up there," Arizona said. "Problem is, we've got no hard evidence yet. I'm stepping up my surveillance work, though. I'll try to get us some pictures that we can take to the media."

"You're a true hero, Arizona." Photon looked at her with unconcealed admiration. "If it hadn't been for you, we wouldn't have had a clue. Who knows how long Project Transfer would have gone undetected?"

Lillian was amazed to see Arizona turn pink.

"Just doin' my duty."

"It's people like you who keep this country safe for democracy," Gabe said.

"Excuse me." Lillian held up her hand. "As the sole representative of the naïve, innocent dupes of Eclipse Bay, I would like to ask a question."

"Go right ahead," Arizona said.

"What, precisely, do you think is going on up at the institute, A.Z.? What is this Project Transfer you mentioned?"

Arizona made a *tut-tut* sound.

The Heralds shook their heads sadly at Lillian's failure to grasp the obvious.

Out of the corner of her eye she saw Gabe hide a quick grin behind his coffee mug.

"Thought it was as plain as the white lines out on the highway," Arizona said. "The secret gov'mint agency in charge of Roswell and the Area 51 facility has decided it's attracting too much attention. The Internet was what did 'em in, I reckon. After those satellite images of the old test site went online, they knew they had a real problem. That's probably when they started making plans."

Gabe nodded knowingly. "Had a feeling those mysterious fires in New Mexico a while back weren't accidental."

"You got that right," Arizona said. "No such thing as an accident where this bunch is concerned."

"Plans to do *what*?" Lillian demanded.

Arizona rocked back and forth in her boots and looked grim. "Pretty clear they're gonna transfer the bodies of those extraterrestrials they've got in deep freeze in Area 51 along with the remains of their spaceship and all that alien technology right here to Eclipse Bay."

# chapter 6

Gabe got into the passenger side of Lillian's car and closed the door. "Makes sense when you think about it."

"What makes sense?" Lillian turned the key in the ignition and checked the rearview mirror.

"Transferring those frozen aliens and their UFO equipment here. Who'd ever think to look for them in Eclipse Bay?"

"I *knew* it, you were enjoying yourself back there, weren't you? You were actually encouraging A.Z. in her idiotic conspiracy theories."

"Not like anything I said would have *discouraged* her. Everyone knows she lives in her own parallel universe."

"Doesn't it worry you that she's glommed onto the Heralds?" Lillian snapped the car's gearshift into reverse and backed out of the parking space. "It was one thing when she was the lone conspiracy theorist in town. But now she's got a bunch of enthusiastic assistants."

"You're right," Gabe intoned darkly. "I don't like the sound of this."

"Oh, for pity's sake." She turned the wheel and drove out of the parking lot. "You're determined to make a joke out of it, aren't you?"

"Look at it from my point of view."

"What is that?"

"Pondering the possibility that some secret gov'mint agency is getting ready to transfer dead space aliens and their technology to Eclipse Bay makes an interesting change."

"Change from what?"

"From thinking about that sixth date you owe me."

"Hmm." She concentrated on the curving sweep of Bayview Drive. "Hadn't thought of that. Dare I hope that you might sign up with A.Z.'s happy little band of conspiracy buffs and forget about trying to make me fulfill the terms of that contract you signed with Private Arrangements?"

"Well, no. Thing is, I never forget about getting what I paid for."

She gripped the wheel. "Gabe, I told you, I'd refund your money."

"It's not the money."

"Hah. With you, it's the money. You've made that very clear from the start. I've never known anyone as paranoid about being married for his money as you are."

"I am not paranoid."

"The heck you aren't. On this particular subject, you're as bad as A.Z. is when it comes to secret government conspiracies."

He settled deeper into the seat and looked out over the gray waters of the bay.

"I'm not that bad," he said.

The dry, sardonic amusement that had infused his voice a moment ago was gone now. She shot him a quick glance,

trying to read the shift in his mood. But his head was
turned away from her. She could discern nothing from
the hard angles of his profile.

She turned off the main road a short time later and went
down the narrow, rutted lane that led to the old Buckley
place. The weathered cottage was hunkered down on a
windswept bluff overlooking a rocky stretch of beach. It
looked as if it had not been lived in for a long time. The
trees grew right up to the edge of the tiny yard. The blinds
in the windows were yellowed with age. The porch listed
a little to the right. The whole structure was badly in need
of a coat of paint.

The only sign of life was Gabe's gleaming Jaguar
parked in the drive.

She brought her compact to a halt in front of the sagging porch.

"Thanks for the lift into town." Gabe stirred and unfastened his seat belt.

"You're welcome."

He opened the car door and paused, gazing straight
ahead through the windshield.

"You really think I'm a full-blown paranoid?" he asked
quietly.

This was not good. No doubt about it, Gabe was sinking deeper into a very strange mood.

"Let's just say I think you're a little overly concerned
about the issue of being married for your money," she
said gently.

"Overly concerned."

"That's how I would characterize it, yes."

"And you're not."

"Not what?"

"Paranoid. About being married because of your connection to Harte Investments."

She took a deep breath. "I won't say that I don't think about the possibility once in a while. As I told you, I have dated a few men who gave me some cause for concern. But I try to employ my common sense in the matter. I don't obsess on the idea that every man I meet is only interested in me because of my family's company."

"Can't help noticing that you still haven't married, though."

She felt her jaw tense. "The fact that I'm still single has nothing to do with being secretly paranoid about being married for my inheritance."

"So, why are you still single?"

She frowned. "Why do you care?"

"Sorry. None of my business." He pushed the door open and got out. "See you later."

"Gabe?"

"Yeah?" He paused and leaned slightly to look at her.

"Are you, you know, okay?"

"Sure. I'm swell."

"What are you going to do today?"

"Don't know. Haven't decided. Maybe take another walk on the beach. Check my e-mail. Do some research." He paused. "What are *you* going to do?"

"Paint. That's why I came here."

"Right." He made to close the door.

She hesitated, trying to resist the impulse that had just struck her. She failed.

"Gabe, wait a second."

"What now?"

This was stupid, she thought. Just because Hannah was married to Rafe, it did not follow that she herself had to assume any responsibility for members of the Madison family. Gabe was perfectly capable of taking care of himself. If she had any sense she would keep her mouth shut.

But she could not get past the feeling that something was not as it should be with Gabe. The way he had tried to amuse himself with Arizona's conspiracy theories and now this swing to another, darker mood did not seem right. He was definitely not in a good place.

Burnout was a form of depression, she reminded herself.

"What about dinner?" she asked before she could give herself any more time to think.

"What about it?"

"I'm going to drive back into town later this afternoon to do some serious grocery shopping. If you don't have any plans for tonight, I could pick up something and bring it over here. We can fix it together."

"I'm no gourmet chef like Rafe," he warned.

"Few people can cook as well as Rafe, but I can find my way around a kitchen. What about it? You interested? Or do you have other plans?"

"One thing I do not have is other plans," he said. "By the way, if you're going to the grocery store, could you pick up some peanut butter?"

"I suppose so."

"Make it chunky style. See you for dinner."

He closed the car door with a solid-sounding *kerchunk*, went up the steps and disappeared into the lonely-looking house before she could figure out how to climb back out of the hole she had just dug for herself.

He heard the sound of a car's engine in the driveway just as the early winter twilight descended. A gut-deep sense of pleasurable anticipation rippled through him. He pow-

ered down the laptop computer, closed the lid and got to
his feet.

He peered out the window, checking the weather. He
could almost feel the weight of the heavy clouds moving in off the ocean. The storm would hit later tonight.

Perfect timing.

He crossed the threadbare carpet, opened the front door
and went out onto the porch. The little rush of excitement faded at the sight of the vehicle coming toward him.
It was a late-model Mercedes. Not Lillian's Honda.

The Mercedes halted in front of the steps. The door on
the driver's side opened. An attractive, athletic-looking
woman with stylishly cut honey-brown hair got out. She
wore a pair of expensively tailored trousers and a pale
silk shirt. Silver gleamed discreetly in her ears. A designer
scarf in a subdued mauve print framed her long neck.

Marilyn Thornley hadn't changed much since she had
been Marilyn Caldwell, he thought. If anything, she had
become more striking and more self-confident with the
years. There was an invisible aura of authority and importance about her. When she walked into a room, you
knew it.

She saw him watching her from the porch and gave
him a glowing smile.

He did not take the smile personally. Marilyn always
glowed like this whenever they occasionally encountered
each other at one of the social events they both were
obliged to attend. As Rafe had reminded him, he had a
lot of what politicians loved most. Money. Marilyn had
been a tireless fund-raiser for Trevor Thornley for years.
Now she was firing up her own campaign.

Under the circumstances, he was not real surprised to
see her, he thought.

"Gabe." She came around the front of the Mercedes

with long, purposeful strides. "I heard you were in town for a while."

She was moving more quickly now, coming up the steps, heading toward him.

Belatedly he realized her intention and took a step back. But he didn't move fast enough. She had her arms around his neck, her face tilted for a welcoming kiss before he could dodge. Reflexively, he turned his head at the last instant. Her lips grazed his jaw.

The mouth thing caught him off guard. It was the first time she'd pulled that stunt. But then, this was the first time he'd seen her since she and Thornley had announced their intention to divorce.

She released him, giving no indication that she had even noticed his small act of avoidance. Politicians had thick skins.

"You look wonderful," she said.

"You're looking great yourself."

She gave him an arch look. "You mean for a woman whose husband humiliated her by withdrawing from a senatorial campaign and who is in the midst of a nasty divorce?"

"You've had a busy year."

"You can say that again. Talk about stress. Life's been a little rough lately." She opened the front door of the house. "Come on, let's go inside. It's cold out here. Another storm's coming."

He checked his watch. "I've got company scheduled to arrive at any minute."

"Lillian Harte?"

*Should have known,* he thought.

Marilyn gave a throaty laugh. "Don't look so surprised. It's all over town that you walked into Incandescent Body bakery with her first thing this morning."

"It wasn't first thing."

"How serious is it? You two sleeping together?"

The ease with which she asked such a personal question was a forcible reminder of just how personal their own relationship had once been. He found himself wanting to protect Lillian from some vague menace that he could not quite define. Or maybe it was just the residual effect of Mitchell's notion of early-childhood education kicking in. Madison men did not kiss and tell. Mitchell had drummed that basic principle of proper masculine behavior into Rafe and Gabe early in life.

Besides, he had nothing to kiss and tell about, Gabe reminded himself.

"No," he said. "We just happened to come out here to the coast at the same time. Found ourselves at loose ends today. We both wanted some company for breakfast. No big deal."

Marilyn winked. "Don't worry, I won't cramp your style. I just wanted to say hello to an old friend."

She swept through the door of the cottage.

He glanced once more back along the drive. There was no sign of Lillian's car. Reluctantly he followed Marilyn into the small house.

"Good lord, couldn't you find a better rental?" Marilyn surveyed the dilapidated interior with a grimace. "Not exactly your style, is it?"

"Until Rafe and Hannah get Dreamscape open there isn't a lot of high-end rental housing available around Eclipse Bay. You know that as well as I do. It was either here or my grandfather's house." He allowed the door to close slowly behind him. "Knew that wouldn't work so I picked this place. It's got everything I need."

"Like what?"

"Privacy."

"Okay, I get the point. You've got a hot date with Lillian Harte and I'm in the way." She settled on the arm of the shabby sofa with a regal grace. "I won't stay long, I promise. I need to talk to you, Gabe."

He did not sit down. He didn't want to encourage her. Instead, he propped one shoulder against the wall and folded his arms. "What's this all about, Marilyn?"

"Do I have to have a special reason? You and I go back a long way. We have a history."

"History was never my best subject. I was a business major in college, remember?"

"I hear you signed up with Lillian's matchmaking agency."

"Who told you that?"

"Carole Rhoades. I got to know her when she did a little fund-raising for Trevor at her law firm last year."

He identified the name immediately. Carole Rhoades was one of the five women Lillian had matched with him.

"Portland sure is a small town in some ways, isn't it?" he said. "Almost as small as Eclipse Bay."

"It's not the size of the town, it's the size of the universe in which you move." She swung one long leg. "People who run companies like Madison Commercial tend to circulate in certain limited spheres."

"I can see I need to get out more. Broaden my horizons."

She chuckled. "I hear the date with Carole was a bust."

"And here I thought we'd had a very pleasant evening."

"She said she was home by ten o'clock and you didn't even try to invite yourself in for a nightcap. She said it was obvious that you would much rather have been at your desk."

"Damn. Women talk about stuff like that?"

"Of course they do."

"I'll have to keep that in mind." He turned his wrist slightly to check his watch. "You want to tell me why you're here?"

Her smile stayed in place but he thought he saw it tighten a notch or two.

"You make it sound as though the only thing that might bring me here is business."

"Whenever we've run into each other during the past few years, you've usually hit me up for a campaign donation for Trevor."

"Which you have always declined to give."

"Madisons aren't real big on political campaign contributions."

"I realize that you never supported Trevor but things have changed—"

A brisk knock on the back door interrupted her before she could finish the sentence.

Gabe straightened away from the wall. "Looks like my guest decided to walk instead of drive this evening."

He went through the ancient kitchen and opened the back door.

Lillian stood inside the glass-enclosed rear porch, a large, well-stuffed grocery bag in her arms. She wore the hooded iridescent rain cloak he'd seen in Portland, although it had not yet begun to rain. The cloak was unfastened, revealing the black turtleneck and black trousers she had on underneath. The tunic-length top was slashed with a lightning bolt of intense turquoise.

"I thought you were going to drive over," he said.

"Walking seemed faster."

"It's almost dark."

"So what? This is Eclipse Bay, not the big bad city."

"Listen, tough lady, you ought to know better than to

run around an unlit, sparsely inhabited stretch of coast-
line after dark."

"You want to help me with this grocery sack or would
you rather stand there and lecture me for a while?"

"Give me the damn sack."

"My, you're in a swell mood tonight."

"Uninvited company." He took the sack from her and
stood back. "Marilyn Thornley. She won't be staying
long."

"That's good, because I didn't bring enough food for
three."

The weight of the grocery sack belied that claim, but
he did not argue the point. He set it on the counter without comment.

Marilyn appeared in the kitchen doorway. She gave
Lillian the same glowing grin she'd used on Gabe.

"Lillian. It's been ages. Good to see you again."

"Hello, Marilyn. Been a while," she responded sweetly.

"I didn't mean to intrude on your little dinner party,"
Marilyn said. "I heard Gabe was in town. Thought I'd
stop in and say hello."

"Doing a little fund-raising?" Lillian asked smoothly.
"Rumor has it that you're going into politics on your own,
now that Trevor is no longer in the picture."

There was a short, brittle silence during which neither
woman's smile faltered.

"Gabe and I were just talking about how fast word
travels in this town," Marilyn said with a slight edge on
her voice.

"I ran into Pamela McCallister at Fulton's Supermarket this afternoon," Lillian said. "Her husband, Brad, is
on the faculty at Chamberlain but he has a joint appointment at the institute. He says you've already got your

campaign staff organized and that you've put Claire
Jensen in charge."

"You know Claire?"

"Yes. I haven't seen much of her in recent years but
we worked together at a local restaurant one summer when
we were both in college. She always said she wanted to
go into politics."

"Claire worked very hard on Trevor's staff. She's had
a lot of experience. I think she's ready to head up a campaign."

"I hear you've got your sites on a seat in the U.S. Senate."

There was another brittle pause. Gabe helped Lillian
with her rain cloak.

"Yes," Marilyn said.

"Expensive," Lillian murmured.

"Yes," Marilyn said again. "Politics is an expensive
pursuit."

Lillian went to the counter, reached into the grocery
sack and removed a plastic bag containing a head of dark-
green broccoli. "Probably not a lot of money left over
after Trevor bowed out of the race last fall."

"No."

"The Thornley campaign did a lot of media, as well.
The television commercials must have cost a fortune."

"You're right," Marilyn said in a low voice. "The ads
wiped out most of the war chest. We knew going in that
they would be expensive, but you can't win elections without television." She paused. "There were also some additional, unplanned expenses toward the end."

The sudden anger in her voice made both Gabe and
Lillian look at her.

"We were so close. So damned close," Marilyn said
bitterly.

"I'm sorry it all fell apart," Lillian said quietly. "I know it must have been a blow."

"You don't have to pretend that you don't know what happened," Marilyn said. "I'm sure you heard the rumors about the videos."

Gabe exchanged a glance with Lillian. They were both aware of the story behind the videos that had disappeared when the former editor of the *Eclipse Bay Journal* had been arrested a few months ago. The missing films purported to show Trevor Thornley cavorting in high heels and ladies' undergarments.

"I heard that those tapes, assuming they ever actually existed, were destroyed," Gabe said neutrally. "No one I know has ever seen them."

"That bastard, Jed Steadman, lied about having destroyed them without looking at them. He made copies." Marilyn's voice roughened with tightly controlled rage. "He blackmailed Trevor from jail. Said he needed the money for his trial."

Gabe exhaled slowly. "That was the unexpected additional campaign expense you mentioned? Blackmail payments to Jed Steadman?"

"Steadman was too smart to approach me," Marilyn said. "He contacted Trevor. And that idiot *paid* him off. I couldn't believe it. When I discovered that he was actually making blackmail payments I knew the campaign was finished. But Trevor thought he could keep it all hushed up. He did not even begin to comprehend what we were up against."

"You walked out and Trevor was forced to quit the race," Lillian said.

"There wasn't any other viable option. It was obvious that Trevor was going down, but that didn't mean that I had to go down with him." Marilyn looked at Gabe. "Politics is a lot like any other business. You have to know when to cut your losses."

"Sure," Gabe said, keeping his voice very even. "I can see the parallels."

Marilyn blinked rapidly once or twice, realizing she'd gone too far. "So much for catching up on my personal news. It's getting late. I'll leave you two to your private little dinner party. Nice to see you both."

She turned away from the kitchen and started toward the front door.

Gabe looked at Lillian. She raised her brows but said nothing.

"I'll walk you out to your car," he called to Marilyn.

He caught up with her and together they went out onto the porch. The fast-moving storm clouds had cut off what little was left of the sunset's afterglow. He switched on the porch light. The wind had grown stronger while they had been inside the cottage. The limbs of the fir trees at the edge of the drive were stirring briskly.

Marilyn put up a well-manicured hand to keep her hair in place. She looked at her Mercedes, not at him.

"Do you ever wonder how things might have worked out for us if we hadn't broken up?" she asked in a pensive voice.

" 'Never look back' is about the closest thing we Madisons have to a family motto."

"You've never married."

"Been busy for the past few years."

"Yes, I know. So have I. Sure wish I could adopt your family motto." Her mouth twisted sadly. "When I think of all the time I invested in Trevor's career, I feel almost physically ill. Looking back, I can't believe I made such a huge mistake. How could I have been so stupid, Gabe?"

"We all make the best choices we can with the information we have available at the time we have to make them. None of us ever has enough information to be absolutely sure we're making the right choice."

"We've followed separate paths for a while," she said. "But now we seem to be circling back toward each other. Strange how life works, isn't it?"

"Strange, all right."

She unfolded her arms and reached up to touch his cheek very lightly with her fingertips. "Enjoy your dinner with Lillian."

"Thanks. I will."

"You know, if anyone had suggested a few days or months or years ago that you might find her attractive, I would have laughed. But now that I'm going through the breakup of my marriage, I view male-female relationships in a different light."

"Light is funny. Did you know that if you put it into corn bread dough, it makes terrific muffins?"

"I understand the appeal that Lillian has for you, Gabe."

"You might want to take it easy on the way back to the main road. The rains must have been heavy last month. They washed out a chunk of the drive."

"Your family and hers have a very tangled history."

"I think I hear my cell phone ringing." He patted his pockets.

"Don't forget, I know you well from the old days. I remember very clearly how you measured your own success against that of Harte Investments. I can only imagine how tempting it would be for you to marry Lillian and graft a third of her family's company onto Madison Commercial. In a way, it would be the ultimate triumph for you, wouldn't it?"

"Must have left the damn thing in the house."

He took a step back toward the partially opened door.

"I know you probably aren't interested in any advice from me," Marilyn said. "But for the sake of the past we share, I'm going to give you some, anyway. Don't marry just to prove something to yourself or because you think it would be worth it to add a chunk of Harte Investments to your empire. I married Trevor for reasons that had nothing to do with love. It was the biggest mistake of my life."

She went down the steps, got into the Mercedes and drove away.

He watched the taillights until they disappeared, listening to the wind, aware of the oncoming storm.

"Going to donate to her campaign?" Lillian questioned.

He turned around slowly, wondering how long she had been standing there on the other side of the screen door.

"Don't think so." He opened the door and walked into the warmth of the house. "Ready to work on dinner?"

"Sure. I've worked up quite an appetite. Spent the day setting up my studio in the spare bedroom at the cottage. I'm starving."

She turned and disappeared into the kitchen.

Had she overheard Marilyn's crack about marrying her to get a chunk of Harte Investments?

He went to stand in the doorway of the kitchen. A variety of vegetables, including the broccoli, stood on the counter. A wedge of parmesan cheese wrapped in plastic and a package of pasta were positioned nearby.

"Looks like some assembly required," he said.

"We're both smart people. I think we can get this done." She picked up a small knife and went to work on a yellow bell pepper. "Why don't you pour us a glass of wine? Probably make things go more smoothly."

"Good idea." He moved out of the doorway, opened a drawer and removed a corkscrew.

Lillian concentrated on the bell pepper.

He should probably say something, he thought. But he wasn't sure what she expected from him. How much had she overheard?

"Marilyn just showed up a few minutes before you got here," he said. "Out of the blue."

"She'll be back. You've got something she wants."

"I know. Money. You're not the first one to warn me."

Lillian dumped the sliced pepper into a bowl. "It's not your money she wants."

"Sure it is. She needs cash to fuel her campaign."

"I'm not saying that she wouldn't find your money useful. But what she really wants is someone she can trust completely, a man who will support her ambitions. She wants someone who will add strength and influence to her power base. Someone whose goals won't conflict with hers and who will not try to compete with her."

The cork came out of the bottle with a small pop. "You could tell all that in the five minutes you spent talking to her?"

"Sure. I'm a former matchmaker, remember?"

"Oh, yeah, right. I keep forgetting about your famous matchmaking intuition."

"Go ahead, mock me at your own peril. But I'm here to tell you that you've got a lot of what she's looking for in a husband." Lillian paused, head tipped slightly to the side. "And you know what?"

"What?"

"She's got a lot of what you stated you wanted on the Private Arrangements questionnaire. Say, maybe you were a tad more honest in your responses than I thought."

He poured two glasses of the cabernet, grimly pleased that his hand remained steady. "Marilyn and I already tried the couple thing. It didn't work out."

"I'm serious." Lillian put down the knife and picked up one of the wineglasses. "Marilyn meets a lot of the requirements you listed. There's money in her family. Even if they have cut off her campaign allowance for the moment, she'll inherit a nice bit of the Caldwell fortune someday. She's not an elitist academic or a fuzzy-brained New Age thinker." She paused a beat. "And she's not the *arty* type."

He leaned against the refrigerator and swirled the wine in his glass. "You didn't answer my question. Think she and I would be a good match if we gave it another try?"

She reached for the box of pasta. "No."

"Decisive. I like that in a matchmaker. Why don't you think she and I would be a good match?"

"Because you lied on the questionnaire."

"In your opinion."

"Mine is the only one that counts here," she said coolly. "I'm the professional, remember?"

# chapter 7

The storm crashed ashore shortly after ten o'clock. Time to go, Lillian thought. The edgy intimacy that had been thickening the atmosphere all evening was getting to her. She could no longer ignore the vibes. If she hung around any longer she might embarrass herself by making a pass at Gabe.

She put down her cards. "Gin."

"Damn. Not again." Gabe tossed his cards onto the cushion between them. He sprawled against the back of the sofa and regarded her with a malevolent expression. "Didn't realize you were the competitive type."

"I'm a Harte, remember? We're all competitive in some ways. Besides, it was your idea to play gin rummy."

"I wasn't concentrating. Had my mind on other things."

"Yeah, sure. They all say that when they lose to me." She looked out the window into the heavy darkness. "I'd better be on my way. That rain is going to get worse before it gets better."

He uncoiled from the depths of the sagging sofa. "I'll drive you back to your cottage."

He didn't have to sound quite so eager to get rid of her, she thought. But it was probably for the best. At least his mood seemed lighter now. Her mission of mercy was accomplished.

"Thanks." She rose quickly, a sense of urgency pulsing through her.

She had left it too long, she thought. It was *past* time to leave. She was not sure when or how it had happened but she was suddenly, intensely aware of the heavy blanket of sensual awareness that enveloped her. It had settled around her slowly and lightly over the course of the evening, the warm, thick folds practically weightless until now.

She wondered if Gabe felt anything at all. If he did, he was doing a terrific job of concealing it.

He was already at the door, her rain cloak in his hand. Obviously she was the only one who could feel the energy of the storm gathering here inside this room.

The smartest thing she could do tonight was leave right now and go straight home to her own bed.

She touched the back of a chair briefly to steady herself, took a deep breath and walked deliberately toward him.

"One thing I've been meaning to ask you," he said when she reached the place where he waited with her cloak.

She turned her back to him so that he could help her into the garment. "What's that?"

"Did you invite yourself over here tonight just because you thought I needed cheering up or did you have something else in mind?"

She froze, her hands slightly raised to take the edges of the cloak from him.

"Not that I don't appreciate the neighborly gesture," he said.

"We were both at loose ends this evening." She was irritated now. "And we *are* neighbors. Sort of. And you did seem a little moody this morning. Dinner together sounded reasonable. If you've got a problem with that, I'll make sure it doesn't happen again."

"Ouch. You've got teeth, don't you?"

"I'm a Harte."

"Right. I just wanted to let you know that I don't need any do-gooder nurturing. I'd much rather you had another agenda."

He draped the cloak around her shoulders. When he was finished he did not release her and step back. Instead he stayed there, so close that she could feel the heat of his body. He rested his hands on her, letting her feel the weight and strength of them.

"Another agenda?" She twitched the cloak into place, fussing with it a bit to cover her awkwardness. "Such as exploring various strategies we can use to help A.Z. prove that a secret government agency is planning to move frozen space aliens into the institute?"

He tightened his hands on her shoulders. "I was thinking more along the lines of you seducing me."

She opened her mouth. And closed it immediately when she realized she did not know what to say.

"You know, just to help lift my mood." His voice roughened a little. Getting dangerous. "Wouldn't be too much different from inviting yourself over for dinner so that I wouldn't be alone. Just another little act of charity."

"I already gave at the office."

"So much for small acts of random kindness."

His lifted her hair aside and kissed the nape of her neck. Electricity went down her spine. The room dissolved into a thousand different hues. She was inside the rainbow.

"Gabe."

"And here I thought you felt sorry for me," he said against her nape. "I thought you were genuinely concerned about my burnout problem."

"Look, Gabe—"

"Got another question for you," he said.

"Forget it."

"Can't. It's been eating at me for weeks. I've got to know. Did you ever fill out one of your own questionnaires and run it through your computer program to see if you could find the perfect match for yourself?"

The question blindsided her. It caught her up with the force of a heavy wave, sweeping her off her feet and roiling her senses. She pulled herself together with an effort.

"You're very chatty all of a sudden, aren't you?" she muttered.

"You didn't answer my question."

She felt the heat rise in her face. *Damn.* "I don't owe you any answers."

"Ah. So you *did* try to match yourself. I had a hunch you might have done it. Who could resist? There you were with your program and all those potential dates. What happened? No good candidates on your list of clients? Hard to believe."

"I told you," she whispered, "the program is not foolproof."

"Maybe not, but it's got a very high degree of accuracy. You assured me of that when I signed on. What went wrong? Didn't like the matches it selected for you?"

She put out her hand and closed her fingers around the doorknob. "Take me home, Gabe."

"Or did you lose your nerve? It's one thing to use intuition and the results of a questionnaire to help other people make a decision that will affect them for a lifetime." He turned her slowly around to face him. "It's another thing altogether to use them to make a choice that will affect your own life."

"Gabe—"

"Maybe your mistake was in looking too far ahead," he said softly. "Hell, maybe I was making the same mistake. Maybe we should both stop obsessing on the long term and focus more on the short term."

She swallowed. "How short a term are we talking about here?"

"Let's start with tonight." He kissed her throat. "We'll reassess matters in the morning."

She stiffened. "I don't do one-night time frames."

"There you go, trying to think too far ahead again."

"Goading me will not work," she said. "I do not respond to taunts or dares."

"Of course you don't. You're a Harte." He leaned his forehead against hers. His thumb moved along the line of her jaw. "What *will* work?"

She took a deep breath, inhaled some of the dancing storm energy that swirled around them and used it to fortify herself.

"You have to admit that you cheated on the Private Arrangements questionnaire," she said.

"What the hell does that damned questionnaire have to do with what's happening between us?"

"I ran the one you filled out through my program. Compared it with one that I had filled out on myself. If you were completely honest in all your responses on that form, I have to tell you that we are definitely not a good match, Gabe. Not even in the short term."

For the space of two or three heartbeats, he went utterly motionless.

"And if I did shade some of the answers?" he asked.

"Then the conclusions were invalid, of course."

He smiled slowly. "I lied through my teeth on most of them."

She touched the tip of her tongue to her lower lip. "Honest?"

"I swear it on my honor as a Madison," he said against her mouth.

"I *knew* it." Satisfaction unfurled within her. She put both arms around his neck. "I was sure of it. Even the one about—?"

His mouth closed on hers before she could finish the question. He kissed her, long and hard and deep; so deep that she forgot everything else.

The colors of the rainbow that surrounded her grew brighter, becoming almost painfully intense. She had to close her eyes against the shattering brilliance.

She kissed Gabe back, full on his warm, hard, incredibly sexy mouth. She gave it everything she had, moving into the moment the way she did when she was painting all out; flying with the vision, trying to get it down on the canvas before it evaporated.

Rain pounded on the roof of the cottage. Wind lashed at the windows. Electricity arced in the atmosphere. The night was alive and so was she.

She was vaguely aware of the rain cloak sliding off her shoulders. And then she realized that her feet no longer touched the floor. Gabe had picked her up in his arms.

She turned her face against his chest, savoring the scent of his body and the strength of his arms. She spread the fingers of one hand across the expanse of his chest. Beneath the fabric of his pullover, he was hard and sleek.

He carried her into the cottage's tiny bedroom and tumbled her down onto the old-fashioned four-poster. Her shoes thudded softly on the old rug. He straightened, peeled off his pullover in a single, sweeping motion and tossed it carelessly aside. It caught on a bedpost.

He never took his eyes off her as he stripped off his trousers and briefs. His hands were quick and ruthlessly efficient. The sight of his heavily aroused body elicited an immediate reaction far inside her. She was suddenly aware of a liquid heat pooling in her lower body.

He paused long enough to open a drawer in the nightstand. She heard foil tear in the darkness.

And then he was on the quilt with her, looming over her, caging her between his arms. The ancient bed squeaked beneath his weight. If she had tried to sketch him at that moment, she knew the result would have been a picture composed of dark light, strong shadows, and fathomless pools of mystery.

He tugged the tunic off over her head. Unfastened the satin bra. Excitement sent another flood of brilliant colors through her when he touched her breasts. She could hardly breathe. All of her senses sharpened and focused.

Gabe slid one leg between her thighs. He shifted his mouth back to hers in a heavy, drugging kiss.

She gripped his shoulders, digging her fingers into his bare skin. His hard body cut off what little light came through the doorway from the main room. She could hear the storm swirling outside the cottage, weaving a magic force field that held the rest of the world at bay. At least for now.

His hands moved on her again. Her trousers disappeared. They were soon followed by her panties.

He moved his hand across her stomach and down to the place where she was hot and wet and full. He stroked her as if he were now the painter, applying colors with lavish passion and precision. Getting into his art.

She wanted to tell him to slow down. She needed time to adjust to this unfamiliar level of raw, physical sensation; time to savor the sweep and nuance of the hues of this amazing rainbow.

But time was out of her control, along with everything else tonight. When he found her again with his fingers, she screamed. It was too much.

Her body clenched violently. The rainbow pulsed. Neon brights, effervescent blues and glorious, eye-searing reds filled the shadows with light. She could not think; could not sort out impressions or emotions.

He surged into her at that moment, spilling a whole new palette across the canvas. These were the mysterious, unnamable hues that she had seen only in her dreams.

She felt the rigid tension in the muscles and bone beneath his skin and knew that he was no longer in control either. His release crashed through both of them.

The first thing she noticed when she awoke a long time later was that she could not move. Gabe had her pinned to the bed with one heavy arm wrapped around her midsection and a muscular leg thrown across her thigh.

The second thing she became aware of was that the storm winds had died down. She could still hear gentle rain on the roof, and the darkness on the other side of the window remained immutable. But the world outside was a much quieter, calmer place than it had been earlier.

She lay still, partly because she knew that if she tried to move she would awaken Gabe and she was not at all certain she wanted to do that. Not yet, at any rate. She had things to think about and she needed to think without distractions.

Now that the chaos of passion had resolved itself, the first thing she ought to do was take a cold, hard look at what had happened between herself and Gabe. Life had suddenly become extremely complicated.

But she could not bring herself to focus just yet on her new problems. First she would allow herself the pleasure of absorbing the myriad impressions she had not been able to catalog and enjoy in the heat and turmoil of what had happened earlier. She was entitled.

Memories and impressions stirred her senses. Sex with Gabe had been as disorienting, thrilling, and ultimately as disturbing as that flash of recognition that sometimes struck while she was in the process of trying to translate a vision onto a canvas. In those rare moments of acute awareness she could *see* the whole picture in her mind. But the images came so swiftly, so relentlessly, that it was impossible to paint fast enough to keep up with them. She had learned to concentrate on the critical elements, the core of the vision, knowing that she could go back later to fill in the less essential parts.

Now she tried to do just that, calling up the little details that she had missed during the passionate encounter. The way his fingers had closed around her thigh. The way his teeth had grazed a nipple. The way his tongue—

"You awake?" Gabe asked.

"Yes."

He shifted a little, settling her more comfortably into the curve of his body. "What are you thinking about?"

She smiled into the pillow and said nothing.

He nibbled gently on her shoulder. "Tell me."

"I was just wondering why you lied on the Private Arrangements questionnaire."

"Can't let it go, can you?"

"Nope."

"Going to throw it in my face again and again, aren't you?"

"Yep."

"Okay, why do you think I lied?"

She propped herself up on one elbow and looked down at him, trying to read his expression in the shadows. Impossible. "I think you fiddled with the responses because subconsciously you didn't want me to find you a perfect match. You set things up so that failure was the only option."

"Huh. Why the hell would I do that after paying you all that money for some good matches?"

She put her hand on his bare chest. "Probably because, when crunch time came, your Madison genes just couldn't tolerate the idea of applying such a sensible, logical, rational approach to an intimate relationship with a woman."

"Screwed by my genetic predisposition to do things the hard way, you think?"

She drew her fingertips through the crisp, curling hair. "Madisons are known for doing things the hard way."

"True." He stroked the curve of her head. "There's just one point I want to make before we get up in a few hours and fix breakfast."

"And your point is?"

"Tonight does not qualify as my sixth date."

For an instant, she did not understand. Then the meaning of his words shot through her brain, charring the semi–dream state she had been enjoying.

She sat bolt upright. His arm slid down to her hips.

Aware that she was nude, she grabbed the sheets and held them to her breasts.

"I've got news for you," she said, "we had dinner and sex. If that doesn't qualify as a date in your book, I'd like to know what does. It's certainly a heck of a lot more than any of my other dates have involved in a very long time."

"You came over here tonight because you felt sorry for me, remember? Being neighborly doesn't qualify as a date."

Anger, pain, and outrage slammed through her without warning. She found herself teetering on an invisible emotional cliff that she had not even noticed a few seconds ago.

"I certainly didn't sleep with you just to jolly you out of your brooding mood."

"It worked, though." He closed his palm around her hip, squeezing gently. "I'm feeling a lot more cheerful than I did earlier."

"Damn it, Gabe, don't you dare imply that having sex was no different than . . . than playing gin rummy together. One is a game. The other is not."

There was a short silence. Was he actually having to think about her comment? She went cold. Maybe he didn't believe that there was any major difference between sex and gin rummy. Maybe to him they both ranked as nothing more than casual pastimes.

Maybe she had been a complete fool.

"One is a game, the other is not," Gabe repeated very deliberately. "This is a test, right?"

"Yes," she said through her teeth. "And if you get it wrong, you're a doomed man."

"Okay, okay, just give me a minute." He sounded as serious and intent as a game show contestant who had a hundred thousand dollars riding on the outcome. "One is a game. The other is not. One is a game. The other—"

"Gabe, so help me—"

"I'm thinking, I'm thinking."

There was an odd ringing in her ears now. Surely she could not have been dumb enough to go to bed with a man who treated sex as entertainment for a rainy night in a small town where there was very little in the way of nightlife. She could not have misjudged Gabe Madison so badly. She was a professional matchmaker, for heaven's sake.

He moved his warm palm up over her hip, along the curve of her waist, and pulled her down across his chest. One of her legs lodged between his thighs. She felt a familiar pressure and knew that he was getting hard again.

He cupped her buttock in one hand. "I'm ready."

The sensual laughter in his voice jolted her back to reality. He was teasing her. She was overreacting. Time to get a grip. Act mature and sophisticated.

With an act of will she forced herself to step back from the invisible emotional precipice. Her ears stopped ringing. She took a deep breath and managed a cool smile.

"I'm waiting for your answer," she said.

"Gin rummy is the game, right?"

"Congratulations. Right answer."

He slipped his fingertips along the rim of the cleavage that divided her derrière. Without warning, he rolled her onto her back and came down on top of her.

"What do you think you're doing?" she whispered.

"Collecting my prize."

A long time later she stirred again and leaned over him.

"You know," she said, "there was another reason I decided to stay tonight."

He smiled in the darkness. His hand moved in her hair.

"What was that?" he asked.

"I was curious to see what you do with the peanut butter."

"I'll show you."

"Now?"

"This is as good a time as any. I seem to have worked up an appetite."

# chapter 8

The sound of a heavy engine lumbering down the drive toward the house woke him. He opened his eyes. The gray light of a rainy morning illuminated the window. Beside him, Lillian did not stir.

What he wanted most in the world at that moment, he thought, was to stay right where he was with Lillian's beautifully curved bottom nestled against his midsection. But the rumble outside made that a non-option.

With deep regret, he eased himself cautiously away from her warmth. She wriggled a little, as though in protest. He leaned over and kissed her shoulder. She sighed and snuggled deeper into the pillow.

He studied her as he rose and reached for his pants. She looked very good lying there in his bed. Like she belonged there.

Outside the large vehicle had come to a halt. The motor shut down.

He made himself go out into the hall, pausing long

enough to close the bedroom door firmly. Then he went into the main room.

He glanced around quickly on his way to the front door, checking to see if there was any evidence of Lillian's presence. A glimmering pool filled with shifting lights on the floor caught his eye. He scooped up the iridescent rain cloak and crammed it into the hall closet.

By the time he got the front door open and saw the familiar SUV hulking in the drive, his grandfather was already on the porch.

"What the hell is going on here," Mitchell roared. He thumped his cane on the boards for emphasis. "Just what are you up to, Gabe Madison?"

*Damn.*

Gabe reassessed the situation quickly. Lillian had walked to his place. Her car was not in the drive. Mitchell could not possibly know that she had spent the night here.

Could he?

Small towns had some serious drawbacks when it came to privacy issues.

When in doubt, stall.

"Good morning to you, too," he said easily. "When did you get back into town?"

"Last night. Late."

"Where's Bev?"

Bev Bolton, the widow of a former editor of the *Eclipse Bay Journal*, was the woman Mitchell had been seeing for several months She had accompanied him to Hawaii. Bev lived in Portland. Mitchell had been so discreet about the relationship that for several extremely uneasy weeks Gabe and Rafe had both feared that his frequent trips to the city had been for the purpose of seeing a specialist. They had leaped to the conclusion that he was suffering from some dire medical condition that he was trying to keep from them. The truth had come as an enormous, if somewhat startling, relief.

"Bev went on down to California to visit her grand-kids," Mitchell said. "Now tell me what's happening here."

"Not much." He yawned and absently rubbed his chest. It was cold out here. Should have grabbed a shirt out of the closet. "Been raining a lot."

"Don't try to change the topic. This is me, your grand-father, you're talking to. I had coffee in town at the bak-ery. Must have been at least half a dozen folks who couldn't wait to tell me that Marilyn Thornley's car was seen turning into your driveway last night around sup-pertime."

Gabe drew a slow, deep breath. Relief replaced some of the tension that had tightened every muscle in his belly. Mitchell didn't know about Lillian. He was here because of Marilyn's car.

"Well, it's gone now, isn't it?" Gabe said.

He moved farther out onto the porch, pulling the door closed behind him. Rain dripped steadily from the edge of the porch roof. The temperature had to be in the very low fifties. Maybe the high forties. He tried to ignore the chill. How long did it take to contract a case of hypothermia?

He'd just have to tough it out. He could not risk going back inside to get more clothes. Mitchell would follow him into the hall and the commotion would awaken Lil-lian. She would probably come out of the bedroom to see what was going on and all hell would break loose. A real doomsday scenario, if ever there was one.

He needed to think and he needed to do it fast.

Priorities, priorities.

The first order of business was to get rid of Mitchell. He glanced at the SUV and raised a hand in a casual salute to Mitchell's faithful factotum, Bryce, who waited stoically behind the wheel. Bryce nodded once, acknowledging the greeting with a military-style inclination of his head.

Gabe turned back to Mitchell. "So, how was Hawaii?"

"Hawaii was fine." Mitchell scowled. "Hawaii is always fine. I didn't come here to talk about my vacation."

"I was trying to be civil."

"Bullshit. You're trying to slip and slide around this thing. Don't waste my time. I didn't just fall off the turnip truck yesterday. I want to know what's up with you and Marilyn Thornley."

"Absolutely nothing of any great interest to anyone, including me." Gabe folded his arms. Nothing like a clear conscience when dealing with the old man.

The tension that simmered between the two of them lately was a new element in their relationship. Gabe could not pinpoint when it had first begun to emerge. Sometime during the last two years, he thought. It had grown remarkably more acute since Rafe's marriage, however.

In the old days, after he and Rafe had gone to live with Mitchell following the death of their parents, there had been relatively few conflicts between Gabe and his grandfather. Rafe had been the rebel, the one who had gone toe-to-toe with Mitchell at every turn.

But looking back, Gabe knew that he had taken the opposite path, not because he had wanted to please Mitchell but because he was committed to his future goal. All he had cared about was his dream of proving that a Madison could be a success. In high school he had charted a course that he had calculated would enable him to achieve his objective and he had stuck to it. He had been the one who had gotten the good grades, stayed out of trouble and graduated from college because he could see that was how the Hartes did things. They had been his role models. It was clear to him, even as a boy, that the traditional Madison approach to life led to poor outcomes.

In the end, he had achieved his objective. He had put together a business empire that rivaled Harte Investments. One of these days, it would be even bigger than Harte.

He knew that now, although he had not built Madison Commercial with the conscious intention of pleasing his grandfather. Mitchell's approval had been one of the satisfying side effects of success. He had taken it for granted for some time.

The realization that nothing he had accomplished seemed to matter to Mitchell anymore left him with a peculiar, empty feeling deep inside. This morning, for the first time, he realized that anger was seeping in to fill the void.

What right did the old man have to give him advice on how to run his life?

Mitchell squinted, searching Gabe's face. Whatever he saw there appeared to reassure him somewhat.

"Marilyn didn't hang around?"

"Not for long," Gabe said mildly.

"She and Thornley are calling it quits, you know," Mitchell said.

"I heard."

"Word is, she's got her own plans to go into politics."

Gabe dropped his arms and wrapped his hands around the wet railing. Damn, it was cold. In another few minutes his teeth would probably start to chatter. "She told me that much yesterday when she stopped by to see me. Probably do okay."

"You know what she's after, don't you?"

"Sure. Don't worry, Mitch, I didn't just fall off the

turnip truck either. It's obvious that Marilyn is looking for someone to help finance her political career."

"I hear her father is a little pissed because she blew so much cash on Thornley's campaign. They say Caldwell isn't real eager to pump more money into another political race, even if it is his daughter who is running this time."

"The Caldwells will come around. Eventually. They always do for Marilyn."

Mitchell nodded. "That woman always did have a way of getting what she wanted, even when she was a little girl. Still, no politician ever has enough cash. She could use a rich husband with connections. Looks like you're back on her radar scope."

"I'm not interested in being married to a politician. If she doesn't know that already, I think she'll figure it out real quick. Marilyn is smart."

"The two of you had something going there for a while. Maybe she figures she can relight some old flames."

Gabe shrugged. "Whatever we had was over a long time ago."

"Don't count on her giving up easily."

"Okay, I won't count on it."

Mitchell's hawklike face tightened in a shrewd expression. "You know, things would be a whole lot simpler if you got married."

Gabe gripped the railing and said nothing.

"Marilyn Thornley wouldn't be hanging around here at suppertime if you had a wife," Mitchell said.

Gabe looked at him. "Don't start."

"A man your age oughtta be married. Hell, I was married at your age."

"Would that have been Alicia or Janine? No, wait, Alicia was number three, wasn't she? So was it Susan? It can't have been Trish because I'm sure you told me once that Trish was number one. Must have been Janine."

Mitchell hammered the cane against the boards. "The point is, I was married."

"And divorced. A couple of times, at least at that point. Two down and two more to go."

"So I screwed up once or twice."

"Four times in all."

"Shoot and damn." Mitchell's voice went up a few decibels. "You're supposed to learn from my mistakes."

"Madisons never learn from their mistakes. Family tradition."

Mitchell raised the cane and leveled it at him as if it were a rapier. "You know what your problem is? You're going about this marriage business all wrong."

"You're certainly an authority on the subject."

Mitchell snorted. "Should have known you couldn't go after a woman the way you go after investment prospects for Madison Commercial."

"I did manage to figure that out. That's why I signed up with Private Arrangements."

"What the hell kind of results do you expect from a computer?" Mitchell shot back. "I'm not saying Lillian Harte isn't a smart lady. No such thing as a stupid Harte. And I'm not saying she doesn't know how to run her business. But the fact is, you aren't going to have any luck finding a wife with a computer."

"Why not?"

"Because you're a Madison, that's why not. When it comes to women, a Madison relies on his gut, not his brain."

"And look where it's gotten us," Gabe said. "Three generations of screwed-up relationships."

"Rafe broke that jinx." Mitchell lowered the cane with

grim dignity. "I expect you to do the same, by God. But you're gonna have to stop fooling around with Madison Commercial for a while and pay attention to what's important."

That did it.

Gabe felt his Madison temper flash through him with all the stunning heat of summer lightning. It crackled and flared, surging forth from the windowless vault where he kept it locked and chained in the name of establishing total control.

He released the railing and turned on Mitchell.

"Fooling around with Madison Commercial? Is that what you call what I've been doing all these years? *Fooling around with Madison Commercial?*"

Mitchell blinked. Then the lines at the corners of his eyes creased in wary concern. "Simmer down, son. Just trying to have us a reasonable discussion here."

"Fooling around with Madison Commercial? Is that what you call building a major venture capital company that did a few hundred million dollars' worth of business last year?"

"Now, see here, Gabe, this isn't what—"

"Maybe it has slipped your mind that your stock in Madison Commercial is the primary source of your retirement income."

"Shoot and damn, this isn't about money."

"Not about money? All I ever heard from you when I was growing up was how Harte-Madison had been destroyed because you and Sullivan Harte went to war over a woman. How many times did you tell me how you'd been financially ruined because Claudia Banner made fools out of you and Harte? A couple of thousand, maybe?"

"What happened to Harte-Madison all those years ago has got nothing to do with this."

"The Hartes recovered financially because they had the brains and the determination to concentrate on business. You could have done the same thing, but you didn't, did you, Mitch? You preferred to get married. Over and over again."

"This is your grandfather you're dealing with here. Show some respect."

Gabe flexed his hands at his sides. "I proved to you and the whole damn world that a Madison could be as successful as a Harte."

"I'm not saying you haven't been successful with Madison Commercial. But the fact that the company's making a profit isn't what's important here."

"Tell me that the next time you cash your quarterly dividend check."

"Stop talking about money." Mitchell whacked the cane against a post. "We're talking about getting your priorities straight."

"Madison Commercial is a success because I've had my priorities straight all along."

"If you'd had 'em straight, you'd have been married by now. I'd have me some grandkids."

"Don't tell me how to run my life, Mitch."

"Someone's gotta do it."

"And you think you're qualified?"

The door opened.

Gabe went still. He was vaguely aware that Mitchell did the same.

"Good morning, gentlemen," Lillian said from the other side of the screen. "Lovely day, isn't it?"

Gabe shoved his hand through his hair. Just what he needed.

There was nothing but acute silence from his grandfather. He wondered how he was going to take this turn
of events.

Mitchell stood transfixed. He gazed at Lillian as if she
were a mermaid who had just appeared at the edge of the
bay.

Gabe switched his attention back to Lillian and did a
quick assessment. She was dressed in the black trousers
and the turquoise-slashed sweater she had worn last night.
A little dressy for day wear but it just might pass, especially with Mitchell, who didn't pay attention to the nu-
ances of fashion. Her hair was caught up in a neat twist.
She wasn't wearing any makeup, but there was nothing
unusual in that. In his experience she never wore much.

With luck Mitchell would assume that Lillian had just
walked over from her place to join him for breakfast.

She looked out at the two silent men with an expression of amused interest.

"Am I interrupting anything?" she asked politely.

Neither said a word.

"It's a little chilly out there," she said. "Why don't you
both come inside? I'm making coffee." She turned away
from the screen. "Don't forget to bring Bryce with you,"
she called over her shoulder.

Bryce collected his cup of coffee with a short, brusque
"Thank you, ma'am" and went back out to the SUV.

"Bryce isn't real keen on socializing," Mitchell said.

Lillian sank down onto the sofa. "I can tell."

Nonchalantly she watched Gabe where he stood at the
window, his mug gripped in both hands. He had disappeared into the bedroom while she had poured coffee.
When he reappeared a few minutes later he wore a dark
flannel shirt with the sleeves rolled up on his strong fore-

arms. The neckline of a black crew-neck tee was visible at his throat. Must have been a little chilly out there on the porch, she thought.

The tension in the tiny front room was charged with remnants of the quarrel she had interrupted.

When she had awakened to the sound of the heated argument, her first instinct had been to get dressed and slip out the back door. She was fairly certain that was the course of action Gabe would have preferred.

She might have done just that, sparing everyone, including herself, this awkward scene. But halfway down the hall she had overheard Gabe. *Fooling around with Madison Commercial? Is that what you call what I've been doing all these years?*

The frustration and stark pain in his words had stopped her in her tracks, canceling all thought of disappearing out the back door.

Mitchell studied Lillian. "Heard you were in town. Going to be here for a while?"

She took a sip of coffee. "Yes."

"Your family's place isn't far from here."

"No. A short walk along the bluffs."

A speculative gleam appeared in Mitchell's eyes. "So, you walked on over here for coffee, is that it?"

"I walked over here, yes," Lillian said.

At the window, Gabe tensed a little, as though preparing himself for battle.

Lillian pretended to ignore him. What she had told Mitchell was the truth as far as it went. Admittedly, it was the truth unencumbered by pesky little details such as those pertaining to the exact time and day she had made the trek, but that was not her problem. Mitchell had obviously decided to play inquisitor, but he was a Madison and she was a Harte. She was under no obligation to tell him everything he wanted to know.

Mitchell angled his chin toward the gray mist outside the window and looked concerned. "Pretty wet out there to be taking a walk."

"Yes, it is quite damp this morning," she agreed. "But what else can you expect this time of year?"

Gabe took a swallow of coffee. He did not speak, but she knew that Mitchell's blunt questioning was stoking the flames of his anger. She could only hope that he would have enough sense not to lose his temper again.

"A real coincidence, you and Gabe both deciding to take a little vacation here in Eclipse Bay at the same time, isn't it?" Mitchell said.

"Just one of those things," Lillian said.

"How long you going to be here?" Mitchell asked.

Gabe turned around at that. "What business is it of yours how long she intends to stay here?"

Mitchell glowered. "Just trying to make polite conversation."

"Sure," Gabe said. "That's you, all right. Polite."

Lillian cleared her throat. "As a matter of fact, I'm going to be here for quite a while, I've closed my business in Portland."

Mitchell's attention snapped back to her. "You shut down your matchmaking operation?"

"Yes."

Mitchell looked thoughtful. "So you're the one."

"I beg your pardon?"

Mitchell shrugged. "The one your dad's going to groom to take over Harte Investments. Never figured it would be you. No offense, but you always seemed to be a little on the flaky side."

"And here we thought my flakiness was a closely held family secret."

Mitchell ignored that, busy with his own logic. "Well, makes sense, when you think about it. I reckon you're the only choice left now that Hannah's fixin' to open the inn with Rafe, and your brother quit the company to write those mystery novels."

"As a matter of fact, I'm not going to go to work for my father. I closed Private Arrangements so that I could paint full time."

"Paint what?" Mitchell looked nonplussed. "Houses? Cars?"

"Pictures."

*"Pictures."* If he had looked nonplussed a moment ago, he was clearly floored now. "You mean real paintings? The kind they put in museums?"

"I should be so lucky." Lillian drummed her fingers on her mug, aware that Gabe was watching her with an odd expression. "Octavia Brightwell is going to give me my first show in Portland in a few weeks."

Mitchell shook his head. "Well, shoot and damn. If that don't beat all. Bet your folks and your grandfather are climbing the walls about now. Bad enough having a writer in the family. Now they've got themselves a real live artist."

"I haven't told them yet that I plan to paint full time," Lillian said carefully. "In fact, they don't even know that I've closed Private Arrangements."

"Don't worry, they won't hear it from me," he said. "But I sure would pay big bucks to be a fly on the wall when you tell 'em that you're going to quit working to paint pictures."

Lillian stiffened. "They'll understand."

"They may understand, but they sure as hell aren't

going to be real thrilled about it." Mitchell was almost chortling. "Sullivan sweated blood putting Harte Investments together after our company went under. And your father has worked in the business his whole life. Everyone figured one of you three kids would take over and manage it for another generation. Now, one by one, you're all peeling off to do your own thing."

He was right, she thought. But she didn't need the guilt trip this morning.

"Nick's son, Carson, may develop an interest in the business when he gets older," she said.

Mitchell snorted. "Your brother's boy is only, what? Four? Five?"

"Five."

"It'll be twenty years at least before he's even ready to think about taking on a job like running Harte Investments, assuming he wants to do it in the first place." Mitchell squinted. "Your dad's in his early sixties. He can't wait that long to turn the company over to the next generation."

"It's no secret that Dad plans to retire sometime in the next couple of years," she admitted. "He and Mom want to establish a charitable foundation aimed at teaching disadvantaged young people how to run a business."

"If he wants out, he'll have to sell or merge the company." Mitchell pursed his lips. "Probably make a truckload of money, but for all intents and purposes, Harte Investments will come to an end with this generation."

"It's just a business," Lillian blurted.

"Just a business, my left, uh, foot." Mitchell took another sip of coffee and lowered his mug very slowly. "This is Harte Investments we're talking about."

Lillian became aware of the fact that Gabe had turned away from the window. He was watching her intently.

She looked at him and then back at Mitchell. Both pairs of green eyes were identical. It sent a chill down her spine.

It occurred to her that the success of Harte Investments over the years had been more of a thorn in the sides of the Madison men than anyone in her family had ever fully understood.

Ten minutes later, Gabe stood with Lillian on the front porch and watched Mitchell climb into the SUV. Bryce put the behemoth into gear and drove off toward the main road.

They watched the rain fall for a while.

"I'm thinking about giving you a break," Gabe said.

Lillian folded her arms. "What kind of a break?"

"You know that sixth date you owe me?"

"That sixth date is a figment of your obsessive imagination. It will never happen."

"I'm serious."

"So am I."

He watched the SUV disappear into the trees. "I need a date for that banquet in Portland I mentioned the other night at dinner. The one scheduled to honor a former professor of mine. Are you free?"

She turned halfway around, searching his face with an unreadable expression. "This is your idea of a real date? A rubbery-chicken business dinner complete with long, boring speeches?"

"I'll be giving one of those long, boring speeches. Do you want to come with me or not?"

"I'll think about it."

"Think fast. I'm going to drive into Portland Monday morning so that I can get some time in at the office before the dinner. I plan to stay overight and drive back here Tuesday."

"Hmm."

"What does that mean?"

She shrugged. "Going into Portland for the night would give me a chance to stop by my studio and pick up some odds and ends that I left behind. Yes, I can see where the trip might be marginally worthwhile for me."

"Okay, I get the point. It wasn't a real romantic invitation, was it?"

"I can live with the unromantic part. Just so we're clear that this is not to be considered as your sixth, contractually arranged, bought-and-paid-for Private Arrangements date."

"Call it whatever you want."

"I'll do that," she said curtly and opened the screen door. "And another thing you should know before we drive into Portland for this big evening on the town."

"What's that?"

"I feel that we both need to give ourselves a chance to evaluate the future direction of this relationship."

He stilled. "What the hell does that mean?"

"In simple terms?"

"Yeah, I do best with simple terms."

"It means no more sex, at least not for a while. I want some time to think about what's going on here. I believe that you should do some thinking about it, too."

He said nothing. Just looked at her.

"Is that a problem for you?" she asked.

"Hell, no. I can think. Do it all the time. Sometimes I have two or three whole thoughts in the course of a day."

"I thought you could probably handle it."

"What I'm thinking now is that this decision not to

have any more sex for a while has something to do with that scene that just took place with Mitchell."

She hesitated. "Maybe his sudden appearance on the doorstep first thing this morning did help to put some things into perspective. But don't blame him. They were things that I should have thought about last night."

"Like what?"

"Do you have to get obsessive about this, too?"

"I just want some answers."

She put one hand flat on the screen. "I want us both to be sure that we know what we're doing."

"Does that mean you don't know what you're doing? Or that you don't think I know what I'm doing?"

"I came here to Eclipse Bay to paint. You came here to recover from a bad case of burnout. Neither of us planned to get involved in a relationship."

Understanding hit him.

"What happened between us last night scared the hell out of you, didn't it?" he asked softly.

Her nails made little indentations in the screen.

"Maybe we should both be a little scared, Gabe."

"If it's Mitchell you're worrying about, forget it. I'm pretty sure he bought that story you gave him about walking over here for coffee this morning. He doesn't know you spent the night."

She looked down the long drive to the place where Mitchell's SUV had disappeared.

"He knows," she said.

"Where's that damn cell phone?" Mitchell asked.

Bryce took one hand off the wheel long enough to reach into the small space between the seats. He picked up the phone and handed it to Mitchell without comment.

Mitchell found his reading glasses, fished a notebook

out of his pocket, flipped it open and located the number he wanted. He carefully punched the digits on the phone, peering carefully at the display to make sure he'd struck the right ones. It wasn't easy. The arthritis made some things harder than they had been in the old days.

"Why do they make these buttons so damn tiny?" he asked.

"People like small phones," Bryce said. "Small phones require small buttons."

"That was what they call one of them rhetorical questions." Mitchell listened to the phone ring. "You weren't supposed to actually answer it."

"You ask me a question, you get an answer," Bryce said.

"You'd think I'd know that by now."

"Yes, sir, you would think that."

The phone rang a third time.

"Shoot and damn," Mitchell said. "He'd better be there. I don't have time—"

The fourth ring was cut short.

"Hello?" Sullivan Harte said.

Mitchell grunted with satisfaction at the sound of the cool, graveled voice. He and Sullivan hadn't had much to do with each other in the years since the destruction of Harte-Madison and the infamous brawl in front of Fulton's Supermarket. They hadn't even had a civil conversation until Hannah and Rafe's wedding a few months ago. But some things you didn't forget, he reflected. The voice of the man who had fought alongside you in the green hell of jungle warfare was one of those things.

"This is Mitch."

"What's wrong?" Sullivan asked immediately.

"Your granddaughter is shacking up with my grandson."

There was a short silence.

"Got news for you, Mitch." Sullivan chuckled. "It's okay now that they're married."

"I'm not talking about Hannah and Rafe."

There was another brief pause.

"What the hell *are* you talking about?" Sullivan no longer sounded amused.

"Lillian and Gabe."

"Sonofabitch," Sullivan said very softly.

"You referring to me or my grandson?"

"Sonofabitch."

"You've made your opinion real clear," Mitchell said. "Point is, what are you gonna do about it?"

"Gabe is *your* grandson."

"And Lillian is *your* granddaughter. I fixed things last time. It's your turn."

"You *fixed* things? What the hell do you mean, you—"

Mitchell punched the button to end the call, cutting Sullivan off in midsentence.

He looked at Bryce and grinned.

"This," he said, "is gonna be downright entertaining."

# chapter 9

Claire Jensen dropped an overstuffed leather briefcase onto the vinyl seat and slid into the booth across from Lillian. She was flushed and a little breathless.

"Sorry I'm late," she said. "Marilyn wanted to go over some talking points for an interview she's doing tomorrow and we had to make some last-minute changes in the schedule for the Leaders of Tomorrow open-house event. Hey, you're looking great, Lil."

"Thanks. So are you. It's good to see you again. Been a while."

"Too long."

Claire laughed and Lillian felt the years fall away. Claire had always been fun. She was a bright, high-energy woman who bubbled with personality and plans.

"You're right," Lillian said. "Much too long. Where did the time go?"

"Life happens. Not like we both haven't been busy for the past few years."

They had met when Claire had been a student at Chamberlain College. Lillian had been attending a college in Portland but she had always spent her vacation breaks with her family in Eclipse Bay. She and Claire had both gotten jobs as waitresses at a pier restaurant one summer. Claire had needed the money. Strictly speaking, Lillian had not needed the income but she had needed the job. The Harte family believed very strongly in the work ethic. All Harte offspring were expected to work during summer vacations.

Initially she and Claire had had little in common, but the long hours spent dealing with stingy tippers and rude tourists had forged a bond between them. They had hung out together after work and talked a lot about the important things: guys and the futures they were planning for themselves.

Claire was the first person and, for a long time, the only person to whom she had confided her dream of becoming an artist. In what some would call typical Harte fashion, she had been very focused on her goal but, acutely aware of her family's opinion on the subject of art as a career, she hadn't discussed it much. It had been exciting to share her secret with someone who understood an impractical dream.

Claire had had some very impractical dreams of her own in those days. She had wanted to go into politics.

"This place certainly hasn't changed much, has it?" Claire commented. "Snow's Café looks just like it did when we used to come here back when we were in college."

The décor of Snow's Café had always reflected Arizona Snow's unique view of the world, Lillian thought. The walls were hung with a mix of faded rock band posters and enlarged satellite photos of the terrain around Area 51 and Roswell, New Mexico. The clientele consisted mostly of students from nearby Chamberlain College.

"What about the menu?" Claire asked. "Is it still the same?"

"Let's see." Lillian plucked the plastic laminated menu out from its position between the napkin holder and the little carousel that held the condiments. She surveyed the offerings. "Still heavy on veggie burgers, french fries, and coffee drinks."

"The three basic food groups for college students. Arizona knows her clientele," Claire mused. "I'm so glad you called. How did you know where to find me? I didn't even know that you were in town."

"I saw Pamela McCallister in Fulton's Supermarket. She mentioned that you were up at the institute, plotting Marilyn Thornley's campaign. How's it going? Think she can step into Trevor's shoes?"

"No problem," Claire assured her. "One thing's for certain, she'll look a whole lot better in them than he did."

"I beg your pardon?"

"Didn't you hear the rumors that went around after Trevor pulled out of the running?" Claire leaned forward and lowered her voice. "Word has it that Trevor liked to have sex in high heels and women's lingerie."

"Oh, *those* rumors."

Claire sat up and settled back against the seat. "Gossip among the campaign staff has it that he was forced to quit the race because he was being blackmailed with some old videos that showed him prancing around in frilly underwear. It was a shock, you know?"

"The campaign staff never had a clue?"

Claire sighed. "Of course not. The staff is always the last to know."

"What made Marilyn decide to become a candidate?"

"She's always been extremely ambitious. But I think that until recently she saw herself in the role of the candidate's wife. The power behind the throne, as it were."

"I heard she put a lot of her family's money into Trevor's campaign."

"True." Claire made a face. "Between you and me, when Trevor imploded, she was absolutely furious. I've never seen anyone in such a rage. I overheard a massive fight between the two of them one afternoon. She told Trevor that she could do a better job of running for office herself and that she was going to prove it. Said a lot of things about how much time she had wasted on him. She dropped the divorce announcement on the staff the next day."

"How did you end up as her campaign manager?"

"I was in the right place at the right time. She and I had worked together a lot in the course of Trevor's campaign. She knew me. Knew what I could do. Most of all she wanted someone she could trust to head up her campaign. When she offered me the job, I jumped at the chance. That woman is going places."

"And you're going to go with her, is that it?"

Claire laughed. "You got it." Her grin faded to a thoughtful expression. "You know, it's funny. Back at the beginning, when I used to dream about getting into politics, I pictured myself as the dynamic female senator from the great state of Oregon. Then I found out how much cash it takes just to run for dog catcher, let alone to get a shot at a state or national office. Short of marrying money, the way Trevor did, there aren't a lot of options. So I decided to carve out a career behind the scenes."

"Still dream of becoming a candidate?"

Claire shook her head decisively. "Not anymore. I love what I do. There's real power and a real rush in running a good campaign. And there's very little downside if it fails. The candidate may disappear from the face of the earth after a big loss but a good strategist just moves on to another campaign."

"I'm glad things worked out for you, Claire."

"You and me both. What's up with you? How long will you be in town?"

"I'm here for a month."

"A whole month?" Claire asked in surprise.

"I've made the big move. I closed down Private Arrangements. I'm going to devote full time to my painting and see what happens."

Claire's lips parted on a silent *wow*. "Good for you. No risk, no glory, I always say. Staying at your folks' cottage?"

"Yes."

"Funny how you Hartes and Madisons keep coming back to Eclipse Bay, isn't it?" Claire commented. "Hannah and Rafe are full-time residents now."

"They love it here."

"I'll tell you one thing, those of us up at the institute can't wait until they get Dreamscape open. As it is now, when people come for seminars and receptions like the Leaders of Tomorrow event, we're forced to put them up in one of those low-budget motels out on the highway."

"They're planning to open in the spring. Assuming the Willis brothers cooperate, of course."

Claire grinned. "What a pair. I practically had to get down on my knees and plead with them to come out to my place a couple of weeks ago just to unclog a toilet. They charged me a small fortune. I didn't have any choice but to pay it, of course, and they knew it."

# chapter 10

Gabe dropped Lillian off at the entrance to her apartment building shortly before ten o'clock on Monday morning.

"I'll pick you up at seven," he said when she made to slide out of the Jag.

She stood and looked at him through the open door. Tension coiled in the pit of her stomach. He was dressed for business once again in the legendary Gabe Madison war armor: steel-gray jacket and trousers, charcoal-gray shirt secured with silver-and-onyx cuff links, silver-and-black striped tie. When he moved his hand on the wheel, the dark-gray edge of his shirt cuff shifted, revealing the gleaming stainless-steel watch on his left wrist.

He looked good, she thought. Exciting. Powerful and predatory and wholly in control. You'd never guess that he was suffering a bad case of burnout. But, then, what did burnout look like?

"Fine," she said. "I'll be ready."

She hurried toward the building's secured entrance and punched in the code. Gabe waited until she was safely inside the lobby before he drove off in the direction of his downtown office.

He was wrong to accuse her of being nervous about their relationship, she thought a few minutes later when she twisted the key in the lock of her apartment door. She had spoken the truth the other morning when she had tried to explain herself to him. They both needed to think things through. Neither one of them could trust their own judgment at the moment.

A man dealing with burnout was certainly not in the best position to make sound decisions regarding his personal relationships. As for herself, she had arrived at a major turning point in her life. Getting involved in an affair with a man who was going through his own emotional crisis was the last thing she needed.

Probably be best to write off that night at his cottage as an ill-advised one-night stand.

It all sounded so logical. Why did she feel depressed by her own clear reasoning?

She opened the door and walked into the apartment. They had made good time on the long drive from Eclipse Bay this morning. She had most of the day ahead of her to tidy up some of the loose ends that she had left dangling when she had rushed out of town a few days ago. She had a number of things on her agenda, not the least of which was deciding what to wear to the dinner tonight.

The atmosphere of the apartment had the closed-up feeling that accumulates quickly when a residence has been uninhabited for a few days. She walked through the rooms, cracking open windows to allow fresh air to circulate.

She did the living room first and then went down the hall to her bedroom. At the entrance, she paused. A tingle of eerie awareness drifted through her.

There was something different about the room. Something wrong.

She looked around with her artist's eye, noting the small details. The bedding was undisturbed. The closet doors were firmly closed. The dresser drawers were shut.

The closet doors were closed. Completely closed.

Her attention snapped back to the mirrored closet. She stared at it for a long time.

She was certain that she had left it partially ajar because of the way the slider got hung up when it was pushed fully closed.

Almost certain.

She had been in a hurry the other morning when she had left for Eclipse Bay, she reminded herself. Perhaps she had forced the door closed without thinking about it.

She crossed the room, gripped the handle and tried to open the slider. It stuck. Just as it had been sticking for the past two months. She took a firmer grasp, braced herself and forced it open.

The slider resisted for a few seconds and then reluctantly moved in its track. She stood back and surveyed the interior of her closet. The clothes on the hangers seemed to be in the same order they had been in when she had packed. The stack of plastic sweater boxes on the shelf looked untouched.

This was ridiculous. She was allowing her imagination to get carried away.

She reached for the handle of the slider again, intending to close the door. She went cold when she saw the smear on the mirrored glass at the far end next to the metal frame.

She allowed her hand to hover over the smear. It was right where the heel of a palm would rest if one were to take hold of the frame at the far end in an attempt to force the slider closed. But the mark was a little higher than one she would have left if she had grasped the frame.

Right about where a man or a woman a couple of inches taller than herself might put his or her palm.

She stepped back quickly.

Someone had been in this room.

Take deep breaths. Think about logical possibilities.

Burglary.

She whirled around, examining the scene once more. Nothing appeared to be missing.

She rushed back out into the living room and threw open the doors of the cabinet that housed her entertainment electronics. The expensive equipment was still safely stowed in place on the shelves.

She went cautiously down the hall to the small second bedroom that she used as a study. Halting in the doorway, she studied the interior. The most valuable item in this room was the art glass vase her parents had given her for her birthday last year. It glowed orange and red on the shelf near her desk.

She was definitely overreacting here. Maybe she was on edge because of the tension of dealing with Gabe.

More deep breaths. Other logical possibilities.

*The cleaning people.*

She had canceled the weekly appointments until further notice. But there could have been a mix-up about the dates. The cleaners had a key. Perhaps they had come in last Friday on the usual day.

It made sense. One of them might have tried to close the closet door. But surely a professional housecleaner would have wiped off the smear on the mirror?

Then again, perhaps the cleaner had been in a hurry and hadn't noticed the smudge.

The light winked on the phone, snapping her out of

her reverie. Belatedly it occurred to her that she hadn't checked her messages during the time she had been away in Eclipse Bay. She pulled herself out of the doorway, crossed to the desk and punched in the code.

There had been two calls. Both had been received the night before last between ten and eleven o'clock. In each instance the caller had stayed on the line long enough for the beep to sound. But no one had left a message.

A shiver went through her. She listened to the long silence before the hangup and fancied she could hear the unknown caller breathing.

Logical possibilities.

Two wrong numbers in a row. People rarely left messages when they dialed a wrong number.

This was crazy. She needed to get a grip and fast.

She grabbed the phone and dialed the number of the agency that cleaned regularly. The answer to her question came immediately.

"Yes, we sent the crew in last Friday," the secretary said apologetically. "Sorry about the mix-up. We'll give you a free cleaning when you restart the service."

"No, that's all right. I just wanted to know if you had been into the apartment, that's all."

She put the phone down and waited for her heart to stop pounding. It took a while.

She did the little black dress bit for the dinner. The darkened hotel banquet room was filled to capacity with members of both the business and academic worlds. She sat at the head table, next to the wife of the guest of honor, and listened, fascinated, to Gabe's introductory remarks. She had known this event was important to him but she had not been prepared for the deep and very genuine warmth of his words.

". . . Like so many of you here tonight, I, too, was profoundly influenced by Dr. Montoya . . ."

He stood easily in front of the crowd, hands braced on either side of the podium frame, speaking without notes.

". . . I will never forget that memorable day in my senior year when Dr. Montoya called me into his office to discuss my first five-year plan, a plan which, in all modesty, I can only describe as visionary . . ."

Laughter interrupted him for a moment.

". . . 'Gabe,' Dr. Montoya said, 'with this plan, I sincerely doubt that you could attract enough venture capital to put up a lemonade stand . . .' "

The audience roared. Beneath the cover of applause, Dolores Montoya, a lively woman with silver-and-black hair, leaned over to whisper in Lillian's ear.

"Thank goodness the committee chose Gabe to make the introduction. At this kind of event half the crowd is usually dozing by the time the guest of honor gets to the podium. At least he's keeping them awake."

Lillian did not avert her attention off Gabe. "Trust me, he won't let anyone fall asleep. This is important to him. I hadn't realized just how important until now."

"My husband has told me more than once that Gabe was the most determined student he ever had in the classroom," Delores told her.

At the podium, Gabe continued his remarks.

". . . I'm happy to say that I finally got my lemonade stand up and running . . ."

This understatement was greeted by more chuckles from the crowd. Likening Madison Commercial to a lemonade stand was somewhat on a par with comparing a rowboat to a nuclear submarine, Lillian thought.

". . . in large part because of what I learned from Dr.

Montoya. But looking back, I can see that it wasn't just his nuts-and-bolts advice on how to survive market downturns and nervous investors that I took with me when I left his classroom." Gabe paused for a beat. "He gave me something much deeper and more important. He gave me a sense of perspective . . ."

The crowd listened intently.

". . . Dr. Montoya gave me an understanding not only of how business works in a free country but of what we who make our living in business owe to our communities and our nation. He showed me the connections that bind us. He gave me a deep and lasting appreciation of what it takes to maintain the freedoms and the spirit that allows us to succeed. He taught me that none of us can make it in a vacuum. And for those teachings, I will always be grateful. I give you now, Dr. Roberto Montoya."

The gathering erupted once again as Dr. Montoya walked to the podium. This time the applause was led by Gabe. It metamorphosed into a standing ovation. Lillian got to her feet and clapped along with everyone else.

No wonder Dr. Montoya was important to Gabe, she thought. This was how a kid from a family that could not provide any successful male role models became one of the most successful men in the Northwest. He found himself someone who could teach him how to get ahead and he had paid attention.

"I'm the one who's supposed to be crying." Dolores handed her a tissue.

"Thanks." Lillian hastily blotted her tears, grateful that the lights were all focused on the podium.

The applause died away and the members of the audience took their seats again. The spotlight focused on Roberto Montoya. Gabe made his way back through the shadows to the chair beside Lillian. She felt his attention rest briefly on her profile and sensed his curiosity. She hoped he hadn't seen her dabbing at her eyes with the tissue.

He started to lean toward her, as if about to ask her what was wrong. Fortunately his attention was distracted a moment by Dr. Montoya, who had just launched into his own remarks.

"Before I get to the boring parts," Dr. Montoya said, "there is something I would like to clarify. I taught Gabriel Madison many things, but there is one thing I did not teach him." He paused to look toward the head table. "I did not teach him how to dress. That, he learned all on his own."

There was a startled silence and then the crowd howled with delight.

"Oh, hell," Gabe muttered, sounding both resigned and amused.

Dr. Montoya turned back to the audience. "Five years ago when I approached Gabe to try to talk him into participating in a program that would place college seniors in local businesses during their final semesters, he said—and I recall his exact words very clearly—he said, what the hell do you expect me to teach a bunch of kids about business that you can't teach them?"

There was a short pause. Montoya leaned into the microphone.

" 'Teach 'em how to dress for success,' I said."

When the fresh wave of laughter had faded Montoya continued. "He took me seriously. Every semester when I send him the current crop of business students, he takes them to meet his tailor. What's more, he quietly picks up the tab for those who can't afford that first all-important business suit. Tonight, some of his protégés have prepared a small surprise to thank him for what he taught them."

The spotlight shifted abruptly to the far end of the stage. Two young men and a woman stood there. All three were dressed in identical steel-gray business suits, charcoal-gray shirts, and black-and-silver striped ties. All three had their hair combed straight back from their foreheads. Three sets of silver-and-onyx cuff links glinted in the light. Three stainless-steel watches glinted on three wrists.

The Gabe Madison clone on the right carried a box wrapped and tied in silver foil and black ribbon.

They walked forward in lockstep.

The audience broke out in another wave of laughter and applause.

Gabe dropped his face into his hands. "I will never live this down."

The young woman in the Gabe suit assumed control of the microphone. "We all owe Mr. Madison a debt of gratitude for the opportunities he provided to us during our semester at Madison Commercial. Most of us came from backgrounds where the unwritten rules of the business world were unknown. He taught us the secret codes. Gave us self-confidence. Opened doors. And, yes, he introduced us to his tailor and offered us some advice on how to dress."

One of the young men took charge of the microphone. "Tonight we would like to show our gratitude to Mr. Madison by giving him a helping hand with a concept that he has never fully grasped . . ."

The clone holding the silver foil box removed the lid with a flourish. The young woman reached inside and removed a scruffy-looking tee shirt, faded blue jeans, and a pair of well-worn running shoes.

"... The concept of casual Fridays," the clone at the microphone concluded.

The banquet room exploded once again in laughter and applause. Gabe rose and walked back to the podium to accept his gift. He flashed a full laughing smile at the three clones.

It struck Lillian in that moment that Gabe looked like a man at the top of his game—a man who enjoyed the respect of his friends and rivals alike, a man who was comfortable with his own power in the business world, cool and utterly in control.

He sure didn't look like a man who was going through a bad case of burnout.

# chapter 11

An hour later Gabe bundled her into the Jag and made to close the passenger door. Impulse struck. She gave into it without examining the decision.

"Would you mind if we stopped at my studio on the way back to the apartment?" she said. "I forgot a few things this afternoon when I went there."

"Sure. No problem."

He closed the door, circled the car and paused long enough to remove his jacket. He put it down in the darkness of the backseat and got in behind the wheel. She gave him directions but she had the feeling that he already knew where he was going. He drove smoothly out of the parking garage and turned the corner.

A short time later he stopped at the curb in front of the brick building in which she rented studio space.

"This won't take long," she said.

"There's no rush."

He got out of the car and opened her door for her.

She walked beside him to the secured entrance. He waited while she punched in the code.

They went up the stairs to the second-floor loft in silence. When she inserted her key into the lock she realized that her pulse was beating a little too quickly. A sense of anticipation mingled with unease quickened her breathing.

Why had she brought him here? she wondered. Where had the urge come from? What was the point of showing him the studio tonight? He was a businessman with no use for arty types.

She opened the door and groped for the switches on the wall to the right. She flipped two of the six, turning on some of the lights but not all, leaving large sections of the loft in shadow.

Gabe surveyed the interior.

"So this is where you work." His voice was completely uninflected.

"Yes." She watched him prowl slowly forward, examining the canvases propped against the walls. "This is where I paint."

He stopped in front of a picture of her great-aunt Isabel. It showed her seated in a wicker chair in the solarium at Dreamscape, looking out to sea.

Gabe looked at the painting for a long time.

"I remember seeing that expression on Isabel's face sometimes," he said finally. Absently he loosened the knot in his tie and opened the collar of his shirt. He did not take his gaze off the picture. "As if she were looking at something only she could see."

Lillian crossed to the large worktable at the far end of the room, propped one hip on the edge and picked up a sketchpad and a pencil. "Everyone has that look from time to time. Probably because we all see something a little different when we look out at the world."

"Maybe."

He removed the silver-and-onyx cuff links and slid them into the pocket of his trousers. Again, his movements were casual and unself-conscious; the easy actions of a man relaxing after a formal evening.

He moved on to the next picture, rolling up the sleeves of the charcoal-gray shirt as he crossed the space, exposing the dark hair on the back of his arms.

She watched him for a moment. He looked rakish and extremely sexy with his tie undone and his shirt open at the throat. But what compelled her was the way he looked at her paintings. There was an intensity in him that told her that he made a visceral connection with the images she had created. He might not like the arty type but he responded to art. Unwillingly.

She began to draw, compelled by the shadows in her subject.

"You meant everything you said about Dr. Montoya tonight, didn't you?" she asked, not looking up from her work.

"He was the closest thing I had to a mentor." Gabe studied a picture of an old man sitting on a bench in the park. "I was a kid from a small town. I didn't know how to handle myself. Didn't know what was appropriate. I had no polish. No sophistication. No connections. I knew where I wanted to go but I didn't know how to get there. He gave me a lot of the tools I needed to build Madison Commercial."

"Now you repay him by allowing him to send some of his students into Madison Commercial every year."

"The company gets something out of it, too. The students bring a lot of energy and enthusiasm with them. And we get first crack at some bright new talent."

"Really? I've heard my father talk about what a nuisance student interns are for a busy company. They can be a real pain."

"Not everyone is cut out to work in a corporation."

Her pencil stilled for an instant. "Me, for instance."

He nodded. "You, for instance. And apparently your sister and brother, too. You've all got strong, independent, entrepreneurial streaks. You're all ambitious and you're all talented but you don't play well with others. At least not in a business setting."

"And you think you're so very different? Give me a break. Tell me something, Gabe, if you were only a vice-president instead of the owner, president, and CEO of Madison Commercial, would you still be on the company payroll?"

There was a short pause.

"No," he said. Flat and final.

"You said that not everyone is cut out to work in a large corporation." She moved the pencil swiftly, adding shadows. "But not everyone is cut out to run one, either. You were born for it, weren't you?"

He pulled his attention away from a canvas and looked at her down the length of the studio. "Born for it? That's a new one. Most people would say I was born to self-destruct before the age of thirty."

"You've got the natural talent for leadership and command that it takes to organize people and resources to achieve an objective." She hunched one shoulder a little, concentrating on the angle of his jaw. Going for the darkness behind his eyes. "In your own way, you're an artist. You can make folks *see* your objective, make them want to get there with you. No wonder you were able to get that initial funding you needed for Madison Commercial. You probably walked into some venture capitalist's office and painted him a glowing picture of how much money he would make if he backed you."

Gabe did not move. "Talking her out of the venture capital funds I needed wasn't the hard part."

She glanced up sharply, her curiosity pricked by his words.

"Her?" she repeated carefully.

"Your great-aunt Isabel is the one who advanced me the cash I needed to get Madison Commercial up and running."

She almost fell from her perch on the worktable.

"You're kidding." She held the point of the pencil in the air, poised above the paper. "*Isabel* backed you?"

"Yes."

"She never said a word about it to any of us."

He shrugged. "That was the way she wanted it."

She contemplated that news.

"Amazing," she said at last. "Everyone knew that it was her dream to end the Harte-Madison feud. Hannah figures that's the reason she left Dreamscape equally to her and your brother in the will. But why would she back you financially? What would that have to do with ending the old quarrel?"

"I think she felt that the Madisons got the short end of the stick when Harte-Madison went into bankruptcy. She wanted to level the playing field a little for Rafe and me."

"But when Harte-Madison was destroyed all those years ago, everyone lost everything. Both the Hartes and the Madisons went bankrupt. That's about as level as it gets."

"Your family recovered a lot faster than mine did."

He concentrated on the painting in front of him. "I think we both know why. So did Isabel."

She flushed. There was no denying that the tough, stable Harte family bonds, not to mention the Harte work ethic and emphasis on education, had provided a much stronger foundation from which to recover than the shaky, shifting grounds that had sustained the Madisons.

"Point taken," she agreed. "So Isabel, in her own quiet way, tried to even things up a bit with money."

"I think so, yes."

"What was the hard part?"

"The hard part?"

"You said that getting the backing from her for Madison Commercial wasn't the hard part. What was?"

His mouth curved reminiscently. "Structuring the contract so that Isabel got her money back plus interest and profit. She didn't want to do things that way. She wanted me to take the cash as a straight gift."

"But you wouldn't do that."

"No."

*Madison pride,* she thought, but she did not say it out loud. She went back to work on her drawing. Gabe moved on to another picture.

"I was wrong about you, wasn't I?" She used the tip of her thumb to smudge in a shadow.

"Wrong?"

"Watching you at the banquet tonight, it finally hit me that I had leaped to a totally false conclusion about you. And you let me do it. You never bothered to correct my assumption."

He gave her his enigmatic smile. "Hard to imagine a Harte being wrong about a Madison. You know us so well."

"Yes, we do. Which is why I shouldn't have been fooled for even a minute. But I was."

"What was the wrong conclusion you leaped to about me?"

She looked up from the sketch and met his eyes. "You aren't suffering from burnout."

He said nothing, just watched her steadily.

"Why didn't you set me straight?" She returned to her sketch, adding more depths and darkness. "Because it suited your purpose to let me think you were a victim of stress and burnout? Did you want me to feel sorry for you?"

"No." He started toward her down a dim aisle formed by unframed canvases. "No, I sure as hell did not want you to feel sorry for me."

"What did you want?" Her pencil flashed across the paper, moving as though by its own volition as she worked frantically to capture the impressions and get them down in all the shades of light and dark.

He came to a halt in front of her. "I wanted you to see me as something other than a cold-blooded machine. I figured that if you thought I was a walking case of burnout, you might realize that I was human."

She studied the sketch for a moment and then slowly put down the pencil.

"I've always known that you were human," she said.

"You sure about that? I had a somewhat different impression. Must have been all those comments you made about how I wanted to date robots."

He reached for the sketchpad. She let him take it from her fingers, watching his expression as he looked at the drawing she had made of him.

It showed him as he had appeared a few minutes ago, standing in front of one of her canvases, his hands thrust easily into the pockets of his trousers, collar and cuffs undone, tie loose around his neck. He stood in the shadows, his face slightly averted from the viewer. He was intent on the painting in front of him, a picture that showed an image that only he could see. Whatever he saw there deepened the shadows around him.

She watched his face as he studied the drawing. She knew from the way his jaw tightened and the fine lines that appeared at the corners of his mouth that he understood the shadows in the picture.

After what seemed like an eternity, he handed the sketch back to her.

"Okay," he said. "So you do see me as human."

"And you saw what I put into this drawing, didn't you?"

He shrugged. "Hard to miss."

"A lot of people could look at this sketch and not see anything other than a figure standing in front of a canvas. But you see everything." She waved a hand at the canvases that filled the studio. "You can see what I put into all of my pictures. You pretend to disdain art but the truth is you respond to it."

"I spent a lot of the first decade of my life in an artist's studio. Guess you pick up a few things when you're surrounded by the stuff during your impressionable years."

"Yes, of course. Your father was a sculptor. Your mother was his model." She put the sketch down on the worktable. Guilt and dismay shot through her. "I'm sorry, Gabe. I know you lost your parents when you were very young. I didn't mean to bring up such a painful subject."

"Forget it. It's a fact, after all, not something you conjured up out of your imagination. Besides, I thought I made it clear that I don't want you to feel sorry for me.

Sort of spoils the Harte-Madison feud dynamic, you know?"

"Right. Wouldn't want to do that." She hesitated. "Gabe?"

"Yeah?"

"When you stated on the Private Arrangements questionnaire that you didn't want any arty types, you were telling the truth, weren't you?"

"I thought we'd decided that I pretty much lied through my teeth on that questionnaire."

"I don't think you lied on that issue. Did you make a point of not wanting to be matched with so-called arty types because of your parents? Everyone knows that they didn't give you and Rafe what anyone could call a stable home life."

He was silent for a moment.

"For years I blamed most of what wasn't good in my childhood, including my parents' deaths, on the fact that they were both involved in the world of art," he said finally. "Maybe, in my kid brain, the mystique of the wild, uncontrolled, temperamental, artistic personality was convenient. Better than the alternative, at any rate."

"What was the alternative?"

"That we Madisons were seriously flawed; that we couldn't manage the self-control thing."

"But you've proved that theory wrong, haven't you? I've never met anyone with more self-control."

He looked at her. "You don't exactly fit the image of the temperamental, self-centered artist who has no room in her life for anything except her art, either."

"Okay. I think we've successfully established that neither of us fits whatever preconceptions we might have had."

"Why did you bring me here tonight, Lillian? I know it wasn't because you needed to pick up some supplies."

She looked around at her paint-spattered studio. "Maybe I wanted to find out how you really felt about arty types."

He raised one hand and traced the cowl neckline of her black dress. His finger grazed her throat. "Let's see where we stand here. We've established that you don't think I'm a machine."

She caught her breath at his touch. "And you don't think I'm typical of what you call the arty type."

"Where does that leave us?"

"I don't know," she whispered.

He lowered his head until his mouth hovered just above hers. "I think we ought to find out, don't you?"

"Sex is probably not the best way to explore that issue."

He kissed her slowly, lingeringly. When he raised his head she saw the hunger in him. She felt her blood heat.

"Can you think of a better way to explore it?" he asked.

She swallowed. "Not right at the moment."

He put one hand on her knee just beneath the hem of the little black dress. His smiled slowly and eased the skirt higher. She caught the ends of his silk tie in her hands and drew him closer.

He took the invitation the way a shark takes prey; smoothly and swiftly, leaving her no time to consider the wisdom of moving back into shallower waters.

Between one heartbeat and the next, he was between her knees, using his thighs to part her legs and open her to him. The black dress was up to her hips now, leaving only a scrap of midnight-colored lace as a barrier to his hand. It proved woefully inadequate to the task. She felt the silk grow damp at his touch.

She gripped the ends of the necktie and hung on for the ride.

He roused himself a long time later, sated and content. For the moment, at any rate. He sat up on the edge of the worktable. Beside him Lillian was curled amid scattered sheets of drawing paper, brushes, and tubes of paint. Her hair had come free from the sleek knot in which it had been arranged earlier in the evening. The little black dress that had looked so elegant and tasteful at the head table was now crumpled in an extremely interesting, very sexy and no doubt less-than-tasteful manner. But it looked terrific on her that way, he thought.

His tie was now looped around her throat instead of his own. He grinned, remembering how it had gotten switched in the middle of the lovemaking.

She stirred. "What are you staring at?"

"A work of art."

"Hmm." She nodded once in appreciation. "A work of art. That was pretty quick, Madison."

"Pretty quick, you mean for a man who is still recovering from a truly mind-blowing experience?"

"Gosh. Was that your mind?" Her smile was very smug. "I didn't realize."

He grinned. "I handed you that line on a platter. Admit it."

"I admit it. You're good, you know that?"

"At the moment, I'm a lot better than good." He leaned down to kiss her bare hip. "I'm terrific. What about you?"

"I think I'll survive." She hauled herself up on her elbows and surveyed herself. "But the dress is dead meat."

"I'm sure there are plenty more where it came from."

"Probably. Department stores are full of little black dresses." She noticed the tie around her neck and frowned. "How did that get there?"

He eased himself off the table, stood and stretched. "Some questions are better left unanswered."

He studied a canvas propped against the wall directly across from him as he zipped his trousers and buckled his belt. It was another one of her unique, riveting creations, all hot, intense light and dark, disturbing shadows. He felt it reaching out to pull him into that world, just as her other works did. He had to force himself to look away from it.

He turned his head and saw that the sensual, teasing laughter that had gleamed in her eyes a moment ago had evaporated. She was watching him in the same way that he had looked at the painting, as if she were wary of being sucked into his universe.

"Does this mean we're having an affair?" she asked. Curious. Polite. Very cool. Just asking.

Her deliberately casual air wiped out a lot of the satisfaction that he had been enjoying. Whatever was going on here was a long way from settled.

"Yes," he said. I think we'd better call this an affair. I don't see that we have any real choice."

She sat up slowly and dangled her legs off the edge of the worktable. "Why is that?"

She had small, delicate ankles and beautifully arched feet, he noticed. Her toenails were painted scarlet. And here he'd never considered himself a foot man.

He walked back to the table, fitted his hands to her waist, lifted her and set her on her feet. He did not release her. "Be sort of awkward to have to admit that we're into one- and two-night stands, wouldn't it?"

"Might make us both look extremely shallow and superficial."

"Can't have that," he said easily. "Come on, let's go back to your apartment. We need some sleep. Got a long drive back to Eclipse Bay tomorrow morning."

# chapter 12

A deceptively bright sun supplied light but very little heat to Eclipse Bay. Small whitecaps snapped and sparkled on the water. The brisk breeze promised another storm soon. They drove through the community's small business district on the way back to the cottage. Lillian noticed that the handful of men standing around a truck at the town's only gas station were huddled into goose-down vests and heavy windbreakers.

Sandy Hickson, the owner of the station, spotted Gabe's car and waved a casual greeting. His companions turned to glance at the vehicle. Even from where she sat, Lillian thought she could see the open speculation in their eyes.

A Harte and a Madison could not even drive through Eclipse Bay together without drawing interested gazes.

"Small town," Gabe said. He sounded completely unruffled by the attention.

"Very."

"Not like there's a heck of a lot to do around here in

the middle of winter. It's almost like we've got a social obligation to bring a little excitement to town."

"Since when did Madisons worry about their social obligations?"

"Since we started hanging out more with you Hartes. You're a bad influence on us."

She noticed the illuminated message indicator on the answering machine when she walked into the Harte family cottage a short time later.

Gabe saw it too. "Got a hunch Mitchell ratted us out."

"Looks that way. Probably my mother. Great." She put down the carton of painting supplies she had carried in from the car. "I'll deal with it later."

"Thought you said your folks were on a business trip in San Diego."

"They are. But you know as well as I do that gossip travels fast among the Hartes and the Madisons, especially since the wedding."

"Well, we both knew we wouldn't be able to keep this a secret. And it's not as if we're not all adults here."

He sounded a little too philosophical, she thought. Downright upbeat, in fact. As if the prospect of explaining away a red-hot affair between a Harte and a Madison was no big deal. Just a walk in the park.

"Yeah, right," she said. "We're all adults here."

He set her suitcase in the hall and looked at her, brows raised in polite inquiry. "Need backup?"

"From a Madison? That would be like pouring oil on a burning fire."

"We Madisons are good at that."

"I'll remember that the next time I'm trying to start a blaze instead of putting one out."

"This is going to be a tough fire to put out," he said softly.

She did not know if she ought to take that as a warning or just another teasing remark. Upon brief reflection, she decided it would be best to assume the latter.

"I'm an adult," she said. "I make my own decisions. My parents know that."

"Uh-huh." He looked unconvinced but he turned to walk toward the door. "Well, if you don't need my assistance in pacifying your mother, I'll be on my way. See you for dinner."

He said it with such breathtaking casualness, she thought. Taking the concept of dinner together for granted. The unspoken expectation of spending the night was very clear. He was moving right into her daily routine, making himself comfortable.

Well? They had both agreed that they were starting an affair, hadn't they? Why the sudden qualms?

But the answer was there in the next heartbeat. For all her fine talk of being a grown-up, the bottom line here was that getting involved with Gabe was a dangerous business.

"Why don't we go out tonight?" she said on sudden impulse.

Dining out in public would be more like a date. She could handle a date with him. Dates were more structured, more ritualized. They were not infused with quite the same degree of casual intimacy as cooking dinner together and eating it at the kitchen table. A date allowed her to keep a little distance. So what if they went back to his place later and made wild, passionate love. Some people did that after a date. Or so she had heard.

"Fine."

Something told her that he had guessed what was going through her mind. But he did not argue. Instead, he walked out onto the porch.

"I'll pick you up. Six-thirty okay?"

"I can meet you at your place." She went to stand in the doorway. "It's a short walk."

"No. It'll be dark. I don't want you walking alone after dark."

"There's nothing to worry about. We're not exactly crime central around here. Especially in the dead of winter."

"Eclipse Bay isn't the same town it was when you and I were kids. It's not just the summer tourists who cause trouble around here now. Chamberlain College is expanding and so is the institute. I'd rather you didn't stroll around on your own after the sun goes down."

She propped one shoulder against the door frame, amused, and crossed her arms. "Are you always this bossy?"

"I'm cautious, not bossy."

"And maybe a tad inclined to be overcontrolling?"

"Sure, but hey, isn't everyone?" He brushed his mouth across hers. "Humor me, okay?"

"Okay. This time."

He nodded, satisfied and went down the steps. "See you later. Good luck with your painting."

"What are you going to do this afternoon?"

He paused and looked back over his shoulder. "I'm going to go online to do some deep background research on a potential Madison Commercial client. Why?"

She made a face. "Have fun."

"I thought I explained to you that what I do at M.C. is called work, not fun." He gave her his slow, sexy Madison smile. "Fun comes later, after work. I'll show you."

He walked to the Jag, opened the door and got behind the wheel.

Back at the beginning she had made the mistake of

assuming that he was a victim of burnout because he claimed that running Madison Commercial was not fun for him. In one sense, she thought, he was right. But work wasn't the correct label, either, although it was the one he preferred. The truth was, Madison Commercial was his passion.

Passion wasn't fun. Passion was serious stuff.

She had always understood that distinction intuitively when it came to her painting. Now she was starting to understand it about her relationship with Gabe, as well. Serious stuff.

She went back into the house, closed the door and crossed to the phone to listen to her messages. There were two, she noticed. The first was, as she had expected, from her mother.

Might as well get this over with fast. She braced herself and dialed the number of the hotel room in San Diego.

*We're all adults here.*

Elaine Harte answered on the second ring. In typical maternal fashion, she did not take long to come to the point.

"What in the world is going on up there in Eclipse Bay?" she asked without preamble.

"Long story."

"Your grandfather phoned yesterday. He and your father talked for a very long time. It was not what anyone would call a cheerful, lighthearted conversation. I haven't heard those two go at it like that in years. Sullivan says that you've closed Private Arrangements for good. Is that true?"

"Yes."

"But, darling, why?" Elaine's voice rose in that practiced wail of dismay that is unique to mothers around the world. "You were doing so well."

Elaine did not actually add *at last* but it was there, silently tacked on to the end of the sentence.

"You know why, Mom."

There was a short silence, then Elaine sighed.

"Your painting," she said.

The whining tone had vanished from her voice as if by magic, Lillian noticed. Smart moms also knew when to abandon a tactic that no longer worked.

"I've been thinking about this for a long time, Mom. I need to see if I can make it happen."

"Can't you keep Private Arrangements going while you find out if you can make a living with art? You've always painted in the evenings and on weekends."

Lillian flopped down on the sofa and stacked her heels on the coffee table. "I feel that the time has come to put my art at the top of my agenda. I need to concentrate on it. The fact is, after a full day at Private Arrangements, I'm tired, Mom. I don't have a lot of energy left for my work."

My *work*. She was using the word, herself, she realized, mildly astonished. The same way Gabe used it, to describe the important thing that she did. Painting wasn't a hobby. It wasn't fun. It wasn't entertainment. It was her passion.

"And if the painting doesn't go well?" Elaine said. "Will you reopen Private Arrangements? You still have your program and your client list, don't you?"

"I can't think about that now, Mom. I have to stay focused."

"You sound just like your father and your grandfather when you say things like that." Elaine hesitated and then probed further. "Sullivan told your father something else.

He said that you and Gabe Madison are seeing each other . . . socially."

Lillian laughed in spite of tension. "I'll bet he said a lot more than that."

Elaine cleared her throat. "I believe he used the phrase 'shacking up together.'"

"I *knew* it." Lillian took her heels off the table and sat up on the edge of the sofa. "Mitchell Madison did squeal to Granddad. Interesting that he went straight to Sullivan with the news, isn't it? I wonder why he did that."

There was another brief pause.

"So it's true?" Elaine asked, her voice grim.

"Afraid so." Lillian hunched around the phone in her hand. "But I prefer the phrase 'seeing each other socially' to 'shacking up together.'"

"Men of Mitchell's and Sullivan's age have a different view of these matters. And a different vocabulary to describe them."

"Guess so."

"If you don't mind my asking, how does Gabe describe your, uh, relationship?"

*We're all adults here.*

"I haven't actually asked him that question. Not in so many words. Look, Mom, I know you mean well, but this conversation is getting a bit personal. I'm perfectly capable of handling my own private life."

"When Hartes and Madisons get together in Eclipse Bay, there is no such thing as a private life," Elaine said.

"Okay, I'll give you that. But I'm still capable of dealing with things here."

"You're sure?"

"Of course, I'm sure. Mom, I'm not in high school anymore. Or even college, for that matter. I've been get-

ting by out there in the big bad world all on my own for
quite a while now."

"You haven't had to deal with the complications of
having a Madison in your life."

"Gabe is a different kind of Madison, remember? He's
the one who made it through college and built a very successful business. When I was a kid, I recall Dad saying
that Gabe was the one Madison who proved the exception to the rule that all Madisons were bound to come to
a bad end."

"Yes, dear, I know." Another short silence hummed on
the line. "But between you and me, Gabe was the one I
worried about the most."

That stopped Lillian cold. "You did?"

Elaine was quiet for a moment. Lillian could almost
hear her thinking about the past.

"I wasn't the only one who was concerned about him,"
Elaine said eventually. "Isabel and I discussed him often.
Even as a little boy, Gabe always seemed too self-
contained, too controlled. He never lost his temper, never
got in trouble at school. Always got good grades. It just
wasn't natural."

"You mean for a Madison?" .

"No, I mean for a little boy. Any little boy."

"Oh."

"It was as if he always had his own private agenda.
Looking back, I can see that he must have been driven,
even then, by his vision of building a business empire."

"I think you're right," Lillian said. "He needed to prove
something to himself. But he accomplished his goal."

"People who are compelled by a lifelong ambition do
not change, even after it appears to everyone else around
them that they have achieved that ambition. In my expe-

rience they remain driven. It's a deeply imbedded characteristic."

A Madison and his passion.

"Mom, listen, I really don't—"

"I don't want to intrude on your personal life, but I *am* your mother."

"I know." Lillian sighed. "You gotta do what a mom's gotta do."

"I think you should assume that nothing has changed with Gabe."

"What?"

"Madison Commercial was always the most important thing in his life. It still is. If anything, all that single-minded determination and willpower he used to get to where he is today has only become more honed through the years."

"Meaning?"

"Meaning," Elaine said bluntly, "that if he has decided to see you socially, as you call it, he very likely has a reason."

She felt her stomach tighten. "Is this where you tell me that the only thing Gabe wants from me is sex?"

"No." Elaine paused. "To be frank, I expect that, given his money and position, Gabe can get as much of that as he wants."

Lillian winced. She had a feeling her mother was right. "Please don't tell me that you think he's getting some sort of perverse satisfaction out of having an intimate relationship with a Harte. I refuse to believe that he's so warped or so immature that he sees seducing me as a form of one-upsmanship."

"No."

She felt her stomach unknot. "He wouldn't stoop to such a thing just to score points off a Harte. Heck, his brother is married to one now. Even Granddad couldn't possibly believe—"

"No," Elaine said again, soothing now but firm. "I don't think Gabe would seduce you just to score points in that ridiculous old feud. He's a long-term strategist, not a short-term opportunist."

She let herself relax a little more. "So, what are you trying to say, Mom?"

"I just want you to be careful, dear. Your father and I have been talking a lot lately. It is clear that Harte Investments will have to be sold or merged when Hampton retires in a couple of years. None of you three kids wants to take over the company, nor does your father want you to feel that you must."

"I know. He's been great about not pressuring us."

"Lord knows he experienced enough pressure when he was your age. He refuses to put any of you through it, regardless of what Sullivan wants."

"What?" Lillian froze. "Are you telling me that the only reason Dad took over Harte Investments was because Granddad pressured him to do it?"

"In the years following the breakup of Harte-Madison, your grandfather put everything he had into building Harte Investments. It was always understood that Hampton would be his heir apparent. Your father went along with Sullivan's dreams but they were never really his dreams."

"I see."

Lillian got to her feet and stood in front of the window, the phone clutched very tightly in her hand. She looked out at the white ripples on the bay and knew a strange sense of sudden understanding. It was as if a veil had been pulled back. She had just gotten a fleeting glimpse of a piece of family history that she had never even suspected existed.

"Hampton did not want any of you three to feel you had to live someone else's dreams," Elaine said. "He made that clear to your grandfather years ago."

"Dad took the heat for us? I always wondered why Granddad didn't make a bigger issue out of the fact that none of us showed much interest in Harte Investments. We all thought that Sullivan had just mellowed with the years."

"Fat chance." Elaine gave a soft, ladylike snort. "Your father went toe-to-toe with Sullivan more than once over that issue. He warned your grandfather that he would not permit any of you three to be coerced into turning the company into a family dynasty. Hampton wanted each of you to feel free to choose your own paths in life."

"But Dad never felt that he, himself, had that option?"

"Not in the early days," Elaine said. "But things have changed. Hampton and I agree now that life is simply too short to spend it maintaining someone else's vision. Your father has plans for his future and he's going after it with both hands. Sullivan has called the shots in this family long enough. He can do whatever he wants with Harte Investments. Hampton and I are cutting loose."

There was no mistaking the steely satisfaction and determination in her mother's voice. This was, Lillian thought, a whole new side of Elaine.

"You're talking about the charitable foundation you two plan to set up, aren't you?" Lillian asked.

"Yes. Your father can't wait to get started on it."

"I see." Lillian blinked away the moisture that was blurring her view of the bay. "Guess Hannah and Nick and I all owe Dad big-time for keeping Sullivan off our backs, huh?"

"Yes, you do," Elaine said pointedly. "But that's not the issue here. What I want you to understand is that Gabe

Madison is one very smart, very savvy CEO. Rumors travel like wildfire in his world. He has to be aware of the situation at Harte Investments. He must know very well that the company probably won't continue as a privately held family business much longer."

"So what?"

"I suspect he's working on the assumption that H.I. will either be merged or sold soon. But if he marries you—"

*"Stop."* Lillian could hardly breathe. "Stop right there. Don't say it, Mom. Please don't tell me that he's sleeping with me just because he thinks he can get his hands on a third of Harte Investments that way."

There was a heavily freighted pause on the other end of the line.

"He'd have to do more than sleep with you to get his hands on a large piece of the company," Elaine said finally. "He'd have to marry you to accomplish that goal, wouldn't he?"

Through the window Lillian could see that another new storm was moving in quickly. The winds were snapping and snarling beneath the eaves of the cottage. An ominous haze was forming out on the bay. The water was turning steel gray.

"Look on the bright side, Mom. Gabe hasn't said a word about marriage. I have it on good authority that, when you get right down to it, I'm not his type."

She went through the motions of making a pot of tea while she dealt with the floodtide of restless thoughts that cluttered her brain after she hung up the phone. By the time the water boiled, she had managed to regain some perspective.

Get a grip, she told herself as she poured the brewed

green tea into a cup. What she had said to her mother was true. Gabe had not even hinted at marriage. He seemed quite satisfied with the prospect of having an affair with her, but that appeared to be his only goal.

On the other hand, she did not have a great track record when it came to applying her intuitive abilities to Gabe Madison. For some reason, her normally reliable sensors always seemed to get scrambled when it came to analyzing his vibes. Until last night, for example, she had been laboring under the assumption that the man was suffering a severe case of burnout.

She wandered into her studio, mug in hand, and looked at the blank canvas propped on the easel. She had come here to Eclipse Bay to paint, but thus far she had done little more than unpack her paints and brushes. She had made some sketches but she had not done any serious work. The relationship with Gabe was proving to be a huge distraction.

She fiddled with a pencil for a while, doing a little drawing, trying to get into the zone where the vision of the picture took shape around her, forming an alternate universe.

But she couldn't concentrate, so she headed back toward the kitchen to refill her tea mug.

She saw the light on the telephone answering machine when she was halfway across the living room. Belatedly she remembered that there had been two messages. She had only listened to the one from her mother.

She changed course to play the second message.

". . . This is Mitchell Madison. We gotta talk."

Just what she needed to round out her day and ensure that she got absolutely no painting done whatsoever.

•    •    •

That afternoon, she walked into Mitchell Madison's garden and looked around with interest. She had heard about this fantasyland of lush ferns, exotic herbs, and exuberant roses for as long as she could recall. For years it had been generally accepted in Eclipse Bay that Mitchell's garden was far and away the most spectacular in town. Even now, in the heart of winter when all of the blooms had disappeared, it was an earthly paradise. But, then, they said gardening was Mitchell's passion and everyone knew how it was with a Madison and his passion.

She followed the graveled path that led past banks of thriving ferns and through a maze of exquisitely maintained plant beds. The recent rains had released rich scents from the ground. At the far end of the walk a large greenhouse loomed. She could see a shadowy figure moving behind the opaque walls.

She opened the door and stepped into the fragrant, humid warmth. Mitchell was working intently over some clay pots arrayed on a waist-high bench. He had a pair of small shears in one hand and a tiny trowel in the other. The pockets of his heavy-duty, dirt-stained apron were filled with gardening implements. He appeared to be totally engrossed in his plants.

"I got your message, Mr. Madison," she said from the doorway.

Mitchell looked up quickly, gray brows bristling above his fierce, aquiline nose. "There you are. Come in and close the door. It's cold out there today."

She stepped farther into the greenhouse, allowing the door to swing shut. "You made it sound urgent. Is something wrong?"

"Shoot and damn, course there's something wrong." He put down the shears and the trowel and stripped off his gloves. "I turned this thing over to Sullivan but as far as I can see, he hasn't done a blame thing to straighten up this mess. Looks like I'll have to take a hand."

"Situation?"

"First things first. You serious about Gabe or are you just havin' yourself some fun?"

She came to an abrupt halt. This was going to be worse than she imagined. For an instant she was afraid the thick air would suffocate her. With an effort of will, she managed to resist the temptation to flee back outside.

"I beg your pardon?"

"Don't play games with me, young woman. You know what I'm talkin' about here. If you're fixin' to break Gabe's heart, I want to find out now."

"Me? Break Gabe's heart?" From out of nowhere, anger surged through her. "What makes you think that's even a remote possibility?"

Madison gave a muffled snort. "You've got him in the palm of your hand and you know it. Question is, what are you gonna do about it?"

"That's ridiculous. Just because we're seeing a lot of each other—"

"Seeing each other? Huh. Appears to me that the two of you are doin' a heck of a lot more than just lookin' at each other. You think no one would notice if you just up and ran off to Portland together for a night? Shoot and damn, you aren't even trying to keep things a secret."

"You know as well as I do that you can't control gossip here in Eclipse Bay."

"When I was your age most folks had the common decency to do their foolin' around out of sight."

He was genuinely irate, she realized, as if this mess were somehow all her fault. His bad temper only served to inflame her own.

"That's not what I hear, Mr. Madison. The way my folks tell it, you were more than a little obvious about your fooling around back in the good old days. In fact, Madisons in general are notorious for keeping the gossip mills humming here in Eclipse Bay."

"Times change. Things are different now."

"The fact that things are different now doesn't change the past."

"We're talking about Gabe." Mitchell planted his hands on his hips. "He's a different kind of Madison."

"People keep saying that, but how do I know if it's true?"

"You're gonna have to take my word for it."

She smiled coldly. "Now why would I do that?"

"Look, I can see where you might not be able to figure him out. Gabe's a little complicated."

"A *little* complicated. That's putting it mildly."

"The important thing here is that I don't want him hurt. If you're not serious about him, I want you to break it off now before he gets in any deeper."

"Just because we're *seeing* each other," she said through her teeth, "it does not necessarily follow that your grandson is in love with me."

"If the two of you were just bouncing around together in a bed in Portland, that would be one thing. I wouldn't pay any attention. But Gabe left Madison Commercial to follow you here to Eclipse Bay. That means he's serious."

"Good grief, you make it sound like the company's his wife and I'm the other woman."

Mitchell nodded. "That's not too far off, when you think about it."

"Look, for the record, Gabe did not leave Madison Commercial for me." She spread her hands. "He's just taking a little vacation, that's all."

"Bullshit. 'Scuse my language. Gabe doesn't take vacations. Leastways, not monthlong ones. He walked out on M.C. because he lost his head over you. That's the only explanation."

"A very romantic notion but that's not what happened. Furthermore, there are any number of people around these parts and several in my own family who will be only too happy to tell you what they believe is the real reason he took a month off from Madison Commercial."

"And just what the heck do they figure that real reason is?"

"I'm sure you've heard the talk. The gossip in certain quarters is that Gabe wants to marry me in order to get his hands on a large piece of Harte Investments."

Mitchell stared at her in astonishment. He looked genuinely thunderstruck. "Are you crazy, woman? Madisons don't marry for money."

"Maybe most Madisons don't marry for money. But everyone has always claimed that Gabe is a different kind of Madison."

Mitchell snorted. "Not that different."

"Look, we all know that Madison Commercial is the most important thing in Gabe's life. It's his creation. Over the years, he has sacrificed for it, fought for it, nurtured it. Why wouldn't he be attracted to someone who could add significantly to his empire?"

"If he'd been the type to marry for money, he'd have married Marilyn Thornley all those years ago. Her family has plenty of cash."

She frowned. "I was under the impression that they broke up because Marilyn ditched him for Thornley, not because Gabe didn't want to marry her."

"Shoot and damn. Can't you figure it out for yerself? They split on accounta Gabe made it clear that Madison

Commercial was more important to him than she was.
That woman likes to be number one."

"So do I, Mr. Mitchell."

"You're a Harte. You understand about business coming first."

"No, as a matter of fact, I do not."

"Sure you do. Look, you know damn well you've got
Gabe's full, undivided attention and that means things are
dead serious. At least they are for him. What I want to
know is, how do you feel about Gabe? You willing to get
married?"

She took a step back and groped for the doorknob with
one hand. "Mr. Madison, this discussion is purely hypo-
thetical. For your information, the subject of marriage has
never come up between Gabe and me."

"Looks like it will. And pretty damn quick, too, if I
know Gabe. He didn't get where he is by letting grass
grow under his feet."

"I really don't think so, Mr. Madison." She found the
doorknob and wrapped her fingers around it very tightly,
using it to steady herself. "For the record, Gabe has made
it very clear that he does not want to marry what he refers
to as an arty type. If you will recall, I'm an artist. That
sort of takes me out of the running, don't you think?"

"Nah. Not with a Madison. Madisons aren't that logical when it comes to love."

She had to get out of here. She was ready to explode.
"Let me make something clear. If, and I repeat, if, Gabe
ever brought up the subject of marriage, I would want to
know that I was more important to him than just another
addition to his empire."

"And just how the hell is he supposed to prove that?"

"Beats me. That's not my problem. It's Gabe's. Assuming you're right, of course, which is highly doubt-ful."

"Shoot and damn, if that isn't just like a Harte. Askin' for hard evidence when it comes to something that's down-right impossible to prove." Mitchell leveled a finger at her. "Know what I think? I think you've just decided to play with him a little. You're havin' yourself some fun, aren't you? You're not serious about him."

She had the door open now but something in his voice made her pause on the threshold. "You're really worried about him, aren't you?"

"Got a right to worry about him. He's my grandson, damn it. I may not have done the best job of raising him and Rafe after their parents died, but I did what I could to make things right. I got a responsibility to Gabe. I got to look out for him."

She searched his face. "He has the impression that you don't care that he's made a success of Madison Com-mercial."

"Course I care," Mitchell roared. "I'm proud of what he's done with that company. He proved to you Hartes and the whole damn world that a Madison can make some-thin' of himself. He proved that a Madison who sets his mind to it can get his act together, that being a member of this family doesn't mean you're doomed to screw up everything you touch the way I did and the way his father did."

There was a short, hard silence.

"Did you ever tell him that?" Lillian asked softly. "Be-cause I think he needs to hear it."

Mitchell's mouth opened again but this time no words emerged.

She turned and walked out into the garden.

•　　•　　•

Gabe dunked a clam strip into the spicy red sauce. "Heard you went out to the house to see Mitchell this afternoon."

Lillian started a little. The fork in her hand trembled slightly. She clenched her fingers around it and stabbed at the mound of coleslaw on her plate.

"Who told you that?" she asked.

Stalling, he thought. Why? What the hell was going on here?

This morning when they had left Portland together he had been feeling good. More settled. Like he finally had a handle on this relationship. He had assured himself that various issues had been clarified.

He and Lillian were having an affair. They both agreed on that. Couldn't get much simpler or more straightforward than that.

But now that they were back in Eclipse Bay, everything was starting to get complicated again.

He pondered that while he listened to the background hum of conversations and the clatter of dishes and silverware. The Crab Trap was a noisy, cheerful place. Until Rafe and Hannah got Dreamscape open, it was the closest thing to fine dining that Eclipse Bay could offer. It boasted a view of the bay, actual tablecloths and little candles in old Chianti bottles. On prom night and Mother's Day it was always fully booked.

It had seemed the obvious choice for dinner tonight.

A little too obvious, he had realized a few minutes ago when Marilyn Thornley had walked in with a small entourage and occupied the large booth at the rear.

"Ran into Bryce at the gas station." Gabe put the clam strip into his mouth, chewed and swallowed. "He mentioned you'd been out to the house. Not like Bryce to say anything about a casual visit. He doesn't talk much. Must have figured it was important."

Lillian hesitated and then gave a tiny shrug. "Your grandfather left a message on my answering machine while we were in Portland. Said he wanted to see me. I drove over to his place. It seemed the polite thing to do under the circumstances."

"What did he want?"

"Seemed to think that I was exerting my feminine wiles on you. Weaving a net of seduction in which to trap you, et cetera, et cetera. Evidently he's afraid that I might break your heart."

He managed to swallow the clam strip without sputtering and choking but it was not easy.

"He said that? That he's worried you might break my heart?"

"Uh-huh."

"Well, shoot and damn."

"He said 'shoot and damn' a lot, too."

"This is a little embarrassing."

"He wanted to know if my intentions were honorable," Lillian said without inflection.

Gabe made himself pick up another clam strip. "What did you tell him?"

"I told him the same thing that I told my mother today when she asked me about our relationship."

Definitely getting more complicated by the minute.

"And what was that?" he asked.

She picked up her water glass. "That the subject of honorable intentions had not arisen and that it was highly unlikely to arise."

"You told both of them that?"

"Yes. Well, it's true, isn't it?"

"Want to talk about 'em now?" he asked.

She flushed and glanced hurriedly around, apparently

making certain that no one had overheard him. "That is not funny."

"Wasn't trying to make a joke."

"For heaven's sake, Gabe, keep your voice down."

"It is down. Yours is starting to get a little loud, though."

"You know, I don't need this. I've had a difficult day. I came here to work. Thus far I have accomplished nothing. Absolutely zilch."

"Painting not going well?" he asked.

"What painting? I'm starting to think I'll have to go back to Portland to get anything done."

"Take it easy. You seem a little tense tonight."

"I'm not tense," she muttered.

"Okay, if you say so, but I gotta tell you that you look tense."

She lowered her fork very deliberately. "If this is your idea of a relaxing evening, I—" She broke off, stiffening in her chair. "Oh, damn."

"What's wrong? Is it Marilyn? I saw her come in earlier. Don't worry about her, she's busy with her staff in the booth at the back. I don't think she'll pester us tonight."

"Not Marilyn." Lillian stared past him toward the door. "Anderson."

"Flint? Here? What the hell?" He turned to follow her gaze. Sure enough, J. Anderson Flint stood in close conversation with the hostess. "Well, what do you know? Almost didn't recognize him in his clothes."

"What on earth could he possibly be doing in Eclipse Bay?"

"I'd say that was obvious." Gabe turned back to his food. "He followed you here."

"There is absolutely no reason for him do that."

"I can think of one."

She frowned. "What?"

"He wants to buy your matchmaking program, remember?"

"Oh. I forgot about that. But I told him I didn't want to sell."

"Probably thinks he can talk you into it."

"Damn. I did not need this."

Gabe turned his head to take another look at Flint. At that moment Anderson caught sight of Lillian. His smile was the sort a man bestows on a long-lost pal. He made a never-mind gesture to the hostess and started across the restaurant.

"He followed you, all right," Gabe said.

Lillian crushed a napkin in one hand. "I can't believe he wants my program that badly."

"You made a lot of money with that program. Why wouldn't he want to do the same?"

Her brows came together in a sharp frown. "You really are paranoid when it comes to money, aren't you?"

"I'm not paranoid, I'm cautious."

"Cautious, my—"

"Lillian." Anderson came to a halt beside the table before Lillian could finish her sentence. He leaned down with the clear intent of kissing her lightly in greeting. "What a pleasant surprise."

Lillian turned her head slightly, just enough to avoid the kiss. "What are you doing here?"

"I'm attending a conference at Chamberlain College. Arrived this afternoon. I'm staying at a motel just outside of town. I remember your saying something about taking some time off here in Eclipse Bay. We'll have to get together while I'm here." He extended his hand to Gabe. "J. Anderson Flint. I don't believe we've met."

"Gabe Madison." He rose slowly and kept the handshake perfunctory. "We haven't been formally introduced but I did see you once. Don't think you would remember the occasion, though. You were a little busy at the time."

"Gabe Madison of Madison Commercial? This is, indeed, a pleasure. Are you one of Lillian's clients?"

"As a matter of fact—"

"We're friends," Lillian interrupted crisply. "We both have roots here in Eclipse Bay. My sister is married to his brother. Our families go back a long way together."

"I see." Anderson kept his attention on Gabe. "How long are you going to be in town?"

"As long as it takes," Gabe said.

There was a stir at the front of the restaurant. He was conscious of a change in the atmosphere of the room. At the door an attractive woman was in heated conversation with the hostess.

"That's Claire Jensen." Lillian sounded concerned. "Marilyn's new campaign manager, remember? Looks like something's wrong."

She was right, he thought. Even from here he could see that Claire's face was tight with fury.

He also noticed that Marilyn had left her booth and was making her way swiftly toward the front of the restaurant. Her mouth was compressed into a tight, determined line.

"Uh-oh," Lillian said. "I don't like the looks of this."

Claire's voice rose above the hubbub. "Get out of my way, I said." She tried to push the hostess aside. "I have something to say to that bitch and I'm not leaving until I've said it."

Marilyn reached the hostess's podium. She gripped Claire's arm.

"I'll take care of this," she said to the hostess.

"Let go of me, you bitch," Claire raged. "Take your hands off me. I'll have you arrested. You can't do this."

But Marilyn already had her halfway through the door. Within seconds both women disappeared outside into the rainy night.

A hush fell over the restaurant. It lasted for all of five seconds. Then the room erupted in a buzz of excited conversation.

"Was that Marilyn Thornley?" Anderson sounded awed. "The wife of the politician who quit the senate race?"

"Soon to be ex-wife." Lillian watched the closed doors at the front of the room. "And something tells me that Claire Jensen is now an ex–campaign manager. Poor Claire. I wonder what happened? I thought everything was going so well for her in her new job."

The front door opened again a short time later. Marilyn strode back into the room, looking cool and unruffled by the skirmish. She paused to speak quietly to the hostess. Then she walked straight toward the table where Gabe sat with Lillian.

"You know her? You know Marilyn Thornley?" Anderson asked urgently.

"Her family has had a summer place here in town for years," Lillian explained. "Gabe is much better acquainted with her than I am, however."

Gabe gave her what he hoped was a silencing glare. He got one of her bright just-try-to-shut-me-up looks in return.

Marilyn arrived at the table.

"Sorry about that little scene," she said. "I had to let Claire go today. She didn't take it well."

"Terminations are always so stressful, aren't they?" Anderson's voice throbbed with compassion. "May I say that you handled that unfortunate scene very effectively. You took complete control before things got out of hand. That's the key. Complete control."

"Someone had to do something before she interrupted everyone's dinner." Marilyn smiled and extended a graceful hand. "Marilyn Thornley."

Anderson looked dazzled. "J. Anderson Flint. In town for a conference at Chamberlain. I'm delighted to meet you, Mrs. Thornley."

"Please, call me Marilyn."

"Yes, of course."

This was getting downright sticky, Gabe mused.

"Got a new campaign manager lined up?" he asked.

"I'm putting together a short list," Marilyn said. "I intend to announce my selection as soon as possible. This problem couldn't have come at a worse time. I can't afford to lose any momentum."

Anderson glanced toward the door, a concerned expression knitting his brows. "I trust your former manager won't cause you any trouble. Disgruntled employees can sometimes be dangerous."

"Claire will behave herself if she knows what's good for her," Marilyn declared. "It was a pleasure to meet you, Mr. Flint. Any friend of Gabe's and Lillian's is welcome at the institute. Please feel free to drop by while you're in town and pick up some of my campaign material."

"I'll do that," Anderson said immediately.

Marilyn inclined her head. "Wonderful. Now I'll let you two get back to your meal. Have a nice evening."

She walked away toward the booth at the rear. Anderson did not take his eyes off her.

"A very impressive woman," he breathed. "Very impressive. So forceful. Dynamic. Authoritative. We need more people like her in public office."

Lillian caught Gabe's eye. She looked amused.

"A perfect match," she murmured beneath the hum of background chatter.

He grinned. "Are you speaking as a professional?"

"Absolutely."

He knew before she started making excuses that she wasn't going to spend the night with him.

"I really need to get some sleep," Lillian said when they walked out of the restaurant some time later. "I want to get up early tomorrow morning and try to do some work."

"Here we go again. It's those conversations you had with your mother and Mitchell, isn't it?" He opened the door of the Jag with a little more force than was necessary. "They messed with your mind."

She slid into the dark cave that was the front seat. "It's got nothing to do with them. I just need some quiet time."

"Sure. Quiet time."

"I told you earlier that I haven't gotten any real painting done since I got here. If I go home with you tonight, I probably won't get to work until noon or later."

"Wouldn't want to interfere with your best painting time."

He closed the door. With a little more force than was necessary.

# chapter 13

"It's just a business," Hampton said on the other end of the line.

"The hell it is." He'd had enough of the familiar argument, Sullivan decided. He ended the call abruptly with a sudden punch of a button.

He ought to be used to this feeling after so many years of butting heads with his stubborn son. It was always like this whenever the subject of the future of Harte Investments arose. Hampton had done a brilliant job with the company, but he flatly refused to be concerned about what happened to it in the next generation. As if it didn't matter a damn.

It had taken him a long time to realize that, to Hampton, Harte Investments was just a business. Running the company was nothing more than a job to him. He had done it extraordinarily well but he could walk away tomorrow and never look back.

In fact, walking away from H.I. was precisely what Hampton planned to do. Sometime in the next two years.

Sullivan swore under his breath and reached for his cane. He still could not believe that after having worked so hard to take the company to another level, his son was looking forward to retiring so that he could start a charitable foundation.

As far as he was concerned, Sullivan thought, charity began at home.

*Just a business.*

What the hell was the matter with everyone else in the family? Didn't they understand that a company like Harte Investments was a work of art? It had required vision and sweat to bring it to life. It was the result of a lot of carefully calculated risks and farsighted strategy. It had heart. It had struggled and fought and survived in a jungle where other businesses, large and small, got eaten alive.

And now, because none of his grandchildren had any interest in the company, it would be sold or swallowed up by some other, larger, predator.

He rapped the tip of the cane sharply against the cool terra-cotta tiles of the living room floor. The small gesture did nothing to release his pent-up frustration.

*Just a business.*

He stopped at the bank of floor-to-ceiling French doors that overlooked the pool.

Rachel was on her last lap. He watched her glide through the turquoise water and felt some of his anger fade. He became aware of the quiet sense of connection that he always experienced when he saw her. It calmed him and gave him a centered feeling that he could not explain. The older he got, the more he realized that Rachel helped define him. A great deal of what he knew about himself he had learned from living with her all these years.

He opened one of the glass-paned doors and went out

onto the patio. It was late afternoon. The long rays of the desert sun were blocked by the walls of the house. The pool lay in comfortable shadow. In the distance the mountains were very sharp against the incredibly blue Arizona sky.

He selected two bottles of chilled springwater from the small refrigerator he had installed near the outdoor grill and lowered himself onto a lounger. He unscrewed the cap of one of the bottles, took a long swallow, and waited for Rachel to emerge from the jeweled pool. Talking to her always helped him put things into perspective.

She reached the steps and walked up out of the sparkling water. He watched her peel her swim cap off her short, silver-blond hair and admired her figure in the black-and-white bathing suit. After all this time he still felt the quiet heat of sexual attraction. She was only five years younger than he but somewhere along the line she had stopped aging, at least to him. He would want her until the day he died. And probably after that, too.

Her mouth curved as she walked toward him across the patio. "I can see that the discussion with Hampton did not go well."

"I don't know where he gets that stubborn streak."

"Certainly not from you."

She picked up her white terrycloth robe, wrapped it around herself and sat down beside him. He handed her one of the bottles of cold water. She removed the cap and took a sip. They sat and watched the sunlight on the mountains. Sullivan relaxed into the lounger.

"Hampton and Elaine think that Gabe will try to marry her in order to get his hands on a chunk of Harte," he said after a while.

"What do you think?"

"No Madison I ever knew had enough common sense to marry for money."

"Good point. But everyone says that Gabe is a different kind of Madison. His company is his passion. He built it to prove something to himself and everyone else. It's as important to him as Harte Investments is to you."

"I know." Sullivan grimaced. "Just wish one or two of my grandkids felt the same way about H.I. It's Hampton's fault that none of them ever showed much interest in the company."

"He didn't want them to feel the same kind of pressure he got from you when he was growing up."

"Pressure, hell. I just guided him a little, that's all."

"You groomed him for Harte from the day he was born. Made him think he owed it to you and that he had to prove he wouldn't turn out to be the same kind of wastrel Mitchell's son was. Hampton took over the firm to please you and you know it."

"What's wrong with that? He's done a damn fine job of growing the company. He couldn't have run it that well if he hadn't had a talent for business."

"Hampton has a talent, all right. But he wants to use it to set up that foundation of his. He's had enough of H.I. and he doesn't want any of our grandchildren to be forced into running it when he steps down."

Sullivan groaned. "I knew Hannah and Lillian probably wouldn't take on H.I. But I had hopes that Nick would take the helm eventually. Why he had to go off on his own to write mysteries is beyond me. Don't know why anyone as smart as he is would want to waste time writing novels when he could be running a company the size of Harte Investments."

"All three of them have followed their own stars and

that's the way it should be." Rachel patted his shoulder. "Besides, you enjoy Nick's mysteries and you know it."

Sullivan brooded on that for a moment. "Little Carson may show some interest in business in a few years," he said hopefully. "He's a bright kid."

"For heaven's sake, he's only five years old. It will be ages before Carson can even think of assuming such a responsibility. You certainly can't expect Hampton to hold the reins for another two decades on the off-chance that your great-grandson might someday want to take over the business."

Sullivan leaned his head against the back of the lounger and considered the problem.

"You're always telling me what people will do and why," he said eventually. "Do you think Gabe Madison would marry Lillian just to get his hands on Harte?"

To his surprise, Rachel hesitated briefly. A troubled frown creased her forehead.

"It's a legitimate concern, under the circumstances," she said finally. "Of the two boys, I think Gabe was more affected by all the baggage Mitchell carried because of the blowup of Harte-Madison. Proving to himself and everyone else that he could compete with a Harte has been a fierce source of motivation for Gabe for years. In addition, H.I. is one of his competitors."

"Only occasionally. H.I. and M.C. have carved out different territories for the most part."

"My point is that if he saw a chance to control a portion of Harte Investments he might not be able to resist for both emotional and business reasons."

"The ultimate revenge for a Madison, hmm?"

"I'm not saying that it would be a deliberate act of revenge on his part. More of a subconscious motivation."

"Subconscious, my sweet patoot." Sullivan took a swig

of his springwater and lowered the bottle. "When it comes to business, Gabe Madison knows exactly what he's doing."

Rachel stretched her legs out on the lounger. "That stupid feud. I can't believe that it's still affecting both our family and the Madisons, too."

Sullivan said nothing.

Rachel studied the pool for a while. "Do you ever think about her?"

When Rachel spoke in that quiet, thoughtful tone he paid attention. It meant that she was very serious.

"Who?" he asked, groping to refocus on whatever this new issue was.

"Claudia Banner. The woman who destroyed Harte-Madison and ruined your friendship with Mitchell. I've always assumed that she was very beautiful."

He summoned up an image of the Claudia he had known all those years ago, contemplated it for a few minutes and then shrugged.

"She was a pretty little redhead. Sharp as a tack, too. Mitch and I were fresh out of the service and eager to make our fortunes. She showed us how to do it. That combination of qualities can make a woman seem pretty damn attractive."

"Were you in love with her?"

He sensed a minefield.

"Thought I was for a time," he said. "Changed my mind real fast when she disappeared with the total assets of Harte-Madison and dumped the company into bankruptcy. But poor Mitch had fallen for her hook, line, and sinker. He refused to believe she'd conned us. He was convinced that I had somehow used her to grab his share of the firm."

"Hence the infamous knock-down-drag-out fistfight in

front of Fulton's Supermarket and the start of the legendary Harte-Madison feud."

"It was a long time ago, Rachel. Mitch and I were young men. Young men do dumb things."

"You said you thought you were in love with Claudia Banner."

"For a time."

"Don't you know for certain whether or not you loved her?"

He gazed out at the mountains. "I now know for sure that whatever the hell I felt for Claudia Banner was not love."

"How can you be so certain of that?"

"I didn't know what love was until I met you."

She turned her head very quickly, obviously startled.

Then she laughed softly, leaned across the small space that separated the two loungers and kissed him lightly.

"Good answer," she said.

"Thanks. I thought it was pretty good, myself."

It was also the truth, he thought. But after all these years he was certain she knew that.

# chapter 14

He dressed carefully before he went to see her, wanting to strike precisely the right note. So much hung in the balance. He contemplated the limited range of clothing in the closet. Unfortunately he had left many of his best shirts and ties behind in Portland. He hadn't expected to need them here on the coast. But he was not entirely unprepared. He was never entirely unprepared. He wanted her to know that.

After due consideration he went with a pale-blue shirt that matched his eyes and an Italian knit sweater that made his shoulders appear a little broader. The trousers and loafers worked well with the sweater.

He stood in front of the mirror studying the effect. Not quite right. He took off the sweater and went back to the closet for a tie and the corduroy jacket. The tie showed respect. The cord jacket said he was a deep thinker.

Satisfied, he left the room and went outside to the parking lot. He got into the car and drove the short distance to the Eclipse Bay Policy Studies Institute.

Ten minutes later he was standing in front of her secretary's desk.

"I'm here to see Mrs. Thornley," he said.

The secretary looked skeptical and apologetic at the same time. It was probably a natural-born talent.

"Do you have an appointment?"

"No, but please give her this card. I think she'll see me."

The secretary examined the card and the note he had jotted on it. She got to her feet, went to the closed door behind her desk and opened it.

He waited until she disappeared inside before checking his reflection in the highly polished chrome base of her name plaque.

He straightened quickly when the door opened again.

"Mrs. Thornley will see you, Dr. Flint."

"Thank you."

He took a deep breath, preparing himself for acute disappointment in case he had gotten the wrong impression about her last night. The scene in the restaurant had happened so quickly.

He went through the door, closed it firmly and stood looking at his fate.

She studied him from where she sat behind her desk, a vision in a fitted red knit jacket that was accented with gold buttons and well-defined, padded shoulders. She toyed with the small card he had sent in a moment earlier.

He gave the office a quick once-over, checking the quality of the furnishings. First class all the way. The lady had style and taste. The room was spacious with a view of the town and the bay spread out below in the distance.

There was another door on the far side of the office.

It stood open a crack. Someone was moving around in the adjoining room. Probably an assistant or a speechwriter. He heard a desk drawer slam.

"Please sit down, Dr. Flint," Marilyn said. Cool self-possessed authority rang in the words.

He felt his blood heat. He had not been wrong. She was magnificent. A goddess.

He lowered himself into one of the sleek black leather chairs.

Marilyn rose, crossed the room to the door that separated her office from the smaller one on the far side of the room and closed it very firmly. She smiled at him.

Absolutely magnificent.

"We need to talk," Anderson said.

"I found out that she had an affair with Trevor," Marilyn said. She went to stand at the window of the cottage and looked out over the bay. "I could hardly keep her on as my campaign manager after I learned the truth."

"Guess it would be a little awkward," Lillian admitted. She glanced at her watch. Another morning's work shot. The last thing she had needed today was to open the front door and find Marilyn Thornley on her front porch. *Why me?* she wondered. She did not relish being a politician's confidant.

"I knew that he was probably screwing someone but I just assumed it was one of his perky little campaign workers. Someone unimportant. Lord knows, it wouldn't have been the first time. Trevor and I had an understanding, you see. As long as he was reasonably discreet about it, I could ignore it."

Marilyn looked different this morning, Lillian thought. No longer the battlefield general with antifreeze running in her veins. More like a woman who has learned the name of her ex-husband's lover. Hurt. Angry. Resentful.

"I've heard about understandings like that," Lillian said neutrally.

Marilyn's mouth twisted. "You sound very disapproving."

"Let's just say I wouldn't want a marriage based on that kind of unwritten contract."

"You'd rather be married for your family's company, is that it?"

It wasn't easy but Lillian managed to hold on to her temper. "I don't know why you came here this morning to tell me this, Marilyn. It's none of my business."

"Don't you understand? I had to talk to someone. I don't know anyone else I can trust here in town. Not with something this personal. I certainly can't talk to anyone on my staff. I would look weak and emotional." Marilyn took a deep breath and exhaled, making a visible effort to compose herself. "I'm sorry. I shouldn't have made that crack about being married for Harte Investments. That was uncalled for."

Lillian lounged back against the counter. "Forget it. Not like you're the first person to leap to the conclusion that Gabe is only interested in me because of Harte."

"Still, it wasn't right. I apologize. I'm not at my best this morning. The thing is, even though I knew Trevor was sleeping with someone, I never dreamed it was Claire."

"You're sure it was Claire who had the affair with Trevor?" Lillian asked.

"Yes."

"How did you find out?"

"Pure accident. I was going through some old expense account statements the other day, gathering data for my divorce attorney. I came across records of some reimbursements Trevor had made to Claire. At first I thought they were legitimate expenses associated with the campaign. Something made me dig a little deeper. Turned out the expenses were incurred at a series of cheap hotels over a period of several months. In each case Trevor and Claire had registered as Mr. and Mrs. Smith. Can you believe it?"

"Tacky."

"Very. Once I started looking, I turned up a few other unusual receipts. When it comes to sex, Trevor has his little, uh, eccentricities. Apparently Claire catered to them."

"I see. What did Claire say when you confronted her?"

"She denied it, of course. Claimed Trevor must have been with some other woman, not her."

"But you didn't believe her."

"No." Marilyn rubbed her temples in a gesture of weariness that seemed uncharacteristic. "Naturally I had to let her go. Wouldn't you have done the same?"

"If I was absolutely sure of my facts."

Definitely should not have answered the door, Lillian thought. At the very least, she ought not to have invited Marilyn inside. But it had been impossible to ignore the bleak pain in the other woman's eyes. The sisterhood thing.

"I really shouldn't have come here," Marilyn said. "I had no right to dump this on you. But I woke up this morning needing to talk to someone and I couldn't think of anyone else. You and I have a common bond."

"I beg your pardon?"

"Gabe."

"*Gabe?* That's stretching the definition of a common bond a bit far, don't you think?"

Marilyn rested a hand on the windowsill. "Don't worry, I'm not even going to try to take him away from you."

"Oh, hey, thanks. I appreciate that."

"I'm a pragmatic woman," Marilyn said. "I don't waste time beating my head against stone walls. You don't have to think of me as your competition."

"Well, as a matter of fact I hadn't thought of you in quite those terms."

"When I saw you two together that night at the old Buckley place I knew that I had no chance of ever resuming my relationship with him. You can offer him something I can't."

Lillian felt her insides tighten. "I suppose you mean Harte Investments?"

"I'm sure it's not just the company," Marilyn said. "He probably finds you attractive, too."

"Gosh. You really think so?"

Marilyn sighed. "You want to know a little secret? I used to blame your family and Harte Investments for the breakup of my relationship with Gabe."

Lillian stilled. "I see."

"A part of me will always wonder what would have happened if he hadn't been so obsessed with competing with you Hartes. Who knows? Maybe he and I could have had something lasting together."

Enough with the sisterhood thing, Lillian thought. She had done her politically correct duty. She straightened away from the counter.

"If you don't mind, I have a lot of things to do this morning, Marilyn."

Marilyn regarded her with an apologetic expression. "Yes, of course. Forgive me. I didn't mean to get into old history."

"Didn't you?"

"No. I just wanted to talk to someone." Marilyn blinked rapidly and wiped moisture away from the corner of her eye with a fingertip. "Things have been a little rough lately, what with the divorce and getting my campaign organized and now finding out that my campaign manager had an affair with Trevor."

Lillian hesitated. "You've been under a lot of stress. Maybe you need to take some time off. Go somewhere quiet and relax before you start your big push for office."

"I can't afford to take that kind of time. Not at this juncture." Marilyn squared her shoulders. "I intend to go to Washington, D.C., one of these days, so I'd better get used to dealing with stress, hadn't I? But I shouldn't have come here. It wasn't fair to you."

"Forget it. That's certainly what I intend to do." Lillian went past her and opened the front door. "Good luck in the campaign, Marilyn."

"Thank you." Marilyn walked out onto the porch and went down the steps to the Mercedes. She paused just before getting behind the wheel. "I hope you'll vote for me."

Lillian watched her drive away and then slowly closed the door. She walked to the table, picked up her mug and carried it into the second bedroom. She looked at the blank canvas propped on the easel.

For a long time she sipped tea and contemplated the empty white space, trying to get back into that alternate reality where she stood within the vision. But it was hopeless. Too many real-world thoughts barred the way.

"... *You want to know a secret? I used to blame your family and Harte Investments for the breakup of my relationship with Gabe.*"

After a while she gave up trying to get into the zone. She went into the kitchen and took a bottle of wine and some cheese out of the refrigerator. She put both into a paper sack.

She went upstairs to her bedroom, opened a drawer, selected a nightgown and a change of underwear, and put them into a leather tote. In the bathroom she quickly packed the basics into a small, zippered case and dropped the case into the tote.

Carrying the tote in one hand, she went back downstairs, collected the sack with the wine and cheese inside and a jacket. She left the cottage through the mudroom door.

Outside she was met with a brisk, bracing wind and the roar of the surf down in Dead Hand Cove. The day was already darkening into night.

She walked across the top of the bluffs to the old Buckley place.

Gabe opened the back door just as she raised her hand to knock. He looked at the bulging tote bag.

"Looks like you plan to stay awhile."

"Thought I'd spend the night if it's okay with you."

He smiled slowly, emerald eyes warm and sensual.

"Oh, yeah," he said.

She walked into the kitchen.

"Don't want to push my good luck but curiosity compels me to ask." He took the tote and the sack from her. "Why the change of heart?"

"Marilyn came to see me today. You know, it's one thing for my mom and your grandfather to mess with my mind. They're family. They got a right, I guess. But having your ex-girlfriend try the same trick is going too far. Got to draw the line somewhere."

He closed the door and looked at her. "Marilyn paid you a visit today?"

"Uh-huh."

"Why?"

"Among other things, she said she needed to talk to someone about the real reason she'd fired Claire."

"And that reason is?"

"She thinks Claire had an affair with Trevor."

"She *thinks* that or she knows it?"

"Let's just say she's convinced of it." She unfastened her cloak. "At any rate she doesn't trust Claire anymore. So she canned her."

Gabe took the cloak. It spilled from his hand in an iridescent waterfall.

"What's the big deal?" he said. "Marilyn is divorcing Thornley. Their relationship was obviously based on Trevor's electability, not true love. Why worry about an affair with Claire that may or may not have happened?"

"For heaven's sake, Gabe. Would you want to employ someone as your close, personal assistant who had slept with your wife?"

He didn't miss a beat.

"I'd destroy any man who slept with my wife."

The absolute finality of that statement made her catch her breath. "I see."

"But I'm not a politician," Gabe continued. "Politicians are different."

She thought about Marilyn's disturbed behavior. "I'm not sure that they're so very different."

"Marilyn mention me?"

"Oh, yes."

"What did she say?"

"What everyone else seems to be saying. Something about your interest in me probably being linked to an obsessive interest in Harte Investments."

He watched her with unreadable eyes. "And that observation is what made you decide to come over here this afternoon?"

"I'm here because I want to be here."

"Glad to hear that. You do realize that you probably won't get home until noon tomorrow."

"Not like I'm getting much work done here in Eclipse Bay, anyway."

# chapter 15

She did not return to the cottage until after lunch the following day, just as Gabe had warned. He walked her back across the bluffs and left her at the front door with a long, lingering kiss.

"I know you need to paint this afternoon," he said. "Why don't I come over here for dinner tonight? I'll bring the wine this time."

She went into the house and smiled at him through the screen. "That'll work."

He raised a hand in casual farewell and went down the steps. She watched him walk away across the bluffs, hands shoved deep into the pockets of his jacket, his dark hair ruffled by the wind. A dark squall line hung across the bay, moving swiftly toward shore.

Memories of last night's lovemaking ignited hot little sparklers of pleasure deep inside her. But there was something else burning down there, too, a long fuse that promised a painful explosion sometime in the future when this very adult relationship blew up in her face.

*Don't look too far ahead. Just take it one day at a time. That's all you can do for now. That's all you dare to do now.*

Gabe was right. She needed to paint.

She hung her jacket in the closet and started toward the hall that led to her makeshift studio. Halfway across the living room she noticed the light on the answering machine and changed course. She went to the table where the phone sat, and punched up the message.

She was startled to hear Arizona Snow's harsh whisper.

> *". . . Being tailed by an institute spy. Bastard's too smart to get close enough for me to get a look at him but I know he's out there somewhere, watchin' me. I can feel him. Must've seen me doin' recon and knows I'm on to the plans for the new wing.*
>
> *"I called you on accounta I don't know Gabe's number. I'm at a pay phone at the pier. Can't risk leaving all the details on that machine of yours. When I leave here, I'll head for my place and hole up there.*
>
> *"I got to talk to you and Gabe. Heard you two are shackin' up together so if this message gets to you, I figure it'll get to him, too. My place is the only safe house in the sector. Appreciate it if you two would come on out as soon as you can. Things are getting hot around here.*
>
> *"Gotta go. Bye."*

There was a muffled crash on the other end of the line. Arizona had hung up in a hurry.

Lillian glared at the answering machine. "You know,"

she said to the universe at large, "I came out here to find a nice, serene place to do some painting."

She picked up the phone and dialed Gabe's cell phone. He answered on the first ring.

"Madison here."

She could hear the muffled sound of the wind and the surf. He was probably halfway back to the old Buckley place.

"Doing anything important?" she asked.

"Depends how you define important. I'm thinking about a proposal from a small startup company that needs five million in cash. That strike you as a weighty matter?"

"Five mil? Sounds like penny-ante stuff to me."

"Appreciate your consulting opinion."

"My bill is in the mail." She watched the dark shadow of the squall line moving across the bay. "Would you like to do something more exciting?"

"Such as?"

"Help defend Eclipse Bay against the spies up at the institute?"

"Does this involve frozen extraterrestrials?"

"Probably."

"Well, it's not like I've got anything else to do now that you've taken all the fun out of my puny little five-mil deal. I'm almost back to the house. I'll get my car and come pick you up."

The squall struck just as he geared down to take the steep, rutted path that led through the woods to Arizona's cabin. He did not want to think about what the rough road was doing to the Jag's expensive alignment.

"She said she was being followed?" he asked.

"Yes."

"Did she give you a description?"

"No." Lillian watched the narrow road. "Just said she thought it was an institute spy. But she sounded nervous, Gabe. That's what worried me. In all the years I've known A.Z. she's always seemed very cool and somehow in full command of her crazy conspiracy theories. I've never heard her sound genuinely scared or even uneasy."

"Maybe she's slipped another cog. Sunk a little deeper into her fantasy world."

"Gone from being seriously eccentric to seriously crazy, you think?"

"It's a possibility."

Lillian folded her arms tightly beneath her breasts. Her body was tense. She was concerned and she appeared to be getting more so as they got closer to Arizona's cabin.

"Take it easy, we both know there's nothing really wrong here," he said.

"It's A.Z.'s state of mind I'm worried about. I wonder if getting involved with that crowd at the bakery is responsible for pushing her over some psychological edge."

"If she has cracked up big-time," he said, "you're right. We've got a big problem on our hands. I doubt if we'll be able to talk her into checking into some nice quiet psych ward for observation."

"She'd never trust a psychiatrist or a sanitarium."

"Probably not." He negotiated another sharp bend in the road. "There's not much you can do for someone who won't go for help unless she is a clear danger to herself or others."

"Let's try to keep some perspective here. We're talking as if A.Z. has gone off the deep end. We have no evidence of that yet. Keep in mind that she hasn't ever hurt anyone in her life."

"That we know of."

She shot him a swift, searching glance. "What do you mean?"

"Just that no one around here knows anything about her past before she showed up in Eclipse Bay. I remember asking Mitchell about her once when I was in high school. He just shrugged and said that she was entitled to her privacy so long as she didn't do anyone else any harm."

"That's the whole point," Lillian said. "To the best of our knowledge or anyone else's she's never done any damage to people or property."

He navigated the last tight curve in the road and saw the cabin. Rain and wind slashed the heavy limbs of the trees that loomed over the weather-beaten structure. Arizona's ancient truck was parked in the small clearing.

He eased the Jag to a halt behind the truck and switched off the engine.

"Well, at least she's here and not out prowling around the new wing of the institute with her VPX 5000," he said.

He unfastened his seat belt and reached into the back seat for Lillian's rain cloak and his jacket.

"She said something about holing up for a while." Lillian put her arms into the sleeves of her cloak and pulled the hood up over her head. "That's not like her, either, when you stop and think about it. She's always out doing recon and surveillance. Says she likes the bad guys to know she's keeping an eye on them."

"True."

He shrugged into the jacket, tugged the hood up over his head and opened the door. Rain driven by rough winds dampened his hair when he got out.

Lillian did not wait for him to come around to her side

of the car. She already had her own door open. A few
seconds later she joined him at the front of the Jag.

They both went quickly toward the shelter of the porch.
Gabe took the steps two at a time and came to a halt at
the front door. Dripping rain from her sparkling cloak,
Lillian stopped beside him.

There was no doorbell. Gabe banged the brass eagle
knocker a few times.

There was no response. No surprise, he thought. No
right-thinking paranoid would open a door without veri-
fying the identity of the person on the other side.

"A.Z.? Gabe and Lillian out here," he called.

The door did not open. He glanced at the nearest window. It was covered with what looked like blinds fashioned from metal slats.

"I got your message." Lillian rapped her knuckles on
the blank window. "Are you okay in there?"

The wind-driven rain whipped around the cabin. He
knew Lillian was getting more agitated. He had to admit
that the utter silence from inside the cabin was starting
to bother him, too.

He tried the heavy, steel-braced screen door. It was
locked.

"She's not a young woman," Lillian said. "I hope something hasn't happened."

"Like what?"

"A heart attack or stroke. Or maybe she fell."

"Calm down. I'm sure she's fine. Probably locked in
her war room and can't hear us."

"Let's try the back door." Lillian turned and disappeared around the corner of the porch.

"Hang on, not so fast, damn it." He went after her,
moving quickly. "The woman's a full-blown conspiracy

theorist, remember? Paranoid as hell. No telling how she's got this place booby-trapped."

"I just want to see if I can find a window that isn't covered with those steel blinds. I don't understand why she isn't—"

She broke off on a strangled gasp. He saw the crumpled body lying on the porch at the same time.

"A.Z." Lillian rushed forward. "Oh, my God, Gabe, I was afraid of this. She's had a heart attack."

She went to her knees beside Arizona, feeling for a pulse at the throat.

He looked at the blood on the wooden boards beneath Arizona's head and went cold.

"Not a heart attack." The cell phone was in his hand. He didn't remember taking it out of his pocket. He punched in the emergency number.

Lillian followed his gaze. "You're right. It wasn't her heart. She fell and hit her head." Her fingers moved gently on Arizona's throat. "She's breathing but she's unconscious. The bleeding doesn't seem to be too bad."

"Better not move her."

Lillian nodded. She stripped off her cloak and arranged it snugly around Arizona's chunky frame while he gave a terse account of the situation to the 911 operator.

He saw the overturned plant stand lying nearby just as he ended the call. The stand was made of wrought iron.

Lillian bent intently over A.Z. "Arizona? It's me, Lillian. Help is on the way. You're going to be okay. Can you hear me?"

Arizona groaned. Her lashes fluttered. She squinted up at Lillian.

"What happened?" she mumbled.

"It looks like you slipped and fell. How do you feel?"

"Bad."

"I'll bet you do," Lillian said gently. "But you're going to be okay.

Arizona closed her eyes again. She mumbled something.

"What did you say?" Lillian asked.

"Said I didn't fall."

"You probably don't remember much," Lillian said soothingly. "I think that's pretty normal when you've had a blow to the head. Don't worry about it."

Arizona's hand moved a little in a small, agitated gesture, but she did not speak again.

Lillian looked up and saw Gabe watching her. She frowned.

"What?"

"I don't think she fell, either," he said.

"Why in the world do you say that?"

"I'm no cop, but it looks to me like someone used that plant stand to hit her on the back of the head."

# chapter 16

They were standing in the busy hallway outside Arizona's hospital room. Monitors beeped and pinged. Lights winked on computer screens. High-tech equipment gleamed. Eclipse Bay Community Hospital had moved with the times, Gabe thought.

He noticed that everyone around him who wore a name tag and a stethoscope appeared purposeful and competent and a little high on adrenaline. Those who were not decked out with a name tag and a stethoscope looked worried. Civilians, Gabe thought. He and Lillian fit into that category. Definitely worried.

Sean Valentine, Eclipse Bay's chief of police, on the other hand, fell into some middle zone. He had the same purposeful, competent air that marked the members of the hospital staff, but he didn't look as if he were enjoying an adrenaline rush. There were deep lines around his eyes and mouth. The marks weren't caused by Arizona's problems. Sean always looked as if he anticipated the worst.

Gabe figured the permanently etched expression was a legacy of his days as a big-city cop in Seattle.

"Probably came home and interrupted some SOB who was trying to break into her cabin," Sean said. "The bastard must have grabbed the first available heavy object and used it on the back of her skull."

"Whoever he was, he can't be from around here," Gabe said. "Everyone in town knows that it would take an armored tank and a battering ram to break into A.Z.'s cabin."

"Could have looked like a challenge to some dumbass kids from Chamberlain who'd had a few beers," Sean speculated. "Or maybe a transient found the place and didn't realize it was actually a small fortress."

"He could have killed her." Lillian's anger vibrated in every word and in every line of her body. She was very tightly wound at the moment.

"The blow was a little off," Sean said. "Fortunately for A.Z. She's concussed but they say she should be okay. They're going to keep her here at the hospital for a couple of days for observation."

Lillian looked at him. "Are you sure we shouldn't take that message she left on my machine seriously?"

"I take everything seriously," Sean said. "Way I'm made, I guess. But I gotta tell you that a call from A.Z. claiming that she was being tailed by an institute spy does not give me a whole heck of a lot to work with. In her world, institute spies are everywhere and they're all trying to follow her."

"There is that," Lillian agreed reluctantly.

"Another thing," Sean added. "There's a small flaw in A.Z.'s logic here. Assuming the institute actually employed spies, none of them would need to tail her in order to find out where she lives. Everyone in town knows where her cabin is located. All anyone looking for her would have to do is ask a few questions down at Fulton's Supermarket or the video rental shop."

"Nobody ever said A.Z.'s logic holds up well under scrutiny," Gabe said.

Sean's face twisted briefly in a wry smile. "Nope."

Lillian gave them both a quelling glance. "A.Z. operates in a parallel universe but within that universe, her reasoning is consistent and logical."

Sean looked wary. "Meaning?"

"Meaning that something scared her enough to make her use a telephone and leave a message on an answering machine. She would never willingly do that if she could avoid it. She's convinced that all phones are tapped. She doesn't even have one in her house."

"Tapped by institute spies?" Sean asked politely.

Lillian exhaled unhappily. "Yes."

"I think I'll go with my theory of an interrupted burglary in progress for now, if you don't mind. But if you get any more useful information from her when you talk to her, let me know."

He nodded to Gabe, then turned and walked off down the hospital corridor. Lillian watched him until he turned a corner and disappeared. Then she looked at Gabe.

"He's probably right, isn't he?" she said.

"Probably." Gabe hesitated. "You have to admit, it's a simpler explanation than one involving vast government conspiracies. When it comes to this kind of stuff, cops prefer simple because most of the time that's the right answer."

"I know. And we are dealing with A.Z. here. Whatever the answer is, it can't possibly be as mysterious as she thinks it is. Come on, let's go see how she's doing."

"Sure."

He walked beside her to the doorway of the hospital

room. Arizona was stretched out on a bed. She looked so
different in a hospital gown, he thought. In all the years
he had known her he had never seen her in anything except military camouflage and boots. She had always
seemed curiously ageless, sturdy and vigorous. But now,
bandaged and helpless, her gray hair partially covered
with a white bandage, she looked her age. A wave of
anger swept through him. What kind of bastard would hit
an elderly woman on the head with a wrought-iron
planter?

A nurse wearing a tag inscribed with the name Jason
leaned over A.Z., taking her pulse. When he was finished
he lowered her wrist very gently to the sheet and moved
toward the door. Behind him, Arizona stirred restlessly
but she did not open her eyes.

"Are you family?" Jason asked quietly.

"No." Lillian looked toward the bed. "I don't think she
has any family. We're friends. How is she doing?"

"She's got a nasty headache and she's confused and
disoriented. Pretty much what you'd expect after a severe
blow to the head."

"A.Z. always seems confused and disoriented to people who don't know her well," Gabe said. "Has she said
anything?"

Jason shook his head. "Just keeps talking about something called a VPX 5000."

"Her new camera," Lillian said. "She was very excited
about it."

On the bed, Arizona moved slightly. She turned her
head on the pillow. Her face was drawn with pain. Her
cheeks were slightly sunken. "Lillian? Gabe?"

"Right here, A.Z." Lillian went to the bed and patted
Arizona's hand. "Don't worry about anything. You're
going to be fine."

"My VPX 5000." Arizona's voice had lost its usual hearty timbre. She sounded a thousand years old. "I can't find it."

"Don't worry about it," Lillian assured her. "You'll find it when they let you go home."

"No." Arizona gripped Lillian's hand with gnarled fingers. "They said someone hit me. Probably the institute spy. I'll bet he took my VPX 5000. Gotta get it back. Can't risk having it fall into the wrong hands. Pictures. Of the new wing. They'll destroy 'em."

Gabe went to stand at the bed. He leaned on the rails. "Tell you what, A.Z., Lillian and I will go back to your cabin and see if we can find the camera. Maybe you left it in your truck."

"Gotta find it." Arizona's eyes fluttered closed. "Can't let the bastards get it."

An hour later, after a fruitless search of the interior of Arizona's aging pickup, he closed the door on the driver's side and pocketed the keys. He watched Lillian come down the cabin's porch steps and start toward him.

"Any luck?" she asked.

"No. What about you?"

"I went over every square inch of the porch and checked the flower beds around it. It's gone, unfortunately. I hate to have to give her the bad news. She was so thrilled with that camera."

"She may be right. Whoever hit her probably stole it. Maybe he figured he could get a few bucks for it."

"If he's got any sense, he won't try to unload it anywhere near Eclipse Bay," Lillian said. "Sean Valentine will be watching for it and so will everyone else in town."

"I'll do some research online," Gabe said. "Maybe I can find another one to replace it for her."

Lillian flashed him a grateful smile. "That would be wonderful."

He liked it when she smiled at him like that, he thought. He liked it a lot. That smile had a very motivating effect on him. He took a long, slow breath and then he took her arm.

"It's getting late," he said. "Be dark soon. Let's go back to your place and get some dinner."

Another squall struck just as Gabe halted the car in front of the cottage. Lillian pulled up the hood of her cloak, opened the door, leaped out and made a dash for the front porch. Gabe was right behind her. She stopped in front of the door, shook rainwater off her cloak and rummaged in her purse for her keys.

When she got the door open, she headed straight for the mudroom, intending to hang up her cloak so that it could drip dry.

Gabe followed, stripping off his jacket. When they reached the mudroom she did not bother to switch on the overhead light. There was enough illumination from the hall to see the row of metal clothes hooks beneath the window.

"I don't know about you," she said, "but I'm starving."

"I'll open the wine. You can do the salad tonight."

"It's a deal." A damp draft sent a chill through her. "It's cold in here. Why don't you start a fire before you—" She broke off abruptly.

"What's wrong?"

"No wonder it's cold in here. The back door is open. I can't believe I forgot to lock up. But I've been distracted a lot lately."

She crossed the small space to push the door closed.

"Wait," Gabe said quietly, pointing to the door.

He reached out to switch on the mudroom light and then moved past her. She watched him lean forward slightly to examine the door frame.

"Damn."

"What is it?" She moved closer. "Something wrong?"

"Yeah. Something's wrong, all right. Looks like A.Z. wasn't the only one who got hit by a burglar today."

She didn't answer him, just stared, disbelieving, at the deep gouges in the wooden door frame and the broken lock.

"You sure there's nothing missing?" Sean Valentine asked for the second time.

"No, not as far as I can tell," Lillian said.

Gabe leaned against the kitchen counter and watched her answer Sean's questions. She sat hunched on the kitchen stool, knees drawn up, feet propped on the top rung.

"I went through the whole house," she added. "Nothing looks as if it's been touched. Of course, we don't keep anything really valuable here because the cottage is empty for weeks, sometimes months, at a time. Still, there's the old television and the new answering machine. And all the stuff I brought with me from Portland. My painting supplies. Some clothes."

"Nothing that would bring a burglar a lot of fast cash, though." Sean looked down at what he had written. "You know, these guys aren't known for neatness. They usually leave the place in a mess. Maybe he got scared off before he could get inside. A car coming down the drive would have done it. Or someone taking a walk along the bluff with a dog."

Gabe considered that. "Think that after he got nervous

here, he went looking for another, more isolated house to break into? A.Z.'s place?"

"And got surprised again. Hit Arizona and took off with her fancy camera." Sean nodded. "Makes sense." He flipped the notebook closed. "I've been interviewing people all day. So far no one has noticed any strangers acting suspiciously. But that still leaves a bunch of college kids and unknown transients. The camera is my best hope. If someone turns up with it, I'll have a lead."

"Otherwise, zip, right?" Lillian asked morosely. "I've heard that these kinds of burglaries often go unsolved."

"That's true in big cities but not so true in a small town where you've got a more limited group of suspects." Sean stuffed the notebook into the pocket of his jacket and started toward the door. "I'll let you know if I come up with anything useful. Meanwhile, get that back door fixed."

Lillian nodded. "I'll ask the Willis brothers to come over here tomorrow and take care of it."

Sean paused at the door. "Folks are usually a little nervous after a break-in." He angled a brief, meaningful glance at Gabe. "Nice for you that you won't be here alone tonight."

Lillian gave him a basilisk stare from her perch on the stool. She did not say a word.

Sean did not move. But, then, that was only to be expected, Gabe thought. A basilisk could turn a man to stone with the power of her gaze.

"I mean, you'll be a lot more comfortable with Madison here," Sean muttered. "Not nervous or anything."

Lillian continued to glare.

"Right, she won't be alone." Gabe pushed himself away from the counter. "I'll walk outside with you."

He did not know why he felt obliged to rescue Sean.

A guy thing, maybe. Or maybe he just didn't like the way Lillian had reacted to Sean's assumption that she was sleeping with him. She looked ticked. For some reason that irritated him.

Sean cleared his throat. "Sure. Got to get going. Things to do."

Gabe crossed the kitchen in a few long strides. He had the front door open for Sean by the time the police chief reached it.

He moved out onto the porch after Sean and closed the door behind them. They stood in the yellow light and looked at the cars parked in the drive.

"Guess I stepped in it back there," Sean said.

"Yeah."

"Sorry about that."

Gabe braced a hand on the porch railing. "Not like it's a big secret."

"Secrets like that are a little hard to keep here in Eclipse Bay. Especially when a Harte and a Madison are involved."

"I know," Gabe said.

Sean looked thoughtful. "Folks in town are sort of assuming that you're planning to marry her in order to get your hands on a piece of Harte Investments."

"Dangerous things, assumptions."

"You can say that again. I generally try to avoid them in my work, but once in a while I slip up." Sean zipped his jacket and went down the steps. "I'll be in touch."

A long time later Gabe awoke to the sound of rain on the roof. He knew at once that Lillian was not asleep.

"You okay?" he asked.

"Yes."

"What's wrong?"

"I'm not sure."

"I was afraid of this." He levered himself up on one elbow and reached for her. "Are you upset because Sean Valentine guessed that we're sleeping together? Honey, this is a small town and we haven't exactly tried to hide."

"It's not that." She locked her hands behind her head and stared up into the shadows. "I mean, I'm not real thrilled with the fact that Sean and everyone else in town thinks you're trying to sucker me into marriage so that you can get your hands on a third of Harte Investments—"

"Valentine didn't say that. He just sort of observed that you and I are having an affair."

"It's what he was thinking. But, to tell you the truth, I'm getting used to people thinking that."

He wondered if that was a good thing. Did he want her thinking that their affair was fine just as it stood? "So, the gossip isn't what's keeping you awake?"

"No."

"All right, why can't you sleep? The break-in?"

"Yes."

He flattened his hand on her soft, warm belly. "There's nothing to worry about. I wired the mudroom door shut, remember? Besides, if the guy didn't find anything worth stealing the first time, he's not likely to come back."

"I know."

He did not like the disquiet that threaded her words. "What is it?"

"Something like this happened to me in Portland."

He stilled. "A break-in?"

"I discovered it when we went into town for the Montoya dinner. I got the feeling that someone had been inside my apartment."

He sat up very fast. "Why the hell didn't you tell me? Did you call the cops?"

"No. There was no evidence. My door hadn't been forced open the way it was here. Nothing was missing."

"You're sure?"

"Yes. I figured it was the cleaning people. I called them and I was right. A schedule mix-up. But there was a smear on the bedroom closet mirror and well—"

"Well, what?"

"I guess that after what happened tonight, I can't help wondering, that's all."

"Remember what I said about the simple answer usually being the right one. Sounds like whoever cleaned your apartment left a smear. It happens. As long as there was no sign of forced entry or theft, I think we can assume that the break-in here had nothing to do with the cleaning day mix-up in Portland."

"I'm sure you're right. Guess I'm just a little nervous after what happened, that's all. You know, what with one thing and another, I'm not getting a lot of painting done lately."

He lay back against the pillows and gathered her against him. She snuggled close. He stroked her slowly, his hand gliding down her spine to the curve of her hip, letting himself enjoy the warmth and the sensual curves of her body.

"What you need is some artistic inspiration," he whispered.

"You may be right." She put an arm around him. "Unfortunately, it isn't always easy to find."

He moved his hand on her again, savoring the shiver that went through her. Then he eased her onto her back and came down on top of her. "Luckily for you, I am prepared to give my all to art."

# chapter 17

Shortly before noon the next day, Lillian stood in the opening that separated the mudroom from the back hall and watched Gabe and the Willis brothers. The three men huddled around the broken lock with a solemn air. Their expressions were grave, their voices hushed and serious. A guy thing, she thought. You saw it whenever the male of the species was in the presence of a nonfunctioning piece of hardware or machinery.

"Looks like the work of an amateur." Torrance Willis bent low to make a closer examination of the gouges in the door frame. "A real pro would have slipped right through this old lock without leaving a scratch. What d'ya say, Walt?"

Walter stooped to get a better look. "Yep. An amateur, all right."

Lillian hid a grin. The Willis brothers were identical twins but in style and appearance they were opposites. With his completely shaved head, precisely pressed work clothes, and neat, mechanical movements, Walter always made her think of an efficient little robot. In contrast, Torrance was a genial slob. His long, straggly hair was cinched in a ponytail at the nape of his neck. His clothes were stained with what looked like several years' worth of oil, paint, grease, and some orange-red stuff that might have been pizza sauce.

"For what it's worth, Sean Valentine agrees with you." Gabe studied the gouges. "Not that it tells us much."

"If whoever broke in here is the same rat who hit Arizona on the head, I reckon he's long gone," Walter said. "Be a damn fool to hang around Eclipse Bay now that the heat is on."

"I hope you're right," Gabe said. "But the important thing is to get something solid on this door. I don't want Lillian spending another night here with a busted lock."

"No problem." Torrance absently scratched the snake tattoo that slithered out from beneath the sleeve of his grimy work shirt. "After you called us this morning, we stopped off at the hardware store. Picked up just what we need. We'll have this fixed in no time."

Walter selected some tools from a polished metal box. "Won't take long. We can fill in those gouge marks and paint 'em out for you, too."

"That would be great," Lillian said. "I really appreciate this. I know how busy you are with Dreamscape."

"Rafe and Hannah would be the first to tell us to take care of this for you," Walter said. "But I got to admit, they're keeping us real busy over there at the inn."

"You got that right," Torrance agreed. There was a groan of metal and wood as he leaned into the task of removing the broken lock. "Walt and me didn't even bother to bid on any of the work on the new wing of the institute. Knew we wouldn't have time."

"Not that we was invited to bid, mind you." Walter removed the new lock from its packaging. "Perry Decatur is runnin' things up there now. Doesn't like dealin' with local business if he can avoid it. Made it real clear he wanted to bring in out-of-town contractors. Said they were more *competitive*."

"Like money's the most important aspect of a good job," Torrance scoffed. "No respect for fine craftsmanship these days."

"So you two didn't even get a slice of the project?" Gabe asked.

"Nope." Walter positioned the new lock. "Not to say we don't get some work on the side from time to time. Lot of the folks employed up there are local. They know us. They call us when they got a plumbing problem or need a hot-water tank replaced. Those fancy out-of-town contractors aren't interested in the small jobs."

"Claire Jensen mentioned that she had you take care of a clogged toilet for her," Lillian said.

"Yep, she did, as a matter of fact." Walter exchanged a meaningful look with Torrance. Both men smirked.

"What's the joke?" Gabe asked.

"Nothing much." Torrance readied a drill. "Just that while Walt and me was in Claire's bathroom we couldn't help noticing that she had some birth control pills and a box of condoms under the bathroom sink."

Lillian frowned. "Don't you think it's a little tacky to snoop in people's bathroom cupboards when they hire you to fix their plumbing?"

Walter had the grace to blush. "You're right. We shouldn't have said nothin' about it."

"Why not?" Torrance said. "Not like it's news. That woman always did have what you'd call an active social life, even back in the old days. Remember how she used to sneak around with Larry Fulton?"

"Sure do," Walter said. "The two of 'em used to crawl into the back of his dad's delivery van and go at it like a couple of bunnies."

Lillian straightened in the doorway. "She ran around with Larry Fulton? But he's married."

"This was back before he married Sheila Groves and took over his dad's grocery store," Walter assured her. "Way back when he was still in college. That sound right to you, Torrance?"

"Yep, sounds about right. Way I hear it, Claire hasn't changed much over the years."

"I think that's enough gossip about Claire," Gabe said.

He spoke quietly, but Walter and Torrance immediately changed the subject. Lillian smiled to herself. Everyone knew that whatever else you could say about the Madison men, they didn't kiss and tell. Apparently, they didn't listen to other masculine gossip about women either. That kind of old-fashioned chivalry was an extremely endearing trait in a man.

# chapter 18

The following morning Arizona held her security briefing from her dimly lit hospital room. She certainly looked the part of the heroically wounded warrior, Lillian thought. The bandages around A.Z.'s head gave her a dashing air. It was clear from the glittering determination in her eyes that she was recovering rapidly.

Lillian was quite relieved to see Arizona looking so much better this morning. She and Gabe had received the phone call summoning them to A.Z.'s bedside half an hour ago, just as they were finishing breakfast.

The only other attendee present today was Photon from the Incandescent Body bakery. He stood in the corner, serene and silent in his strange robes and jewelry. His shaved head gleamed green in the light of a nearby monitor. Could have passed for a space alien, Lillian thought.

"Way I figure it," Arizona said, "the institute spy followed me home because he spotted me taking my routine sector surveillance photos. I cover the whole town right out to the boundaries three mornings a week, you know.

Check up on the institute daily, of course. I must have caught something on film that they didn't want anyone to see. When he saw his chance he knocked me out and stole my VPX 5000."

"Don't worry about it, A.Z.," Gabe said. "You can replace the camera and get back to your daily recon work in no time."

"Forget the camera," Arizona said. "Now that we know for sure that we're on to something, we've got to get inside."

That sounded ominous, Lillian thought.

"Inside?" she repeated cautiously. "Inside what?"

"The new wing, of course. Listen up here." Arizona's voice lowered. "Got no choice now. We need to get a firsthand look at whatever is going on in there. My guess is they've made the big move."

Dread settled on Lillian. "Oh, I really don't think they've had time—"

"Probably brought 'em in with the HVAC equipment," Arizona said.

"If that's the case," Photon murmured, "whoever goes inside will have to search for a large freezer compartment somewhere in the new wing."

"Right." Arizona adjusted her position on the pillows, checked the door and then lowered her voice again, this time to a raspy whisper. She motioned with one hand. "Move in as close as you can. The institute probably has spies out there in the hall. Be easy enough to disguise them as orderlies or janitors."

Lillian suppressed a sigh and obediently leaned over the bed. Gabe and Photon followed suit.

"We all know that they'll never let me or one of the Heralds step foot inside the institute." Arizona gave Lillian and Gabe a meaningful look. "That leaves you two."

Lillian gripped the bed rails. "Wait a second here, A.Z. We're not, uh, trained in this kind of work."

"Don't worry, I'll give you a few pointers before you go in."

"How do you plan to get us inside?" Gabe asked, looking interested.

Lillian frantically tried to get his attention but he pretended not to see her.

"I figure the Leaders of Tomorrow open-house event will give you both the perfect opportunity," Arizona said. "Easy for you to get invites because one of you is a Harte and the other is a Madison. Perry Decatur and the folks who run the institute will fall all over themselves to get you there. You're both potential donors."

Phonton nodded somberly. "An excellent plan."

"Just might work, A.Z.," Gabe said.

"But the new wing won't be open yet." Lillian struggled to bring some common sense to the situation. "We won't be able to get in there."

"Shouldn't be too hard," Gabe said. "Everyone will be busy with the reception. Don't see why we can't slip out at some point and take a look at the area under construction."

"It's settled then." Arizona gave them a thumbs-up. "You two will go in the night of the open house."

"What about a camera?" Lillian said quickly. "I don't have one and I doubt if Gabe has one either."

"Could always get one of those little throwaway cameras they sell at the pier," Gabe said helpfully.

"One of those gadgets won't do it," Arizona said. "I'll give you my old VPX 4000. Fine piece of equipment. Lacks a few of the features of the 5000 but it'll get the job done. Remember, we need hard proof that they've stashed those frozen extraterrestrials in that new wing."

# chapter 19

Gabe gave up trying to work, closed the laptop, grabbed a jacket and went down to the beach. He walked for a long time, trying to make sense of the screwy dream that had awakened him in the middle of the night. It had featured broken locks and the grinning faces of the Willis brothers. Not quite a nightmare but close enough.

He stopped at the edge of the water and watched a gull angle into the offshore breeze. Normally he didn't pay much attention to dreams. He didn't believe in intuition, premonitions, or the like.

But he had a healthy respect for his own hunches. They had served him well in business.

Something J. Anderson Flint had said the other night at the restaurant was running through his brain again and again this morning.

*"Disgruntled employees can be dangerous."*

When he added it to the dream he got a very uneasy feeling.

What if Lillian's first intuitive suspicion had been correct? What if the break-in at her cottage had nothing to do with what had happened to Arizona but was, instead, linked to her fear that someone had intruded into her Portland apartment?

The knock on her front door interrupted her just as she was about to mix some paint. She put down the palette knife with a sense of deep resignation. What had ever made her think she would get some work done today?

She opened the door warily.

Gabe stood there, one hand braced on the door frame. There was no sign of his car. He was dressed in a black-and-tan windbreaker, jeans, and running shoes. His dark hair was tousled from the wind and a little damp from the mist-heavy air.

"We need to talk." He walked into the hall and shrugged out of his jacket.

His cold, grim expression silenced whatever comment she had been about to make on the subject of interruptions.

"What's wrong?" she asked.

"I've been thinking about something Flint said about Claire."

She took the jacket from him. "What was that?"

"He mentioned that disgruntled employees could be dangerous. It occurred to me that maybe disgruntled boyfriends of former clients might fall into the same category."

She stared at him, the jacket clutched in her hand. "Are you talking about Campbell Witley?"

"Yeah." He disappeared into the kitchen. "Got any coffee?"

She draped the jacket over the hanger, jammed it into the closet and hurried to the doorway of the kitchen.

"What are you thinking?" She watched him fill the coffeemaker with fresh water. "That Witley might be responsible for the break-in here?"

He removed the lid of the coffee canister. "It would explain the incident at your apartment."

"Assuming there was an incident."

He nodded. "Assuming that."

A shiver went through her. "But that would make Witley a stalker."

"I know." He finished spooning ground coffee into the filter and switched on the machine. "I don't want to scare you. Sean Valentine probably got it right when he concluded that whoever conked A.Z. on the head was a transient who had tried to break in here, first. But there is a remote possibility that the two incidents are related. Which, in turn, means that the break-in here could be connected to what happened in Portland."

"It would explain why nothing was taken. A stalker probably wouldn't be interested in stealing stuff."

He crossed the kitchen and cradled her face in his hands.

"Look, this should be easy enough to check out," he said. "All we have to do is find out where Witley was when someone here in Eclipse Bay was breaking into your mudroom. Shouldn't be too hard to see if he's got an alibi. If he can account for his whereabouts during that time period, we can go back to Valentine's theory of a transient burglar."

She swallowed. "I never considered the possibility of a stalker."

"Neither did I until I got to thinking about Flint's comments."

"I can call Nella Townsend, the investigator I used to

check out my clients. She might be able to verify Witley's alibi."

"Fine. Call her. I'll speak to Valentine, too. Let him know what's going on. But from what I've read, stalkers can be very slick. Very devious. It's hard to prove that they're doing anything illegal."

She bit her lip. "I know."

"I want to see this guy myself."

*"What?"*

"I want to meet Witley face-to-face. Ask him some questions," Gabe said.

"No." Alarm washed through her. "You can't do that."

"Take it easy, honey. I've done a lot of deals with a lot of people who have things to hide. I'm good at knowing when I'm being lied to."

"Are you nuts?" she yelped. "You can't confront Witley on your own. What if he really is a stalker? He could be very dangerous."

Gabe looked first surprised and then pleased. "Worried about me?"

"Of course I'm worried. No offense, Gabe, but this is not one of your more brilliant ideas."

"I'm just going to drive into Portland and meet the guy. Don't worry, if he is a stalker, I doubt that he's a danger to me. Stalkers are obsessed with their victims, not other people."

"Listen, I don't want you handling this on your own. If you insist on going to Portland to see him, I'll go with you."

"No." There was no give in the single word. "I don't want you anywhere near him."

"Witley is a big man. He's had military training. He works in construction. Get the picture?"

"You think he might beat me to a pulp. Gee. You really don't have much faith in my manly skills, do you?"

"Your manly skills are not the issue here," she said. "I don't want you to take that kind of risk on my account. I mean it. You can't do this by yourself and that's final."

He hesitated. "I guess I could take along some backup."

That stopped her for a heartbeat or two.

"Backup?" she repeated cautiously.

"A guy I know. He's big. Had some military training. Worked construction for a while."

"Do I know this man?"

"Yeah."

"Tell me again why we're going to drive all the way into Portland to see this guy, Witley," Mitchell said, buckling his seat belt.

"Long story." Gabe put on his dark glasses and turned the key in the ignition. "It's just barely possible that Witley is stalking Lillian. She's going to have an investigator check out his movements in the past few days, but I want to talk to him myself. Lillian made it clear that she didn't want me meeting him alone. I refused to take her along. You're the compromise."

"Well, shoot and damn," Mitchell said cheerfully. "This sounds like fun. Any chance of a fight?"

"Probably not. But there's always hope."

# chapter 20

She stared at the blank canvas, knowing that she was even less likely to get into the zone now than she had been earlier in the day when Gabe had interrupted her.

All she could think about was that he and Mitchell were on their way to Portland together to confront Witley.

The phone rang in the living room. She turned away from the canvas and went to answer it.

"Lillian? This is Nella. I got your message. What's up?"

"Thanks for calling me back." She sank down onto the arm of the sofa. "I've got a little problem here. Remember that guy Witley I asked you to check out?"

"Sure." Nella paused. "Something happen?"

"Maybe. Maybe not. Can you find out if he left town sometime during the past few days?"

"Shouldn't be too difficult. What's going on, Lil?"

"I'm not sure." She gave Nella a quick rundown of events.

"I'll get right on it," Nella said. "Meanwhile, watch yourself, okay? These guys tend to escalate."

"What do you mean?"

"The incidents get more serious. It's a progressive thing. Do me a huge favor. Lock all your doors and windows and keep them locked until your friend Madison gets there or until I give you the all-clear. I'll get back to you as soon as I have something solid."

"Thanks."

Lillian ended the call, put down the phone and went back into the studio.

The blank canvas might as well have been sitting in another universe, a place where she could not go today.

A red compact pulled into the drive just as she was about to pour herself another cup of tea. Her fourth that afternoon. She went to the window and saw Claire Jensen, dressed in a navy blue shirt and a pair of jeans, get out from behind the wheel and walk up the front steps.

Just what she needed. Another interruption. She put down the cup and went to open the front door.

"Hi." Claire looked and sounded as if she had not slept much in recent days. "I need to talk to someone. Mind if I come in for a few minutes?"

More sisterhood stuff. How much of this kind of thing was a woman supposed to do to retain her politically correct status?

"No, of course not." Lillian held the door open. "I made tea. Want some?"

"That would be nice. Thanks."

Claire walked into the front hall, took off her coat and gave it to Lillian to hang in the closet.

"Come on into the kitchen," Lillian said.

"I assume you know that Marilyn fired me."

"I heard."

"It's not exactly the end of the world." Claire folded her hands on the table and looked out the window. "Campaign managers get canned a lot. Goes with the territory."

"I'm sure you'll find another position."

"Sure. Something will turn up. That's not what's bothering me. It was the scene in the Crab Trap. It's all over town. I have never been so embarrassed in my life. The worst part is that I have no one to blame but myself."

Lillian took another cup down out of the cupboard. "It'll all blow over in a few days."

"I still don't know what made me track her down at the restaurant and confront her like that. I guess I was just so angry that I wasn't thinking straight. She actually accused me of sleeping with Trevor, can you imagine?"

Lillian poured tea. "I take it you didn't have an affair with him?"

"Are you kidding? I admired Trevor's political agenda, but that was as far as it went. I'm a pro. I don't sleep with my clients."

Lillian set the cup down in front of her. "Probably a good policy in your line of work."

"You bet." Claire blew on her tea. "Besides, according to the rumors, Thornley likes to dress up in women's lingerie and prance around in high heels. Don't know about you, but personally I don't find that type of thing a real turn-on."

"I can see where the lingerie and heels might be a little off-putting. What happens now?"

"I'll be leaving town in a couple of days. I plan to go to Seattle and regroup. I've got contacts there. But I didn't come here to whine today. Well, maybe just a little."

"Why did you come here?"

Claire put down her cup. "Marilyn has always been a little overcontrolling and a bit paranoid. I never worried about it too much. You expect that in a strong candidate. But I have to tell you that after those crazy accusations about Trevor and me, I'm starting to wonder if maybe she's gone off the deep end. If that's the case, I think you should be careful."

"Me? Why should I worry?"

"Because I've noticed that she's become a little fixated on your relationship with Gabe Madison. Maybe it's because she's divorced now. But I think there's more to it than that."

The phone rang. On the off chance that it might be Nella reporting back with the all-clear, Lillian lunged for it.

She heard the muffled noise of a car in motion.

"Hello?"

"Witley is gone." Gabe's voice was very even. Too even. "He told some friends that he was taking a vacation. He's not at his house. No one has seen him for a few days. Heard from your investigator yet?"

"No." Lillian clutched the phone very tightly. "Where are you?"

"We're on our way back to Eclipse Bay. It's almost four o'clock. We should get there around seven."

"I'll hold dinner for you both."

"Now that we know for sure that Witley has disappeared, I don't think it's a good idea for you to be there alone. We don't know where he is or what he's doing."

"I'll be fine until seven tonight, for heaven's sake. Claire Jensen is here with me now, as a matter of fact, so I'm not alone."

There was a murmur of conversation in the background. Lillian realized that Mitchell was speaking to Gabe.

Gabe spoke into the phone again. "Mitchell wants to send Bryce over to baby-sit until we get back."

"That's not necessary." Lillian checked her watch. "Look, I'm going stir-crazy here. I need to run into town and pick up some groceries for dinner. I'll leave the house right after Claire. I'll do the shopping and then I'll stop and see A.Z. at the hospital. That will keep me busy and I won't be alone. Call me at the hospital when you get into town and I'll meet you back here at the cottage. That way I won't be alone for any extended period of time."

Gabe hesitated. "All right. But don't take any long walks on the beach by yourself, okay?"

"I thought you didn't want to scare me."

"I've changed my mind. I figure if you're scared, you'll be careful."

"Don't worry, I won't wander off by myself."

"Good. See you soon."

Lillian ended the call and put down the phone.

Claire gave her a quizzical look. "Something wrong?"

"To tell you the truth, I don't really know. There have been a couple of small incidents lately. Someone broke in here the other day while I was at the old Buckley place with Gabe."

Claire frowned and slowly lowered her cup. "Anything taken?"

"No. Sean Valentine thinks it's the same guy who tried to burglarize A.Z.'s place."

"I heard about that. It's all over town. They're saying it was a transient."

"I know. But the thing that's worrisome is that there was another possible break-in at my apartment in Portland. Nothing taken there, either. Gabe leaped to the conclusion that the culprit might be a guy named Witley."

"Who's he?"

"A former boyfriend of one of my clients."

"But why on earth would he break into your apartment and this place?"

"The theory is that he blames me for ruining his relationship with his girlfriend."

"You mean because you matched her with someone else?"

"Yes."

"Uh-oh. Are we talking stalker here?"

"It looks like a possibility. A remote one, I hope. You know, a friend told me I was courting a lawsuit in the matchmaking business. But I never considered this kind of thing."

"We worry about stalkers when we plan security for candidates. There are always a few nutcases running around. But I must admit, I never thought about it in your line of work."

"My *former* line."

Claire blew out a deep breath. "And I thought I had problems."

"A matchmaker's life is never dull."

"I can see that." Claire got to her feet. "Well, at least you've got Gabe Madison looking out for you. Things could be worse."

"There is that."

"I'd better be on my way. I can see you've got other things to worry about than my little scene in the Crab Trap. Promise me you'll be careful."

"Don't worry, I will." Lillian rose and followed her out into the hall. She got Claire's coat out of the closet and handed it to her. "You said you had something you wanted to tell me."

"What? Oh, yeah." Claire shrugged into her coat. "But it seems a little petty compared to this stalker business."

"What was it?"

"It's about Marilyn. I'm no shrink, but like I started to tell you before Gabe phoned, I really do think she may be a bit paranoid. When you add that to the fact that she's a very determined woman who always gets what she wants, well, I just think you might want to watch your step around her, that's all."

"Why?"

"Because you've got something she wants," Claire said.

"What's that?"

"Gabe Madison."

"Well, shoot and damn." Mitchell watched Gabe disconnect the phone. "We've got ourselves a problem here, don't we?"

"Maybe. I sure don't like the fact that Witley has disappeared."

Mitchell watched him for a moment. He'd seen that same look of focused determination back when Gabe had been a twelve-year-old kid doing his homework at the kitchen table. Nothing had changed, Mitchell thought. Gabe was a different kind of Madison. But not that different.

"Wasn't talking about Witley," Mitchell said. "We'll get that sorted out. Meant this situation between you and Lillian."

"Situation?"

"Way it looks to me, you're in up to your neck and sinking deeper by the minute."

Gabe navigated a turn, accelerating smoothly on the far side. "What are you talking about?"

Mitchell absently massaged his arthritic knee. He tried to remember if he had taken his anti-inflammatory medication. Things had been a little busy today.

"Had what you might call a chat with Lillian," he said.

"I heard about that. Stay out of this, Mitch. My relationship with Lillian is none of your business. You don't have the right to interfere."

"I'm your grandfather. Course I've got the right."

Mitchell watched the road. There was very little traffic now that they had left the city behind. The last of the daylight was evaporating. The white lines on the pavement marked the path into the darkness.

He braced himself for the old memories. No matter where he was or what he was doing, they always came back to haunt him for a while at this time of day; the point when the oncoming night could no longer be ignored. He knew from long experience that once the transition to full dark was made, the specters would fade. They would not return for another twenty-four hours.

When he was home it was his custom to handle the ghosts with a shot of whiskey. But tonight he had nothing to take the edge off. He would just have to deal with it. Wouldn't be the first time.

From out of the depths the phantoms arose, right on schedule. The scene was a twilight-shrouded jungle drenched with the smell of death and gut-wrenching fear. The worst part had been knowing that the night was inevitable and that there was no hope of rescue until dawn.

He and Sullivan had made it through that hellish night together because they had both understood that their survival depended on staying in control of the panic. They had both understood the need for absolute silence and absolute stillness. Side by side in the unrelenting darkness, they had somehow managed to reinforce that grim knowledge in each other without words or movement of any kind. And without words or movement they had managed to keep each other from slipping over the edge into that place where the fear took over and got you killed.

At dawn, he and Sullivan had still been alive. A lot of the others had not been so lucky.

He wondered if Sullivan went through the same ritual every evening. Waiting. Knowing the night was inevitable.

"What, exactly, did you say to Lillian?" Gabe asked.

Mitchell watched the light disappear, unable to look away. "Just told her flat-out that it looked to me like you were fallin' for her in a big way and that I didn't want her to stomp all over your heart."

"Those were your exact words?"

Mitchell thought back to the conversation in the greenhouse. "Pretty close."

"Did Lillian imply that she intended to, uh, stomp all over my heart?" Gabe asked.

What the hell was it about this time of day? The shift from day to night always seemed to take forever.

"In a manner of speaking," he said.

Gabe gazed steadily at the road unwinding in front of the car. "Doesn't sound like something Lillian would say. What were her precise words, Mitch?"

"Well, she got irritated when I told her that I didn't want you gettin' hurt. Said something about how she was the one who stood to get stomped on account of everyone was so sure you were after her because you wanted a chunk of Harte Investments."

Gabe nodded. "I can see where she'd get that impression. Lot of people have been saying that lately."

"Natural assumption, under the circumstances."

"Probably."

"I told her that was garbage. Said you were a Madison and Madisons never marry for money. Not that practical, when you get right down to it."

"Good point." Gabe waited a beat. "So, how did she respond to that observation?"

"She reminded me how everyone said that you were a different kind of Madison. I told her you were different, but not that different."

"What else did she say?"

"Well, let's see. I believe I may have pointed out that Madison Commercial is your passion and that when it comes to a Madison and his passion—"

"Nothing gets in the way. Yeah, right, I've heard that. She say anything else?"

The transition to night was complete at last. The phantom images receded into the darkness.

Mitchell exhaled slowly. "Seemed to think I'd maybe given you the wrong impression."

"About what?"

"About what you've done with Madison Commercial."

Gabe's hands tightened a little on the wheel. "For the past year and a half you've been telling me that I've spent too much time fooling around with the company. Maybe you were right."

Mitchell had to swallow twice to keep from sputtering. "Shoot and damn, son, you built that company from the ground up. You sweated blood to prove something to the whole damn world."

"What did I prove?"

"You know what you proved. Hell, after you created Madison Commercial no one could say that every Madison who came along was doomed to screw up everything he touched."

"You consider that a major accomplishment?"

"Damn right, I do." He stared at the road. "More important than you'll ever know."

"How so?"

"Because after Madison Commercial, folks had to quit sayin' that I had screwed up both my grandsons' lives the same way I had messed up your father's life."

A crystalline silence enveloped the front seat of the car.

"Did people really say that?" Gabe asked after a while. "To your face?"

"Some said it to my face. Most folks said it behind my back. They were all pretty much agreed that I wasn't fit to raise you and Rafe after Sinclair killed himself and your mother on that damn motorcycle."

"Huh."

"They said I set a piss-poor example for a couple of young boys." He rubbed his jaw. "To tell you the truth, they were right. But what the hell was I gonna do? Not like there was anyone else around to take over the job."

"You could have walked out. Disappeared. Let the social workers deal with us."

"Bullshit. You don't turn your grandkids over to the state to raise."

"Some people would."

"Madisons don't do stuff like that."

Gabe smiled slightly. "Got it."

Mitchell suddenly realized that he wanted to explain things, but he didn't know how to go about it. He wasn't good at this kind of situation. He groped for the right words.

"The point I'm trying to make," he said, "is that you were smart enough not to follow my bad example. You made something of yourself, Gabe. When you built M.C.

you broke the Madison curse or jinx or whatever that made us all failures."

"No."

"What the hell do you mean? That's exactly what you did and don't you ever forget it."

"It wasn't me who broke the jinx," Gabe said. "It was you."

*"Me?"*

"Don't you get it? You're the one who changed after Dad's death. And when you changed, you altered the future for Rafe and me."

# chapter 21

Lillian stopped the car in the drive, opened the door and checked her watch in the weak overhead light. Just after seven. There was no sign of Gabe and Mitchell yet but they would be here any minute. Gabe had called her from the outskirts of town a short while ago.

She had left the porch light on as well as several lamps inside the house. The cottage was illuminated with a warm, welcoming glow. Keys in hand, she collected the two sacks of groceries she had picked up at Fulton's Supermarket and went up the porch steps. With a little jockeying, she managed to get the front door open without having to put down one of the grocery bags.

She walked into the front hall, kicked the door shut and wrestled her burdens into the kitchen. The house felt unaccountably cold.

She was certain she had left the thermostat set at a comfortable temperature.

An uneasy feeling drifted through her. There had been

a cold draft in the mudroom the night someone had broken in.

She went to the door and studied the living room. Nothing appeared to be disturbed. Maybe she had left an upstairs window open a crack.

But the draft was not coming from the staircase. It emanated from the downstairs hall.

Her studio.

Galvanized, she rushed toward the guest bedroom. As soon as she turned the corner she saw that the door stood partially ajar, just as she remembered leaving it earlier. But through the narrow opening she could see that something was very wrong inside her studio.

A chill that had nothing to do with the draft of cold air went through her. With a sense of deep dread, she pushed the door open wide.

The studio was in chaos. The blank canvas on the easel had been ripped to shreds. Rags, brushes, and knives were scattered across the floor. There was paint everywhere. The contents of several tubes of paint had been smeared across one wall and the floor. Her palette lay upside down on the bed. Pages of drawings had been ripped from her sketchbook and crumpled into balls.

She finally identified the source of the cold draft. It came through the broken window.

Gabe felt everything inside him turn to stone when he saw Sean Valentine's SUV parked in the drive.

Then he saw Lillian standing on the front porch talking to Valentine, and allowed himself to start breathing again.

He hit the breaks and switched off the engine. "Something's wrong."

"Yeah, I figured that." Mitchell surveyed the scene on

the porch. "Not like Sean to be running around at this time of night unless there's trouble."

Gabe got the Jag's door open. He loped toward the steps. Sean and Lillian looked at him.

"What happened?" Gabe asked.

"Looks like Lillian had another visit from whoever broke in the other night," Sean said.

"He vandalized my studio this time," Lillian said shakily.

Mitchell came up the steps with his cane. He frowned at Lillian. "You okay?"

"I'm fine." She smiled wanly. "But he made a mess. The floor, the bedspread, the wall. Everything's covered in paint."

Sean looked serious. "Didn't think too much of your idea that this guy Witley might be stalking her, Madison. But after seeing what he did to that bedroom, I'm inclined to agree with you. Let's go inside and see what we've got."

"We've got jack squat, that's what we've got," Mitchell announced an hour later when they finally got around to dinner. He squinted at Lillian. "How the heck did you get into so much trouble running a matchmaking business?"

"Darned if I know." She picked up her wineglass. "Friend of mine told me that the business was a lawsuit waiting to happen. But no one warned me about stalkers."

"Well, don't you worry about it too much." Mitchell tackled his stir-fry vegetables with gusto. "One thing to be a stalker in Portland where no one notices a guy hanging around places he shouldn't be hanging around. Another thing to do your stalking here in Eclipse Bay where a stranger gets noticed, especially at this time of year."

"He's right," Gabe said. "If Witley's in town, Sean Valentine will find him quickly."

"Meanwhile, you'll be okay," Mitchell added. "Gabe here will watch over you."

Lillian looked at Gabe.

He gave her his sexy grin. "Won't let you out of my sight."

She contemplated the wine in her glass. "The thing is, even if Sean does find Witley, what can he do? I've heard it's tough to prove a charge of stalking."

Gabe and Mitchell exchanged silent looks.

She frowned. "What?"

Gabe shrugged. "Don't worry about Witley. If Sean can't do anything, Mitch and I will think of something."

Her hand tensed around the glass. "Such as?"

"Us Madisons are pretty creative," Mitchell assured her cheerfully.

She looked at each of them in turn. Another small chill wafted through her. They were both smiling, easy, laid-back Madison smiles. Probably trying to reassure her. But there was something very different going on in their eyes. Something very dangerous.

She did not argue when Gabe suggested that they go back to his place after dinner. The idea of leaving the cottage undefended made her uneasy but the notion of actually spending the night there gave her the jitters. She knew that she would not sleep.

When she emerged from the bathroom she found him standing at the bedroom window, gazing out into the night. He wore a pair of jeans but nothing else. The sleek, mus-cled contours of his bare back and shoulders made her fingers itch for a pencil and some drawing paper. Other parts of her were tingling, too, she noticed.

"What are you thinking?" she asked.

"I had an interesting conversation with Mitch on the way back to Eclipse Bay this evening." He did not turn around. "Apparently Madison Commercial is more important to him than he likes to admit."

"Oh." She tightened the sash of her bathrobe and sank down on the end of the bed. "I could have told you that."

"He said it was proof to the world that he hadn't screwed up completely with Rafe and me."

She thought about it. "I can see where he might view your success as a sign that he hadn't botched the job of raising you. What did you say?"

Gabe let the curtain fall and turned around to face her. "That he was the reason Rafe and I made it at all."

"Ah, yes."

"It's the truth. I've known it for years but I don't think I ever told him."

"Madison Commercial is important to your grand-father, but you and Rafe mean a lot more to him than the company does."

Gabe sat down beside her, leaned forward and clasped his hands loosely between his knees. He contemplated their images in the mirror above the chest of drawers.

"He really is afraid you'll break my heart," Gabe said.

She managed a soft little laugh. "Did you assure him that's not very likely?"

Gabe said nothing.

She stilled. "Gabe?"

"What?"

"You didn't allow him to think that I could really break your heart, did you?"

"Well, sure." He said it carelessly, easily, casually. As if it were an incontrovertible fact. "I'm a Madison."

She stopped breathing altogether for the space of a

couple of heartbeats. With concentration she managed to drag some oxygen into her lungs.

"Is this your subtle, roundabout way of telling me that you see our relationship as something more than just a short-term affair?" she whispered.

"It's been something more than just an affair for me right from the start."

She could hardly speak. "But I thought we had agreed that we aren't a good match."

He shrugged. "You Hartes probably worry about things like that more than we Madisons do."

"You're supposed to be a different kind of Madison."

He straightened and reached for her, pushed her gently down onto the bed. He leaned forward and kissed her throat.

"Not that different," he said.

The following morning they went back to the cottage together to clean up the studio. There was a message from Nella on the answering machine. It was short and to the point.

*"Call me."*

Lillian grabbed the phone and punched in the number.

"What have you got?" she asked without preamble.

"Where have you been? I've been trying to reach you since six o'clock this morning."

Lillian glanced at Gabe. "Out. I was out."

"Is that so?" Nella sounded amused. "Wouldn't have thought there was enough going on in Eclipse Bay to keep a jaded city girl out all night."

"Nella—"

"I found Witley," Nella said, brisk and businesslike now. "He has a rock-solid alibi for the entire time that you've been in Eclipse Bay."

"What is it?"

"He and a pal are down in the Caribbean doing some diving. They're registered at a hotel on Saint Thomas. I checked with some of the local dive shops and I called his room. He was there, Lil. No way he could have flown back to Oregon, driven to Eclipse Bay yesterday and then returned to the island this morning in time to take my call."

"I see." Lillian looked at Gabe, who was listening intently to her side of the conversation. "I'm not sure if that's good news or bad news because it means we have to start from scratch. But thanks for checking him out."

"Sure. By the way, apparently whatever you said to him on the street that day made an impact. I had a long conversation with him. He said he realized that maybe you'd been right about how he needed an outdoor type, not one of those highbrow arty types."

Lillian groaned. "He used the term *arty*?"

"Uh-huh. He now agrees with you that he and Heather Summers were not made for each other after all."

"Well, what do you know."

"Anything else I can do for you?"

"Not just yet, but stay tuned."

Nella hesitated. "Can you think of anyone else besides Witley who might want to harass you? Any old boyfriends hanging around?"

"No."

"You're sure?"

"You know better than anyone else what my social life has been like for the past year, Nella. Boring doesn't even begin to describe it."

Gabe raised a brow. She ignored him.

"We in the investigation business have a saying," Nella continued. "When the picture doesn't make sense, draw a new one. Maybe you should look at these incidents from another perspective."

"Problem is, I can't see any other angle here."

Nella hesitated. "You know, if it weren't for the trashing of your studio yesterday, I'd say that someone had broken into your apartment and your cottage to look for something."

"I can't imagine what it could be. I told you, nothing was taken."

"The pieces of this puzzle aren't fitting well together, Lil. Be careful."

# chapter 22

The darkened hallway was lined with office doors fitted with opaque glass. Gabe could hear the din of muffled voices in the distance. The noise came from the large reception room in the intersecting corridor. The Leaders of Tomorrow open-house event was in full swing.

Lillian stood beside him in the shadows. Her hair was pinned into a sleek, graceful knot at the back of her head. She wore a close-fitting, midnight-blue dress made out of a stretchy, slinky fabric that moved when she did and a pair of sexy, strappy heels.

He could think of a couple of other things he would rather do with her tonight than hunt for frozen space aliens. But duty called.

He checked the bulky camera Arizona had given him. "We're all set."

"I still say this is a really bad idea," Lillian muttered. "What if we get caught prowling through the new wing?"

"If anyone stops us, which is highly unlikely given that they're all very busy with the reception, we'll say we were curious about the new construction. Big deal. You really think anyone would arrest a Harte and a Madison who just happened to wander into the wrong hallway here at the institute?"

"You never know."

"It's a lot more likely they'd ask us for a contribution. Stop worrying. You're a little tense tonight."

"I've had a very difficult week and now I'm getting ready to look for frozen aliens. I've got a right to be tense. I'm supposed to be devoting myself to art, remember?"

"Take it easy," he said. "Think of this as performance art."

"Yeah, right. Performance art."

"We'll get in, take a few shots of empty offices and get out. Tomorrow we'll turn the pictures over to A.Z. and she can weave whatever conspiracy theories she wants. That will be the end of it for us."

"How do we explain the camera if we're stopped by a guard?"

"No problem," Gabe said. "We'll say we wanted some souvenir photos of the reception."

"It's a high-tech spy camera, for heaven's sake. No one's going to buy that story."

"Trust me. I can fake it if necessary."

"All right," she said with annoyance. "Let's get it over with and get back to the open house."

She started off down the hall toward the new wing with long, determined strides. He fell into step beside her, marveling at how well she could move in the sexy shoes. Together they prowled deeper into the bowels of the institute. The sounds of the open house faded into the distance behind them.

At the far end of the dark passage a temporary door

fashioned out of plywood had been installed to separate the uncompleted wing from the main building. A band of loosely draped construction zone tape barred the way. Gabe ducked under the tape and found the partition unlocked.

"We're in luck." He eased the plywood door open and stood aside to allow Lillian to enter. "Ready to boldly go where no Harte or Madison has gone before?"

She moved into the unpainted hall and stopped.

"Shouldn't you start taking pictures?" she said in a low voice.

"Right."

He walked to the nearest door and opened it. There was enough light filtering through the window from the parking lot lamps to reveal the bones of an empty room that was clearly intended to serve as an office.

"No frozen aliens in here," he announced.

"Big surprise." She leaned around the edge of the door. "Hurry up and take a picture. We've got a whole bunch of rooms to cover."

He raised the heavy VPX 4000 and snapped off a shot. The flash flared, brilliantly illuminating the small space for an instant. Darkness closed in again almost immediately.

"Great," Lillian said. "Now I can't see a thing."

"This thing really puts out some wattage, doesn't it?" He blinked a few times to get rid of the dark spots. "Next time close your eyes when I take the picture."

He went to the door across the hall, opened it, and took another picture of an empty, partially painted interior. When he finished, he moved to the next door and repeated the procedure.

After a while, it became routine. Open a door, take a

photo of a bare office, close the door. Go to the next room.

"I don't think A.Z. is going to be real thrilled with these pictures," Lillian said halfway down the hall. "She has her heart set on finding proof that the government has secretly moved frozen extraterrestrials here to Eclipse Bay."

"Don't worry about A.Z. She's a professional conspiracy buff, remember? A pro can always find a way to spin the facts into a new theory."

He opened the next door in line, raised the VPX 4000 and fired off a shot.

A woman yelled at the same instant the flash exploded. Not Lillian, he realized. Someone else. This room was inhabited. Not frozen aliens. Warm bodies.

Two figures were illuminated in the intense light. A man with a serious erection dressed in a pair of red bikini briefs and a woman in a black leather bustier and high-heeled black boots.

J. Anderson Flint and Marilyn Thornley.

"Holy cow," Gabe said. "A.Z. was right. But it's worse than she thought. Wait'll she hears that they've thawed out two of the frozen alien life-forms."

For two or three seconds everyone stared at everyone else. Marilyn, demonstrating the well-honed instincts of a natural-born politician, recovered first.

"Give me that camera," she shouted.

"Sorry, it's not mine to give away." Gabe took a quick step back toward the door. "Private property, you know. A bulwark of our constitutional republic. Wouldn't be right."

"I said give me that damned camera." Marilyn lunged toward him.

"Give her the stupid camera, for heaven's sake," Lillian said.

She grabbed the heavy VPX 4000 out of his hand and hurled it toward Marilyn the way you'd hurl garlic and a silver cross at a vampire.

"Let's get out of here." She seized his arm and hauled him out of the doorway. "Right now."

She broke into a run. Gabe had to stretch a little to keep up with her. He admired her form as they went down the corridor.

"I didn't know a woman could move that fast in high heels," he said.

By the time they reached the main building he was laughing so hard he accidentally went through the construction zone tape, severing it. The ends fluttered to the floor.

"A.Z. was right," he managed to get out between howls. "Strange things going on in the new wing."

Lillian stopped and turned to look at him. She was breathing hard from her recent exertion. She watched him for a long moment, a strange expression on her face. You'd think she'd never seen a man doubled up with laughter, he thought.

"I'd give anything for a picture of you right now." She stepped forward and brushed her mouth lightly against his. "And to think that I once thought you were a walking case of burnout."

The following morning Lillian was still trying to figure out how to deliver the bad news to Arizona. She stood at the kitchen counter in Gabe's house watching him slather peanut butter onto two slices of toasted Incandescent Body sourdough bread, and went through the possibilities.

"We could say we lost her VPX 4000," she said. "Or maybe imply that it was stolen out of the car."

Gabe did not look up from his task. "Could tell her the truth."

"Don't be ridiculous. No one, not even A.Z., would believe it."

"You've got a point." Gabe put the peanut butter toast on a plate. "Some things defy description."

"Some things are also actionable. The last thing we need is a lawsuit from Marilyn's campaign." Lillian poured coffee. "We have to come up with a reasonable story or A.Z. will invent another new conspiracy theory to explain a second missing camera."

Gabe picked up a slice of peanut butter toast and took a bite. "You have to admit that it's pushing coincidence a bit."

"I beg your pardon?"

"Think about it. Two missing spy cameras. One stolen by force. One confiscated by a politician in a black leather bustier. Both cameras belong to a woman dedicated to uncovering the truth about a clandestine government project housed at the Eclipse Bay Policy Studies Institute. I mean, what are the odds?"

"You find this all very entertaining, don't you?"

He grinned and took a swallow of coffee. "Most fun I've had in a long time."

"Great. Wonderful. I'm glad you're amused. But what the heck are we going to tell A.Z.?"

"Leave it to me. I'll handle it. I think I'll go with the truth. By the time A.Z. gets through twisting it, no one will recognize it, anyway."

Lillian took a bite of toast. She chewed on it for a while and then swallowed.

"Something I've been meaning to ask," she said.

"Yeah?"

"Did Marilyn wear black leather bustiers a lot when the two of you were an item?"

"It's been a long time," Gabe said. "My memory isn't so good when it comes to some things. But I'm pretty sure the black leather gear is new. Probably a political fashion statement."

"Probably." She looked at the unfinished portion of her toast. "You're good with peanut butter, you know that?"

"It's a gift."

"Marilyn Thornley confiscated the camera?" Arizona slapped a big hand, palm down, fingers spread, on the laminated map that decorated the table of her war room. "Damn. I was afraid of this. She's either working with them or she's one of their dupes."

Lillian suppressed a groan. This was not going well. The good news was that Arizona appeared to be back to her old self. She still wore a small bandage but there was no sign of any other physical problems resulting from the blow to her head.

"Personally," Gabe said, "I'd vote for the dupe possibility. I can't see Marilyn getting involved in a conspiracy to cover up dead space aliens and high-tech UFO secrets. She's too busy working on the launch of her campaign."

Arizona squinted a little while she considered that angle. "Guess you know her better than anyone else around here does."

"Guess so," Lillian agreed brightly.

"I doubt that she has changed much," Gabe said deliberately. "She's devoted to one cause and that cause is Marilyn Thornley."

"She's been involved in politics for the last few years, though," A.Z. mused. "Makes for strange bedfellows."

A vision of Anderson in his red bikini briefs flared briefly in Lillian's mind. "You can say that again."

"We'll replace the camera, A.Z.," Gabe said. "In the meantime, you have our full report. The bottom line is that there was no sign of heavy-duty lab equipment in the new wing and we found no evidence of frozen extraterrestrials. If those alien bodies were moved into the institute, they've got them well hidden."

"Figures." Arizona nodded sagely. "Should have known it wouldn't be this easy. We'll just have to keep digging. Maybe literally, if they've hidden the lab underground."

"A scary thought," Lillian murmured.

"My work will continue," Arizona assured them. "Meanwhile, thanks for the undercover job. Couldn't have done it without you. Unfortunately, you'll never get the public recognition you deserve because we have to maintain secrecy."

"We understand," Gabe said.

Arizona nodded. "But I want you to know that your names will be legend among the ranks of those of us who seek the truth about this vast conspiracy."

"That's certainly good enough for me," Lillian said quickly. "How about you, Gabe?"

"Always wanted to be a legend in my own time," Gabe said.

"We don't want any public recognition," Lillian added, eager to emphasize the point. "Just knowing that we did our patriotic duty is all the reward we need. Isn't that right, Gabe?"

"Right," Gabe got to his feet. "Publicity would be a disaster. If our identities as secret agents were exposed, it would ruin any chance of us helping you out with future undercover work."

Lillian was almost to the door. "Wouldn't want that."

"True," Arizona said. "Never know when we might have to call on you two again."

She knew that something was bothering Gabe. The amusement that had carried him through last night's investigation and this morning's debriefing with Arizona had vanished. When she had called him to suggest a walk on the beach a short while ago, he had agreed, but she could tell that his thoughts were elsewhere.

He had met her at the top of the beach path. She had noticed immediately that the cool, remote quality was back. At least she had finally figured out that the withdrawn air did not automatically indicate major depression or burnout. It meant that he was doing some heavy-duty thinking.

At last. Progress in the quest to understand the deeper elements of Gabriel Madison's enigmatic nature.

He moved easily beside her, his jacket collar pulled up around his neck, his hands shoved deep into his pockets. She recognized this brooding mood, she suddenly realized. She had experienced it often enough herself. It came upon her at times when she was struggling to find the key to the inner vision of a picture. She wondered why she had never understood the similarity before.

She did not try to draw him out of whatever distant space he was exploring. Instead she contented herself with setting an energetic pace for both of them. The tide was out, exposing small, rocky pools. She picked a route through the driftwood and assorted debris that had been deposited by the last storm.

Gabe did not speak until they had almost reached Eclipse Arch, the rock monolith that dominated the beach.

"How well do you know Flint?" he asked without any preamble.

The question took her by surprise.

"Anderson?" She came to a halt. "Not well at all. He moved into the same office building in Portland about six months ago. Like I said, we had some conversations of a professional nature. That's about it."

"You told me that he wanted to buy your matchmaking program."

She shrugged. "And I explained to him that it wasn't for sale."

"Maybe he figured he could get it another way," Gabe said.

"What other way is there?" Then it hit her. "Good grief. You don't really think Anderson would try to . . . to steal it, do you? But—"

"I checked with the college public affairs office this morning. There is no conference of any kind scheduled at Chamberlain this week or next. Flint lied when he said that he was in town to attend a professional seminar."

"Are you absolutely sure?"

"Yes."

She started walking again, mulling over the possibilities. "Okay, maybe he made up the story about being here for a conference. I can see where he might have followed me to try to talk me into selling him the program. But it's hard to envision him actually breaking into my apartment and the cottage."

"Why? You've got something he wants. You refused to sell it to him. In his mind that might not leave a lot of options."

"Yes, but—" She trailed off, trying to sort out the logic. "Anderson is a sex therapist, for heaven's sake."

"He hasn't been one for long."

That stopped her in her tracks. "I beg your pardon?"

"After I called Chamberlain, I talked to some people I know in Portland and went online for some research. The institution that issued Flint's professional credentials is a mail-order outfit."

"What do you mean?"

"It's a paper mill. You pay them money, they give you a fancy piece of paper."

"In other words, his credentials are bogus?"

"Let's just say that his alma mater is not real rigorous when it comes to academic standards."

She thought about the women she had seen in Anderson's waiting room. A shudder went through her. "Talk about a lawsuit waiting to happen. And I thought I was on dangerous ground."

"Funny you should mention the word *lawsuit*."

"Why?"

"Turns out that Flint reinvented himself as a sex therapist after he got into legal troubles in his former profession."

She groaned. "I'm afraid to ask but I can't help myself. What did he do before he went into the field of sex therapy?"

"He headed up a consortium that invested heavily in some Internet ventures that disappeared into thin air."

"Are you telling me Anderson is a complete fraud?"

"No. From what I could learn this morning, it appears that no one has as yet managed to prove that. Flint appears to have a talent for staying inside the gray area between legal and illegal activities. But a guy like that might not have any qualms about trying to steal a computer program."

"Great." She took her hands out of her pockets and spread them wide. "What are we supposed to do now?"

"I think," Gabe said, "that we should have a conversation with J. Anderson Flint."

The motel was typical of many that dotted the winding coast road that led to and from Eclipse Bay, a little down at the heels and mostly empty at this time of year. The rooms all opened directly onto the outside sidewalk. There were three cars parked in front of three doors. Two of the vehicles were mud-splattered SUVs. The third was a sparkling-clean late-model Lincoln.

Gabe brought the Jag to a halt at the far end of the parking lot and studied the blue Lincoln.

"What do you want to bet that's his car?"

Lillian followed his gaze. Tension angled her shoulders.

"If you're wrong, this could be a little hard to explain," she said.

"I told you to let me handle this on my own."

"I can't do that and you know it. Anderson is my problem."

"Correction." He cracked open the door and got out. "He's *our* problem."

He closed the door before she could argue.

She emerged from the Jag without another word. Together they walked to Number Seven.

Gabe knocked twice. Anderson opened the door immediately. He wore gray trousers and a blue sweater that matched his car and his eyes. He did not look at all surprised to see them standing outside his room.

"I wondered when you two would get here," he said.

Lillian looked at him unhappily. "We came to talk to you, Anderson."

"Obviously." Flint held the door open. "You might as well come inside. I trust this won't take long. I've got a meeting with Marilyn in an hour."

Lillian entered the room warily. "A meeting?"

"I'm going to be taking over as her campaign manager."

"I don't understand." Lillian hesitated for a moment. "You're taking Claire's place?"

"Marilyn made her decision last night," Anderson said.

"Is that what she was doing?" Gabe moved into the small room. "Selecting a new campaign manager? I wondered."

"Save your pathetic little jokes for someone else." Raw anger sharpened the lines of Anderson's face. He closed the door with sudden force. "I don't have time for your crude humor."

"Congratulations, Anderson," Lillian said quietly. "I didn't know you were interested in politics."

"I wasn't until I met Marilyn." An odd light appeared in his eyes. "It's obvious that she needs me."

He means it, Gabe thought. What the hell was going on here?

Lillian watched Anderson closely. "Why do you say Marilyn needs you?"

"She's a brilliant candidate but it's clear from the way she fired Claire Jensen on impulse that she lacks maturity and experience. I can bring those strengths to her campaign."

"I see," Lillian said.

Gabe leaned against the closed door and folded his arms. He took stock of the room. From the thin bedspread to the faded flower-print curtains, it fit in with the rest of the establishment. A bit on the seedy side. He had a hunch it was not a J. Anderson Flint kind of place. But, then, Flint hadn't had a lot of choice when it came to accommodations here on the coast. Too bad Dreamscape wasn't up and running. Hannah and Rafe could have made some money off him.

"If you're going to join Marilyn's campaign, can we assume that you'll be giving up your practice in Portland?" Lillian asked.

"Yes, of course." Anderson sounded impatient.

"What about your clients?" Lillian said. "Are you just going to abandon them?"

"There are other sex therapists. I'm sure they'll be fine."

"Probably no worse off, at any rate," Gabe said.

Anderson scowled. "There are priorities here. The transition to a new campaign manger has to be made without delay. Any loss of momentum at this juncture could be disastrous for Marilyn."

"Sure," Gabe said. "Gotta have a seamless transition. I understand that. Hell of a sacrifice on your part, though."

"Marilyn's candidacy is far more important than my personal business affairs."

"If you say so."

"She has a great deal to give to this country." Anderson's rich voice was laced with what sounded like genuine fervor. "I can help her achieve her full potential."

"Your patriotic duty to get her elected, is that it?" Gabe asked.

Anderson's expression tightened. "I don't have time for this. There's no point expecting you to comprehend what's at stake here. Let's get down to business."

Lillian cleared her throat. "We didn't actually come here to talk about business."

Anderson made a disgusted sound at the back of his throat. "I wasn't born yesterday. I know why you're here. You came to bargain for access."

Lillian looked baffled. "Access to what?"

"To Marilyn, of course." Anderson did not look at her. He kept his attention on Gabe. "We all know that when she's elected, she'll have a great deal of power. You want me to guarantee that you'll have access to her, isn't that right, Madison? A man in your position likes to have friends in high places."

Lillian stared. "You don't understand."

"Of course I do." Anderson flicked a quick glance at her. "What's the matter, didn't Madison tell you how he intended to use those pictures?"

"But we don't have any photos," Lillian said. "Marilyn took the camera, remember?"

"Don't give me that crap. I know you had two cameras last night."

"Why do you say that?" Gabe asked.

"You were too quick to turn the first one over to Marilyn when she demanded it." Flint moved his hand in a small arc. "There's only one reason why you would do that. You knew you had backup."

"That's not true." Lillian was indignant.

"The double-camera routine is as old as the hills." Anderson cut off her protest with a patently bored look. "It buys the photographer some time to escape an unpleasant confrontation. The victim thinks she's confiscated the incriminating film and doesn't realize until too late that there is another set of photos."

"You sound familiar with the technique," Gabe said.

"I didn't tell Marilyn because I knew it would upset her. Now that I'm her manager, it's my job to handle this type of incident. I certainly don't intend to allow her to be destroyed by the same type of cheap blackmail that ruined her husband's campaign."

"How dare you imply that we would do something like that?" Lillian was furious now. "We didn't come here to blackmail Marilyn."

Anderson paid no attention to her. "Just tell me what you want, Madison, and I'll see to it that you get it, provided that you destroy those photos."

"What we want," Gabe said evenly, "are some answers."

Anderson's brows came together in a puzzled scowl. "Answers to what?"

"Did you break into Lillian's apartment in Portland?"

For an instant Anderson appeared frozen in place. Then he came up out of the chair. He was practically vibrating with outrage.

"Are you out of your mind?" he hissed. "Why would I do such a thing?"

"To look for her computer program," Gabe said. "You can save the act. It's good but it's not that good."

"I did not break into her apartment." Each word was pronounced with unnatural precision.

"And what about her cottage here in Eclipse Bay?" Gabe said. "I assume that was you, too, but I'll admit that incident is a little confusing because of the assault on Arizona Snow."

"I don't even know anyone named Arizona Snow," Anderson gritted.

"Maybe that was an unrelated event, after all," Lillian said to Gabe.

He shook his head. "I don't know. I can't get past the coincidence thing."

"Coincidences happen," she pointed out.

Anderson swung around to face her. "Stop it. Both of

you. You can't make false accusations like this. You can't prove a damn thing."

"You're right about not being able to prove anything," Gabe said.

Anderson settled himself, relieved. "I knew it."

"That's why we came here instead of going to the cops. Of course, if you'd rather we went to Marilyn, we can do that. She might be interested to hear about your legal problems back in the days when you were selling online investments."

Shock flashed on Anderson's face. "Marilyn would never listen to you."

"Don't bank on it," Lillian responded. "She and Gabe have a history. They go back a long way, I think Marilyn would listen to him if he told her that he didn't believe that you were a good choice for campaign manager."

"You can't do that," Anderson stammered. "You have no right. Nothing was ever proven."

"All we want is confirmation that you went through Lillian's things looking for her matchmaking program," Gabe demanded.

Anderson abruptly turned away toward the window. He gazed bleakly out at the motel parking lot.

"I did not break into Lillian's apartment or the cottage," he said eventually, again enunciating each word with care.

"Let's not quibble over the details." Gabe watched him closely. "Maybe you didn't *break* into her apartment. Maybe you let yourself inside with keys that you either duplicated from her key ring or conned out of the housekeeping staff or the manager."

Lillian flashed him a startled look. Her mouth opened but she closed it quickly without saying a word.

"The cottage was a problem," Gabe went on, "because

you didn't have a key so you had to pry open the door. The second time you smashed a window. By then you had heard about our theory that Lillian was being stalked. Word of that kind of thing gets around fast in a small town. You trashed her studio hoping to keep us looking in that direction. You didn't want us thinking there might be another motive for the break-ins."

*"I am not a stalker."*

"I didn't say you were," Gabe said. "But I think it's pretty clear that Marilyn can't afford to be connected to a campaign manager who goes around imitating stalkers. Or one who breaks into apartments and cottages, for that matter. Bad for the image, you know."

"It's a lie. I didn't trash Lillian's studio. You can't do this to me."

"All we want is the truth," Gabe said.

"Damn it, I won't let you ruin this for me."

Without warning, Anderson spun away from the window and flung himself at Gabe.

"Anderson, no," Lillian called. "Stop. This won't solve anything."

But Anderson was beyond reason. Gabe managed to sidestep the initial charge but Anderson wheeled with startling speed and came at him again. This time Gabe found himself trapped in the corner, the television set on one side, a lamp on the other.

He took the only way out, going low to duck Anderson's swinging fist. Anderson's hand struck the wall where Gabe had been standing a second earlier. A shuddering jolt went through him. Gabe heard him suck in an anguished breath.

He caught Anderson by the legs and shoved hard. The momentum toppled both of them to the rug. They went down with a stunning thud, Anderson on the bottom. He struggled wildly, fighting back with a reckless fury, completely out of control. He hammered the floor with his heels and managed to slam a fist into Gabe's ribs. He twisted violently, trying to lurch free.

Gabe finally pinned him to the rug, using his weight to force him to lie still.

Trapped, Anderson stared up at him. Gabe felt him go limp as the hurricane of violence dissipated as suddenly as it had appeared.

"I don't want her hurt, do you understand?" Anderson's voice was ragged. "I'll do whatever you want—just don't hurt her."

"Listen to me, Anderson, no one wants to hurt Marilyn. We just want the truth." Gabe tightened his hands on Anderson's shoulders. "Tell me about the break-ins."

"All right. Okay. I did go into Lillian's apartment. But I didn't break in, damn it. I went in with the cleaning people."

"It was that easy?"

Anderson nodded. "It was that easy. Just told them I was there to check out some electrical problems. People trust you when you wear a uniform with your name on it."

Lillian moved closer. Gabe sensed the shock that gripped her. He caught a glimpse of her hands. They were clenched so tightly that her knuckles were white. But her voice was surprisingly steady.

"Did you want the matchmaking program that badly, Anderson?" she asked. "I told you, it wasn't magic. Just a standard personality inventory analysis program that I used together with a dose of common sense."

Anderson looked up at her. "It wasn't the damned matchmaking program I wanted, you little fool. It was the data on your clients."

"My *clients*."

"Don't you get it?" He made a disgusted sound. "Hell, you really don't know what you've got, do you? Don't you have any concept of what that client database is worth? You've got detailed background information on some of the wealthiest, most successful, most powerful people in the city. Hell, in the whole damn state."

"But what would you do with it?"

"Why don't you ask your boyfriend, here. I'm sure he understands what that kind of information is worth these days."

"A fortune." Gabe released Anderson and got to his feet. "Good client data is one of the most valuable commodities on the market today. Businesses, investors, politicians, charitable organizations, you name it, they all want it. They'll all pay big bucks for solid background on people who have a lot of money to spend."

Lillian looked at Anderson. "You never were interested in collaborating on a book, were you? You were after my client roster all along. Who did you plan to sell my files to?"

He sat up slowly, wincing. "I hadn't finalized my list of prospects. I was still working on it when you announced that you intended to close down Private Arrangements. When I realized you were serious, my first thought was to salvage the data. I offered to buy your program, thinking I'd get the client list with it. But you refused to sell."

"So you tried to steal it."

"I didn't intend to steal the damned files." Anderson actually looked offended. "I just wanted to take a copy for myself."

"You don't call that theft?" Lillian asked.

His jaw clenched. "It wasn't like you had any use for that data."

"When you didn't find her files in Portland, you followed her here to Eclipse Bay," Gabe said. "That night in the restaurant you encountered the perfect prospect for the client info. Marilyn Thornley. A politician badly in need of a rich donor list."

Some of the fierceness returned briefly to Anderson's expression. "She needs those names and the background on those people."

Lillian opened her mouth. Gabe didn't know what she planned to say but quite suddenly he had had enough. He shook his head once. She got the message and remained silent.

"Let's get out of here," he said.

She glanced once more at Anderson and then walked to the door.

"Just a minute." Anderson gripped the edge of the television set to steady himself. "What are you going to do? You can't involve Marilyn in this. She had nothing to do with it."

"Don't worry, Flint." Gabe opened the door. "We're not going to do a damn thing. I told you, all we wanted was the truth. It stops here, provided you leave Lillian alone. But if you make another move to get her computer, I'll take the story straight to the cops and to the press."

Anderson looked horrified. "Marilyn's campaign couldn't survive that kind of scandal at this stage. Things are too delicate."

"I know," Gabe said. "You have my word that if you leave Lillian alone, this won't go any further."

"I swear I won't bother her again." Anderson sounded frantic. "I promise."

"It's a deal," Gabe said.

He ushered Lillian through the door and out onto the sidewalk. A chill, damp wind was blowing bits of litter around the parking lot.

"Lillian, wait." Anderson came to stand in the doorway. "If you change your mind, my offer to buy those client files is still good."

"Forget it, Anderson. The files are gone."

"I don't believe you destroyed them. They're too valuable. Think about my offer. You've got in-depth information on guys like Tom Lydd of Lydd-Zone Software and Madison, here. That data is worth a lot of money."

"I don't know about the Lydd information," Lillian said quietly. "But the data on Gabe certainly wouldn't do anyone any good."

Anderson scowled. "What the hell do you mean?"

"Most of it is false," Lillian explained. "He lied through his teeth on the questionnaire that he filled out for Private Arrangements."

# chapter 23

Gabe needed a place to think. And a cup of coffee. So he drove to the nearest restaurant, Snow's Café. They found a booth at the back. Lillian ordered tea. He went for the hard stuff, a double espresso.

There was a sprinkling of Arizona's customary clientele around them, primarily students and faculty from Chamberlain College, but no one bothered them. Arizona was not behind the counter today. Gabe figured she was probably at home in her war room, devising strategy to uncover the secret, underground labs at the institute.

"Do you really think he'll leave me alone now?" Lillian asked after a while.

"Yes."

"He didn't believe me when I told him that I had destroyed the client files."

Gabe sipped the supercharged espresso and lowered the small cup. "Did you?"

"First day I got here. I couldn't figure out how to be absolutely certain that my clients' privacy would be protected as long as the data concerning them was stored in my computer. So I removed the hard drive and tossed it into Dead Hand Cove at high tide. I left the rest of the computer in the trunk of my car. It's still there as far as I know."

"The only copy of those files was on that hard drive?"

"Yep."

"Guess that took care of the privacy issue."

"That was the whole point." She sighed. "Looking back, I suppose I should have realized sooner that Anderson was after those files. But he kept talking about the program so I assumed he wanted to go into matchmaking. It seemed like a logical extension of his sex therapy business."

"He could hardly admit that he wanted the background info on your clients. He knew how strongly you felt about guarding their privacy."

"One thing bothers me," she said slowly. "He acknowledged that he went into my apartment in Portland. Why didn't he admit that he broke into the cottage here in Eclipse Bay, too?"

"He's smart enough to know that he left no proof of illegal entry in your apartment. Like he said, he just walked in disguised as a repairman and looked around. Nothing was taken. No damage done. Hell, he's got witnesses that he didn't steal anything. Your cleaning people will vouch for him. And you never even filed a report with the cops. He had nothing to lose by telling us about that incident."

"But here in Eclipse Bay, he left obvious signs of forcible entry and I did file a report with Sean Valentine."

He nodded. "In addition, everyone knows that Valentine is investigating the assault on A.Z. and that he's working on the assumption there may be a link to at least one of the break-ins at your place. Flint didn't want to take the risk of admitting that he was ever inside your cottage."

"Must have been him, though. He was the only one who knew about the files on my computer."

Gabe contemplated the espresso cup. "And after meeting Marilyn, he wanted those files very, very badly."

"He probably made the deal with her right after he met her and then had to deliver the goods quickly. So he took some chances and used force to get into the cottage."

"Yeah." Absently he touched his side, feeling the sore place around his ribs.

Her gaze followed the movement of his hand. Sudden alarm tightened her expression. "Are you all right?"

"Yes."

"Good heavens, did Anderson hurt you?"

"I told you, I'm fine, Lillian." He put his hand back down on the table.

"You're sure?"

"I'm sure."

"Do you think you should have a doctor check out your ribs?"

"No."

"Okay, okay, no need to snap at me. I was just worried about you."

"Thanks." He took another swallow of coffee.

"It was a little scary there for a while." She shivered. "To tell you the truth, I was completely taken off guard when Anderson turned violent. I never expected him to attack you that way. He seemed the type who would try to talk himself out of trouble."

"People change when they fall in love."

"In *love*." She set her cup down hard on the table and fixed him with a dumbfounded expression. "*Anderson?*

Are you crazy? Who in the world could he possibly—?
Good grief, not Marilyn Thornley."

"Yeah."

"But he just met her."

"Happens that way sometimes."

She flopped back against the vinyl cushions. "It boggles the mind. J. Anderson Flint in love with Marilyn
Thornley."

"You're the one who said they were a perfect match."

"Yes, but I was joking. Sort of."

"It's no joke."

She looked thoughtful. "You may be right. He was
very protective of her, wasn't he? I wonder if she cares
about him?"

"I don't know. But if she's smart, she'll keep him on
as her campaign manager. He's committed. She'll have
his complete loyalty."

"Nice qualities in a campaign manager. And in a husband. Be interesting to see what happens there."

"Yes."

She smiled at him across the table. "Weird, when you
think about it."

"Their relationship?"

"No, the fact that you picked up on it first. I'm supposed to be the expert in that department. What tipped
you off?"

"Male intuition." He drained the last of the espresso
and put down the cup. He certainly wasn't going to tell
her the truth. Not yet at any rate. He had problems enough
dealing with it, himself.

"It bothers you, doesn't it?"

"What?"

"The fact that you found his weak spot and you used
it to apply pressure to get him to confess."

He looked up, surprised. "No."

"Are you sure?"

"Let's get something clear here." He pushed aside the empty espresso cup and folded his arms on the table. "Protecting you is my only priority. I don't give a damn about Flint's finer feelings."

She searched his face. "I see. But if that's true, then why are you acting so weird?"

"I'm not acting weird." He started to extricate himself from the booth. "Are you finished? Let's go."

She reached across the table and covered one of his hands with her own. He went very still, intensely aware of the warmth of her fingers.

"Gabe, I'm sorry. I know you've been through a lot because of me. I'm very grateful."

Anger heated his blood, just as the violence had earlier. He clamped down on the fierce surge of emotion, seeking refuge in that inner space to which he always retreated when things threatened to get out of control.

"The last thing I want is your gratitude," he said.

She recoiled, her hand coming off his so swiftly an onlooker would have thought she had gotten her fingers burned.

"I didn't mean it that way," she said tightly.

He made himself breathe. "I know." He got to his feet and reached for his wallet. "I'll take you home."

"Sure." She slipped quickly out of the booth and hurried toward the front door without looking back.

He watched her rush away. *Nice going, Madison, you really screwed that up, didn't you?*

# chapter 24

Gabe was thinking of shutting down the computer and walking to Lillian's cottage to join her for lunch when he heard the sound of a car in the drive.

He opened the front door and saw a large black Lincoln come to a halt in front of the steps. The man behind the wheel wore a dark, inexpensive suit and a single gold earring. A hired driver.

The rear door of the vehicle opened. Sullivan Harte got out of the car.

This did not look promising.

Sullivan said something to the driver and then started toward the front porch.

"I didn't know you were in town," Gabe said.

The tip of Sullivan's cane hit the first step. "We need to talk."

"I was afraid you were going to say that." He held the door open. "Is this where you tell me that if I manage to sucker Lillian into marrying me you will make certain that she never inherits a dime's worth of Harte Investments?"

"Not quite."

Sullivan went past him into the house.

Gabe glanced at the limo. The driver had pulled out a paperback novel and appeared to be content to remain where he was.

Gabe followed his uninvited guest inside and let the door close behind him.

"Coffee?"

"I could use a cup." Sullivan surveyed the desk where Gabe had left the laptop and a stack of papers. "You really trying to run Madison Commercial from here?"

"I'm not trying to run it. I am running it from here. Technology is amazing." Gabe went into the kitchen.

"How long can you afford to stay away from the office?" Sullivan demanded.

"Long as I want." Gabe poured a cup of coffee and carried it into the living room. "Did you come here to talk about the wonders of modern techniques for long-distance management?"

"No."

"Didn't think so," Gabe said.

Mitchell slammed the newspaper down with such force that the little table vibrated on its spindly legs. He scowled at Bryce, who had just walked into Incandescent Body with the news.

"What the hell do you mean, Sullivan Harte is in town?"

"Saw him sitting in the back of a limo a few minutes ago," Bryce said. "Passed me while I was at the gas station. Must have flown into Portland and hired a car and driver there. Thought you'd want to know."

"Damned right I want to know." Mitchell grabbed his cane and levered himself to his feet. "Where was he headed?"

"Took Bayview Drive. Could be on his way out to the Harte cottage."

"Or he could be headed toward the old Buckley place where Gabe is staying." Mitchell tossed some money on the table. "What do you want to bet that he came here to try to scare off my grandson?"

"Forget it. I never take bets on Hartes and Madisons. Too unpredictable."

Lillian studied the fresh canvas propped on the easel while she finished cleaning the last of her brushes. It was the start of a portrait of Gabe based on the sketch she had made of him in her Portland studio. All brooding shadows and hard, bright light, it was the first real work she had done since she had arrived in town. She was pleased with it. She had been in the zone this afternoon. About time.

She set the brushes in a holder to dry and looked at her watch. She was startled to see that it was nearly two o'clock. Gabe had said he would come over around noon for lunch. As usual, she had lost all track of time while she was in that other place where the vision reigned supreme.

Maybe he had been delayed by business or a phone call.

She looked out the window. There were whitecaps on the bay and no rain in sight. She could use some fresh air after such a long stretch of work. The overstimulated sensation that always followed a particularly good session in the studio was making her restless. She needed to get out and work it off. A walk along the bluffs would do the trick. She would probably run into Gabe on his way here.

She indulged herself in a brief, romantic picture of herself flying into his arms on the top of a windswept bluff. Gulls would be wheeling overhead. His dark hair would be ruffled by the crisp breeze. She would be sexy and free-spirited in a gossamer dress and bare feet.

That image made her wonder if she ought to take time to change out of her paint-stained jeans and long-tailed denim shirt. Then she remembered that it was only about fifty-three degrees outside and that there was a lot of rough gravel on the bluff path. Forget the gossamer dress and bare feet.

She put on a pair of scuffed running shoes, took a black denim jacket out of the hall closet and left the house through the mudroom door.

Outside, the scene on the bluffs was very much as she had envisioned it, blustery and invigorating. The bay was a dramatic sweep of quietly churning seawater. The town was picturesque in the distance. The air was clear and bright. The only thing missing was Gabe. There was no sign of him on the path.

An uneasy feeling coiled around her, pushing aside the zesty anticipation. By the time she emerged from the trees and found herself near the back porch of the old Buckley place a dark foreboding had settled on her.

She walked around the side of the house to see if Gabe's car was in the drive. It was. So was another vehicle, a dark limo complete with a driver behind the wheel. The chauffeur did not notice her. He was deep into a paperback.

She told herself to relax. Obviously business from out of town had caught up with Gabe. But for some obscure reason the anxiety didn't dissipate. Things felt wrong.

She returned to the back door, opened it quietly and moved stealthily into the kitchen. If Gabe was wheeling and dealing with an important client she did not want to interrupt.

The low rumble of voices from the other room made her stop short. She knew those voices. Both of them.

Suddenly everything made sense. Outrage flared. She rushed to the doorway.

Sullivan and Gabe were seated on the sofa. A leather-bound binder and a stack of computer printouts were arrayed on the low table in front of them.

"Granddad, how dare you?"

Sullivan looked up swiftly, peering at her through a pair of reading glasses. She could have sworn that he turned red.

"Lillian."

Gabe said nothing. He took one look at her and lounged back into the corner of the sofa, one arm stretched out along the top of the cushions.

She ignored him. Her entire attention was focused on Sullivan.

"What in the world are you doing?" Her voice cracked. "No, don't bother explaining. I know exactly what you're doing."

Sullivan blinked owlishly behind the spectacles. "You do?"

"It's as obvious as those papers on the table." She walked a few steps closer. "You're here to try to buy off Gabe. Or maybe you want to scare him off. Which is it?"

"Now, honey," Sullivan said in placating tones.

She was vaguely aware of the sound of a large vehicle arriving in the drive. She ignored it.

"You think he wants to marry me so that he can get his hands on a chunk of Harte, don't you? What are you offering him to get out of my life? Or are you threatening him?"

The front door crashed open. Mitchell stormed into the house.

"Who's threatening my grandson?" he roared. He came to a halt, brows bristling, jaw clenched, and glowered at Sullivan. "What do you think you're doing, Harte?"

"Things aren't quite the way they look," Sullivan said.

"I don't believe that for one minute," Lillian declared. "You've been talking to Mom and Dad, haven't you? They told you I was seeing Gabe and you just leaped to the conclusion that he was after me because of H.I."

"Speaking of leaping to conclusions," Gabe said mildly.

She glared at him. "Stay out of this. It has nothing to do with you. This is between me and Granddad."

"And me." Mitchell jabbed a thumb at his own chest. "Don't forget about me. I'm involved in this thing, too."

"Sure," Gabe said dryly. "Don't know what I was thinking."

Lillian whipped her attention back to Sullivan. "I realize you feel you're acting in my best interests. I know everyone believes that Gabe is after a piece of Harte. But that is absolute nonsense."

All three men stared at her.

"Nonsense?" Sullivan repeated carefully.

"Yes. Nonsense." She swept out a hand. "He would never marry for business reasons. He's a Madison. They don't do things like that."

Sullivan cleared his throat. "Always heard that Gabe, here, was a different kind of Madison."

"Not that different," she shot back. "And what's more, you can't buy him off or scare him off. Madisons don't work that way."

"She's right," Mitchell said. "If Gabe wants to marry her, you won't be able to get rid of him with money or threats."

"Which brings up a very crucial issue," Lillian said. "As I told Mom on the phone, Gabe has never asked me to marry him. Isn't that correct, Gabe?"

"Correct," Gabe said.

"What's this?" Sullivan grabbed the handle of his cane and used it to haul himself up off the sagging sofa. He turned on Gabe with a thunderous expression. "I was under the impression that you were serious about my granddaughter. If you think I'm going to stand by while you shack up indefinitely with her, you can think again."

"Wasn't planning to shack up indefinitely," Gabe said.

Mitchell beetled his brows. "Just what are you doing here, Sullivan?"

"Before we were so rudely interrupted," Sullivan said, "I was presenting a business proposition to Gabe. Of course, that was when I was still under the impression that he intended to marry Lillian."

Mitchell eyed him with deep suspicion. "What kind of business proposition?"

Gabe looked at Lillian. "Your grandfather was outlining the financial advantages of marriage to you. You come with one-third of H.I., you know."

"The *advantages*?" Lillian stared at Sullivan. "You mean you're trying to *bribe* him to marry me?"

"I just wanted him to understand that we'd be happy to have him as a member of the family," Sullivan said mildly.

"Well, shoot and damn." Mitchell whistled softly. "Got to hand it to you, Sullivan. Didn't think you had that much common sense."

Lillian was aghast. "You weren't trying to buy him off.

You're here to try to buy him for me. This is the most mortifying thing that has ever happened to me in my entire life."

Sullivan stiffened. "What's mortifying about it? I thought you wanted Gabe."

"For heaven's sake, Granddad. It's like you're offering him a dowry to take me off your hands. If he marries me and gets a chunk of H.I., everyone will say he did it for the money."

"Which is why I turned down the deal," Gabe replied softly.

She swung around to face him. "You did?"

"Shoot and damn." Mitchell waved a hand. "Why did you go and do something dumb like that? You coulda had the lady and one-third of H.I. That's what we call a win-win situation."

"What choice did I have?" Gabe gestured toward the papers on the coffee table. "If I sign those Lillian would always wonder if I married her for her inheritance."

"No, I wouldn't," Lillian said quickly.

Gabe looked at her. "I appreciate your faith in me but I'm afraid I can't accept you and one-third of H.I., too. I just finished explaining that to Sullivan."

"What if I just give up my shares in H.I.?" she asked.

Sullivan glared at her. "I'm not about to let you walk away from your inheritance, young woman. Wouldn't be right. I worked my tail off to build that company. I did it for you and Hannah and Nick."

Her refusing a third of H.I. would be a terrible blow to him, she realized.

"Evidently I'm fated to be doomed by my inheritance," she muttered.

"Depends," Gabe said.

She looked at him, hope rising. "On what?"

"There is a way around this. If you agree to marry me and if your family insists on endowing you, so to speak, you can put your share of your Harte inheritance into a trust for any children we might have. Okay with you, Sullivan?"

Sullivan looked thoughtful. "One way to handle it, I guess."

Joy flowed through Lillian, bringing a rainbow of colors.

"No problem," she whispered.

Gabe got to his feet. "You'll do it? You'll marry me?"

Neither Mitchell nor Sullivan so much as twitched. It was, Lillian thought, as if the whole world was holding its collective breath in anticipation of her answer.

"Well, sure," she said softly. "I mean, what else can I do after you turned down the chance to get your hands on a chunk of my family's company? It's such a truly Madison-style gesture. But I really don't want you to feel that you have to do this. It's not necessary, honest. I know you're not a fortune-hunter."

He gave her his slow smile, showing just a hint of teeth. "Honey, if I want Harte Investments, I'll buy the whole damn company when your dad puts it on the market in a year or two."

Everyone stared at him in dumbfounded silence.

Lillian met Sullivan's eyes. He grinned. She felt the laughter bubble up inside.

"Yes, of course," she gasped between giggles. "Why didn't I think of that. It's no secret that H.I. will be up for sale soon. You can buy it outright when Dad retires. No fuss, no bother, no need to get married."

"Trust me," Gabe said. "it would be a whole lot simpler that way."

Mitchell grunted. "Never thought of that."

"Probably because business is not your forte, Mitch," Sullivan growled. "It was obvious right from the start that Gabe didn't need to marry Lillian to get his hands on Harte. All he has to do is wait a few years and do a buy-out."

Gabe wrapped his fingers around Lillian's wrist. "Come on, let's go someplace where we can discuss our private affairs in private."

He opened the porch door and led her outside into the bright afternoon light. Together they went down the path toward the rocky beach.

Neither of them spoke until they reached the bottom.

"You're serious about this?" she said at last.

"Never been more serious in my life." He tightened his hand around hers. "Did you mean it when you said you'd marry me?"

"Yes. But you don't have to give up a share of Harte Investments for me. I mean, I appreciate the grand gesture but it's not necessary. Really."

"It's necessary."

"Why?"

He stopped and pulled her around to face him. "Because I'm a Madison. A Madison does things like turn down the offer of a third of a multimillion-dollar company for the woman he loves. It's in the genes."

*The woman he loves.*

"Oh, Gabe." The brilliant colors of happiness splashed through her, effervescent and glorious. She went into his arms. "I love you so much."

He kissed her.

Except for a few details such as the fact that they were on the beach, not on the bluffs, and she wasn't barefoot and there was no gossamer gown, the scene was just the way it had been in the romantic fantasy she had conjured up when she had set out to meet him on the path.

Perfect.

Sullivan surveyed the seating options in Mitchell's living room and chose the recliner that provided a view of the bay. He lowered himself into it with a long sigh and looked out at the water. The light was starting to go. He never liked this time of day.

"We came mighty close to screwing that up pretty bad, didn't we?" he said.

"What's with this *we* business?" Mitchell settled into the other well-worn recliner. "You're the one who damn near screwed things up. What the hell did you think you were doing trying to buy Gabe with a chunk of H.I.?"

"You're the one who told me I was supposed to fix things."

"You don't fix things between a Madison and a Harte with a business contract."

"Seemed like the logical thing to do. Pretty clear that Lillian wanted him and I just wanted to encourage him to see the benefits of marriage to her." Sullivan stretched out his legs, wincing when his joints protested. "How do you stand this damp, cold weather all year long?"

"I'm used to it. You've gotten soft living down there in Arizona."

"Not soft, smart. If you had any sense you'd move to the desert, too."

"I like it just fine here in Eclipse Bay." Mitchell rested his head against the back of the chair. "You figure to drive back to Portland tonight?"

"Had enough driving for one day. Knees stiffen up when I sit in a car for a long period of time."

"Yeah, I know what you mean." Mitchell absently

rubbed one of his own knees. "Occurs to me that if you're gonna hang around town for a while, you might as well stay here with me."

"Why would I want to do that?"

"If you stay at the cottage you'll get in the way of Gabe's courting."

"Maybe I'll take you up on that offer. Don't want to interfere with the lovebirds." Sullivan chuckled.

Mitchell eyed him suspiciously. "What's so funny?"

"Just thinking about what the folks in town will say when they find out that I'm your houseguest."

"Huh." Sullivan grinned. "Probably figure we'll try to knock each other's teeth out."

"Probably."

"Now that's settled, maybe I should fill you in on some of the stuff that's been happening around here."

Fifteen minutes later Sullivan was ready to explode. "Why the hell wasn't I told about the break-ins? I didn't have a clue that Lillian was in danger."

"Take it easy. Like I just said, everything is under control. Gabe took care of Flint for you."

"I should have been informed."

"Gabe put the fire out before anyone realized just how big it was." Mitchell heaved himself up out of his chair. "Bryce will have dinner ready in a while. I generally have a glass or two of something beforehand. As I recall, you used to do the same."

"I haven't changed." Sullivan watched the darkness close in over the bay. "A little something at this time of day helps a man relax."

"That it does."

Mitchell went to a cabinet, hauled a bottle out of a cupboard and splashed whiskey into two glasses. He brought the two drinks back across the room and handed one to Sullivan without comment.

They drank their whiskeys and watched the darkness thicken outside the window.

After all these years, Sullivan thought, it was good to sit here and share the twilight with the one other person in the world who understood why this was such a bad time of day.

"They say the memories fade as you get older," Mitchell said after a while.

"They lie."

# chapter 25

Lillian parked her car in the driveway behind Claire's red compact, got out and walked across the graveled drive toward the porch steps. All four doors and the lid of the compact's trunk were open wide. Two suitcases and a file box occupied the trunk.

The front door of the house banged open just as she reached out to knock. Claire lurched forward, head down, onto the porch, struggling with an oversized suitcase. She was dressed in sweats and running shoes. Her hair was anchored in a ponytail.

The loud, strident voice of a radio talk-show host holding forth on politics poured out of the doorway behind her.

"Need a hand?" Lillian asked above the hammering of the radio pundit.

Claire jolted to a stop, breathing hard. She looked up quickly, startled.

"Lil." She let go of the suitcase. "Sorry, didn't hear you drive up. What are you doing here?"

"You told me you were leaving town today. I came by to see if I could help with the packing."

"Thanks." Claire looked at the compact's trunk and then down at the suitcase that she had angled through the doorway. "I underestimated the job. Guess I hadn't realized how much stuff I had accumulated here in Eclipse Bay. I'm taking the essentials with me in the car. The moving-van people will be here at two o'clock for the rest."

"Point me in the right direction."

"I finished my office. I was just getting started on the bedroom and bath. If you want to take the kitchen, I would be forever grateful."

"No problem." Lillian moved through the doorway.

Claire followed her. She went to the table where the radio blared and turned off the political hot talk. The sudden silence left an uncomfortable vacuum.

"You're a good friend," Claire declared. "Unlike some others I could mention. You will notice how none of the other members of the *team* bothered to show. Turns out they all had something unexpected come up at the last minute. Why am I not surprised?"

"Claire—"

"Getting fired from a political campaign staff endows you with instant invisibility. Did you know that? Like being in the wrong crowd in high school."

Lillian cleared her throat. "Where are the packing cartons?"

"In the laundry room off the kitchen. Help yourself."

Lillian went toward the kitchen.

"There's coffee on the counter," Claire called after her. "And some croissants from Incandescent Body. You know, that bakery is one of the few things I'm going to miss about this place."

"Understandable. It's very good."

Lillian went into the kitchen and opened the cupboard doors. She did a quick survey of the contents of the cabinets, getting a feel for the size of the job, and then went into the laundry room to look for boxes.

The small space was crowded with the usual jumble of odds and ends that tend to wind up in laundry rooms. A long shelf above the aging washer and dryer held a collection of soap, bleach, and dryer-sheet packages, together with squeeze bottles of glass cleaner and stain remover. A mop and a broom were propped in a bucket in the corner. The basket on the floor next to it was filled with rags.

A selection of empty cardboard cartons was stacked on top of the washer and dryer. She chose two and went back into the kitchen. Methodically she began emptying Claire's cupboards.

Impulse had brought her here today. She did not know what she was looking for. She only hoped that she would know it when she saw it.

Half an hour later, the two cartons filled, she went out into the living room and down the hall to the room Claire had used as a second office. The desk and file cabinet were still there but they had been cleaned out.

Claire appeared in the hall, a box filled with bathroom items in her arms.

"Finished with the kitchen already?"

"No. I need some strapping tape."

"On the table in the living room."

"Thanks."

"Don't know what I'd have done without you today." Claire went past her toward the front door. "Next time you're in Seattle, give me a call. I'll take you to dinner."

"I'll do that."

She waited until Claire disappeared outside and then ducked into the bedroom. The closet doors and the drawers in the chest beneath the window stood open, making a quick search easy. She examined an array of shoes first. Ignoring the high heels and pumps, she looked for a familiar pair of loafers.

They were nowhere in sight. Maybe they had already been packed. She opened one of the unsealed cartons.

Claire's footsteps sounded on the porch. Adrenaline surged through Lillian, making her hand tremble.

This was pointless. She was wasting her time. She dropped the lid of the carton and hurried out of the bedroom. She started back along the hall.

Too late. Claire was already in the living room, looking at the strapping-tape device that rested on the coffee table. She turned and saw Lillian. A frown crossed her face.

"Didn't you find the tape?" she asked.

"I stopped to use the bathroom." Lillian kept moving. She went to the coffee table and picked up the tape. Her pulse was pounding. "I'm almost finished with the kitchen."

"Terrific."

She took a deep breath and made herself walk briskly but not too briskly back into the kitchen. She knelt beside the cartons and went to work sealing them.

Claire's footsteps receded back down the hall toward the bedroom.

Lillian wondered if her heart would ever stop pounding. Clearly she was not cut out for this kind of thing. But there would never be a better opportunity to satisfy her curiosity.

She finished taping the boxes, got to her feet and went back into the laundry room for more cartons. Her pulse had finally slowed. She moved two large boxes aside to get at the medium-sized one that looked right for the contents of the silverware drawer.

She noticed the crumpled piece of navy blue cloth on top of the rag basket when she put the boxes down beside it. The blue fabric was not faded or torn. It looked new.

It looked familiar. She had an artist's eye for colors. She remembered them.

Her pulse picked up speed again. Her heart was pounding now.

Don't get too excited. Probably nothing. Just a rag.

Cautiously she reached into the basket, picked up the wad of navy blue cloth and shook it out. It was the shirt Claire had worn the day she had stopped by the cottage to warn her that Marilyn still wanted Gabe.

There did not appear to be anything wrong with the garment. No rips or holes that would have explained how it had come to be relegated to the rag pile. Could have fallen out of the laundry hamper by accident, she thought.

She flipped the shirt around to examine the back.

The smear of dried red paint on the right cuff made her go cold.

"Oh, damn," she whispered.

She had come here this morning on the off chance that she might get some answers. *Be careful what you wish for.*

"How are you doing in here?" Claire came to stand in the doorway of the laundry room. "Need more boxes? I've got some—"

She broke off at the sight of the navy blue shirt dangling from Lillian's fingers. Her eyes went to the paint-stained cuff.

"It was you who trashed my studio." Lillian put the

shirt down on the washer. "I knew there had to be some evidence somewhere. It's almost impossible to work with a lot of paint and not get some on your clothes."

The blood drained from Claire's face. She swallowed twice before she managed to speak.

"You can't prove anything," she stammered. "You can't prove a damn thing, do you hear me?"

"Probably not. Unless, of course, you kept the VPX 5000. But I'm sure you had enough sense to ditch it. Did you throw it into the bay? That's what I did with my client files."

Claire eyes filled with tears. She seemed to collapse in on herself.

"There was no need to injure Arizona," Lillian said. "She had nothing to do with this. Do you realize what might have happened if you had hit her even a little bit harder? She's an elderly woman, Claire. You could have killed her."

"I didn't want to do it but I had no choice."

"No choice? What are you talking about. No one made you hit her and steal her camera."

"I had to get the camera." Claire's hands knotted into fists at her sides. "Don't you understand? She had pictures."

"Pictures of you breaking into my cottage?"

"I didn't see her until I left. I had parked my car in the woods nearby. But when I started to drive away, I saw her truck parked on the opposite side of the road. She wasn't in it so I knew she was probably nearby conducting her idiotic surveillance rounds. I was afraid she might have spotted me coming out of your cottage."

"For heaven's sake, Claire, you know as well as I do that it wouldn't have mattered if she had noticed you in the vicinity of the cottage. No one ever pays any attention to A.Z.'s claims and theories. Everyone knows she's a little weird."

"When she came out of the woods a short time later she was carrying that damn camera. I panicked. Of course, no one would have listened if she had claimed to see me near your cottage on the day a break-in was reported. Everyone knows she's paranoid about people who work at the institute. But they sure as hell would have paid attention if she had produced some time-and-date-stamped photos of me coming out the back door of your place with a tire iron in my hand."

"You followed her home, waiting for an opportunity to take the VPX 5000 from her, didn't you? She knew that she was being tailed."

"I watched her for a while but I realized that sooner or later she would go back to that fortress. I got there ahead of her, hid the car in the trees and waited on her back porch behind the woodshed."

"You planned to attack her."

*"No."* Claire wiped away her tears with the back of her hand. "I didn't know exactly what I was going to do. I couldn't think straight. I guess I had some vague idea of catching her off guard when she went into the house. I just wanted to get that camera."

"But something made her walk around the porch to check the rear door. You saw your chance, grabbed the plant stand and hit her."

"I didn't mean to put her into the hospital." Claire's voice rose on an anguished wail. "You have to believe me. I just wanted to knock her down. Make her drop the camera."

"You gave her a concussion, Claire. You could have killed her."

"I told you, I never meant to hurt her." Claire sniffed.

"What's more, you can't prove that I took the camera. Just your word against mine."

"Sure." Lillian leaned back against the dryer and gripped the white metal edge on either side. "And since its just us girls talking here, I've got some questions. What gave you the idea of going after my client files in the first place? Did you come up with it all on your own or was it something Anderson said?"

Rage infused Claire's face. She turned a shade of red that rivaled the paint on the shirt.

"Flint. I heard that bastard tell Marilyn about your files the day he came to see her at the institute. He actually bragged about them to her. He used them to talk his way into *my job*. Promised her he could get them for her."

"I see."

"Got to give credit where it's due. Marilyn is no fool. She understood the value of those files immediately."

"Did Anderson tell her he planned to steal them?"

"Of course not. He just said he was working an angle to get them. Told her not to worry. He'd handle all the details."

"Where were you when they had that conversation?"

"I was packing up my desk in the adjoining office. Marilyn closed the door but I simply switched on the recording system." Claire smiled bitterly. "That was one of my jobs, you know. Recording Marilyn's meetings and conversations with important people. She plans to publish her memoirs someday."

"Later you decided to see if you could find my client files before Flint got to them, right?"

Claire shrugged. "He said they were on your computer. Sounded easy enough. I could have used them the same way Flint planned to use them."

"To buy your way into another job?"

"Yes. The data on your high-end clients would be worth a fortune to any candidate in the Northwest." Tears welled in Claire's eyes again. "But I couldn't find your computer when I broke into the cottage. And there was Arizona with her damned camera when I came out. Everything went wrong. All that risk for nothing. It's not fair."

"That day you stopped by the cottage to warn me to watch out for Marilyn, you overheard my conversation with Gabe when he was on his way back from Portland. You learned that we had concluded I might be the target of a stalker. That made you very nervous, didn't it? You realized that we were no longer dismissing the break-in as the action of a transient. So you came back to trash my studio to add some credibility to our theory."

"I got scared. Really scared. This is Eclipse Bay. I knew that if a Harte and a Madison were putting pressure on Sean Valentine, he might actually conduct a serious investigation. I didn't know where that would lead. I thought that I would be safe if everyone continued to blame the break-in on a stalker who could conveniently just disappear."

"Oh, Claire." Lillian shook her head. "What were you thinking?"

The bitterness tinged Claire's voice. "How did you figure it out?"

"I suppose you could say it was a process of elimination. Gabe and a private investigator cleared the only real potential stalker we had on our list. When we talked to Anderson, he denied the break-ins here in Eclipse Bay. Adamantly."

Claire widened in scorn. "And you actually believed that bag of sleaze?"

Lillian shrugged. "The forced entry didn't fit with what

I knew about him. Anderson is the sort who tries to talk his way in and out of situations."

"What about Marilyn? She should have been on your list. She was the one who had the most to gain from those files."

"The thing about Marilyn is that she is very up-front about what she wants. She doesn't sneak around. You, on the other hand, have a history of sneaking around."

Claire flinched. "What do you mean?"

"She was right when she said that you had an affair with Trevor Thornley, wasn't she?"

"I told you, I never slept with Trevor."

"I don't believe you."

Claire watched her warily. "Why not?"

"Because I found out that you were sneaking around with Larry Fulton in the back of his father's van the summer that he and I were dating."

"Larry Fulton." Claire's mouth fell open. "But that was years ago. We were in *college*."

"I know. I was pretty sure that he was fooling around with someone else that summer. I just hadn't realized that the other woman was you. The Willis brothers set me straight a few days ago. They gave me a whole new perspective on you, Claire. Once I started asking the right questions, things fell into place."

Claire backed out of the laundry room, never taking her eyes off Lillian. "You can't prove anything."

"You keep saying that." Lillian came away from the washer. "I'm not arguing the point. I came here today for some answers, not to get you arrested."

"Get out."

"I'm on my way." Lillian crossed the living room, paused at the front door and looked back over her shoulder. "Just one more question."

"I said, get out of here."

"You told me that Trevor was into high heels and ladies' lingerie and that his tastes would be a real turn-off. Can I assume you lied about that, too?"

"I hated the dressing up part," Claire explained. "But the man was on track to be a U.S. senator. I figured I could overlook a few eccentricities if it meant I would be a senator's wife."

"Did he really tell you that he would divorce Marilyn and marry you after he was elected?"

"He promised." Claire looked down at the blue shirt crumpled in her hands. "Just like Larry Fulton promised we would get engaged after he broke up with you. Nothing ever works out the way it's supposed to. It not fair, you know? It's just not fair."

Gabe prowled back and forth across the cottage kitchen. "You shouldn't have confronted her on your own."

"You've mentioned that several times already." Lillian propped her elbows on the kitchen table and rested her chin in her hands. "I've explained that I went there on impulse."

"What if she had turned violent?"

"She's not the type."

"You can't be certain."

"Gabe, she knows I can't prove anything."

"Unfortunately."

"I guess this is one of those situations where you have to let karma happen."

"Karma never happens to people like her. Karma is bullshit. The Claires of this world always skate."

Lillian looked out the window. "I wouldn't say that Claire has done a lot of skating in her life. She said that things have never worked out for her. None of her big plans ever jelled. Larry Fulton and I broke up but he didn't marry her. He married Sheila. Trevor Thornley crashed and burned, so she didn't get to marry him and become a senator's wife. She lost her job with Marilyn's campaign. All and all, Claire hasn't been what anyone would call a winner."

They drove into town for warm croissants and coffee the next morning. Gabe parked in the lot in front of Incandescent Body. He studied the warmly lit interior of the bakery through the windows. A handful of people were clustered inside. The array of vehicles standing in the rain outside included Mitchell's big SUV, Arizona's aging truck and Sean Valentine's cruiser.

"Looks a little cozy in there," he said. "Want to go somewhere else?" he asked.

"There is nowhere else where we can get croissants like the ones they make here." Lillian pulled up the hood of her rain cloak and reached for the door handle. "Come on, we can deal with this."

"I don't know about that." Reluctantly he opened the driver's side door. "It's a little early for a Harte-Madison scene."

"Nonsense. Never too early for one of those."

He hunched deeper into his jacket and walked quickly beside her through the drizzle to the entrance.

He opened the glass door and immediately registered the serious tone of the atmosphere inside. The buzz of conversation was more intense than usual. His first thought was that the sight of Mitchell and Sullivan sharing coffee together had electrified the gossip circuit. But then he realized that no one was paying much attention to the pair, who were seated at a small table with Bryce and Sean.

Predictably, everyone looked toward the door when it opened. Lillian pushed back the hood of her cloak and bestowed a bright smile on the crowd. Gabe nodded brusquely and headed for the counter. He needed some coffee before he dealt with Mitchell and Sullivan.

"What's up?" he asked the Herald who took their orders for croissants and corn bread.

"Haven't you heard?"

Before she could explain, the curtain opened behind her. Arizona leaned out and beckoned urgently.

"Come on back here, you two," she hissed. "I'll brief you along with the others."

Gabe looked at Mitchell and Sullivan. They had resumed their conversation with Sean. He was in no great rush to join them, he thought. One of Arizona's briefings promised to be a lot more entertaining. He glanced at Lillian. She shrugged and turned to go behind the counter.

He picked up his corn bread and followed her.

A familiar group of Heralds, including Photon, was gathered at the large worktable. They nodded somberly when Lillian and Gabe joined them.

"'Morning," Gabe said.

"What's going on?" Lillian asked.

Arizona rapped a rolling pin on the floured table. "A very interesting development has just occurred. Course, the mainstream media and the local authorities, including Sean Valentine, have bought into the cover story being handed out by the gang up at the institute. But that's only to be expected." She shook her head. "Poor dupes."

Gabe propped one shoulder against the wall and savored a bite of warm corn bread. "What's the story?"

"Official version is that Claire Jensen was injured in a single-car accident on her way out of town yesterday. She's in the Eclipse Bay hospital as we speak."

"Good heavens." Lillian stared at Arizona. "Is she all right?"

"Sean says she's pretty banged up but she'll be okay. He investigated the crash. Said she was driving like a bat outta hell in the rain. Took a curve way too fast. But we all know the truth."

Heads nodded around the table.

Lillian cleared her throat. "Uh, what is that?"

"It's obvious. She must have seen somethin' she wasn't supposed to see up there at the institute. Probably stumbled into the underground lab. *They* faked an accident to try to get rid of her. Lucky for her they botched the job."

Lillian looked at Gabe. "And you say you don't believe in karma."

"I stand corrected," Gabe said. "Learn something new everyday."

He took her arm and steered her back through the curtain into the main room. Several pairs of eyes followed them as they made their way to the small table where Mitchell and Sullivan sat with Bryce and Sean.

Lillian leaned down to give Sullivan a kiss on his cheek. "'Morning, Granddad."

"Good morning, honey."

Gabe nodded at Mitchell and Sullivan. "Glad to see that the two of you didn't knock each other's teeth out last night."

"When you get to be this age," Sullivan said, "you have to think twice about risking your teeth. Not that many good ones left."

She greeted the others and sat down beside Sullivan.

"Arizona give you her version of the accident?" Mitchell asked Gabe.

Gabe set his coffee and partially eaten corn bread down

on the table and took one of the chairs. "All part of the big conspiracy up at the institute, according to A.Z."

Sullivan chuckled.

"Got to admit that her take on local news is always a lot more interesting than mine," Sean allowed.

"So it was an accident?" Lillian asked.

"Definitely." Sean took a bite out of a large, jelly-filled pastry. "She must have been in a real hurry to get out of town. Had to be doing seventy when she took that curve out by the Erickson place."

Bryce shook his head in solemn disapproval. "Everyone knows that's a real bad curve."

"The medics who pulled her out of the car said she was spittin' mad when they got to her." Sean swallowed the bite of pastry and reached for his coffee. "Kept saying something about how unfair it all was."

# chapter 26

On the night of the reception at the Eclipse Bay branch of the Bright Visions Gallery, Sullivan stood with Mitchell, a glass of champagne in his hand, and watched the large crowd ebb and flow around Lillian and her paintings. Warm pride flowed through him.

"Not like it was in Portland last week," Mitchell observed. "Only press here is from the *Journal*. But, what the heck, Eclipse Bay isn't exactly the art capital of the western world."

"Portland was all about publicity and media coverage," Sullivan reminded him. "It worked just like Octavia Brightwell said it would. It introduced Lillian to important collectors and the museum and gallery crowd. But this event is special for Eclipse Bay."

"And they're lovin' it." Mitchell grinned. "Look at 'em, all dressed up and swilling champagne. I doubt if a lot of these folks know much about art, but they're sure having a good time."

The throng that filled the gallery was composed largely

of local townsfolk. Everyone from the Willis brothers to
the strangely dressed group from Incandescent Body had
turned out. Sullivan had a hunch that it wasn't a keen interest in art that had brought so many of the residents of
Eclipse Bay out on a wet night. The driving motivation
for this crowd was its lively curiosity about Hartes and
Madisons. Everyone knew that both families would be in
town for the event and they were all well aware that Gabe
and Lillian were engaged.

The free drinks and hors d'oeuvres were just icing on
the cake as far as most folks were concerned tonight.

"Who would have thought that a Harte would turn out
to be an artist?" Mitchell said.

"Who would have believed that anyone in your family could create a profitable business like Madison Commercial?"

"Gotta say that Octavia sure knows how to give a
party." Mitchell helped himself to a cheese canapé. "First
class all the way, too. Lot of people here tonight wouldn't
have noticed or cared if she had served cheap champagne
and second-rate food. But she pulled out all the stops,
same as she did for the Portland crowd."

"Showing respect for the locals." Sullivan nodded.
"Very smart. Good public relations."

"She's a smart young woman. But she's real, too, if
you know what I mean. She didn't put on this bash just
for publicity purposes. She did it because she really
wanted to show folks that she appreciates them as much
as she does the Portland crowd."

Sullivan took a sip of his champagne. "I'll buy that."

"Huh."

"What's that supposed to mean?"

"Can't help noticing that she and your grandson, Nick,

are having themselves a mighty serious conversation over there."

Sullivan followed his gaze, searching for the pair over the heads of the crowd. He spotted Nick, dressed in formal black and white, standing with Octavia on the far side of the gallery.

The conversation looked more than serious, he thought. It had a close, intimate quality. Nick had one hand casually flattened on the wall behind Octavia's head. He leaned slightly in toward her, his broad shoulders angled in a way that subtly but effectively cut her off from the crowd around them. Sullivan recognized the body language and knew that every other man in the room understood it too, if only on a subconscious level. It was a clear statement of possession, a this-woman-is-mine-tonight message.

"Oh, brother," he said softly. "Here we go again."

"I wouldn't worry about it, if I were you," Mitchell said cheerfully. "Like I said, Octavia's a nice young woman."

"Red hair."

"So what? You got a problem with red hair?"

"There's something familiar about her, Mitch."

"You've seen her before. She attended Hannah and Rafe's wedding. And you met her at the Portland reception last week."

"No, I mean something *really* familiar."

"Like what?"

"The red hair, the profile. The way she holds herself. Take a good look, man. She remind you of anyone?"

Mitchell studied Octavia for a long time.

"Well, shoot and damn," he said at last. "She's a dead ringer, isn't she? Funny, I never noticed before."

"Might explain why you took to her right off, though."

"Well, shoot and damn," Mitchell said again, this time sounding dazed. "What the hell is going on here?"

"Beats me," Sullivan said. "But I figure this isn't a co-incidence."

"Nope." An expression of bemused wonder gleamed in Mitchell's eyes. "No coincidence. Tell you one thing, Nick better behave himself with her."

"What business is it of yours, how he behaves?"

"Octavia's alone in the world. No family to protect her."

"So you're going to take on the job, is that it?" Sullivan asked.

"Someone's gotta do it. That grandson of yours has a reputation for playing it fast and loose with the ladies."

"He just hasn't found the right woman to take Amelia's place."

"Way I hear it, he's not lookin' real hard for a wife," Mitchell observed. "Seems like he prefers a more casual arrangement with his lady friends, one that doesn't involve rings and a ceremony and a commitment. I hear tell they call him Hardhearted Harte in some circles."

"Damn it, my grandson's love life isn't any of your business."

"I won't let him take advantage of Octavia, got that?" Mitchell set his jaw. "She's not gonna be just another one of his short-term flings. You better set him real straight on that score or there'll be hell to pay."

Glumly, Sullivan studied the pair on the other side of the room.

"This could get complicated," he said.

"Sure could."

Sullivan didn't know precisely what Mitchell was thinking, but he was willing to bet his companion was recalling the same scene he himself remembered so well.

It was a scene out of their shared past: an eerie, unsettling memory of the day a flame-haired woman in a short skirt and high heels opened the door of their little office on Bay Street and told them she would make them both very rich.

They both stared, fascinated at Octavia. No doubt about it, Sullivan thought, she bore an uncanny resemblance to Claudia Banner, the mysterious creature who had blazed through their lives all those years ago, singed them both badly and turned their world upside down before she disappeared with the assets of Harte-Madison.

"Who the hell is Octavia Brightwell and what is she up to here in Eclipse Bay?" he asked very quietly.

# chapter 27

She listened to him climb the stairs and walk down the hall toward her studio. She continued to clean her brushes. His strides were easy, smooth, full of purpose and determination. A lot of the essence of Gabe Madison was distilled in the way he moved.

She put down the brushes and went to open the door. He came to a halt in front of her. He had left his jacket in the car and removed his cuff links. The collar of his charcoal-gray shirt was open, the silver-and-black striped tie loose around his neck. He was not smiling.

"You're late." She stood on tiptoe to kiss him.

"Ummm." He wrapped an arm around her when she made to pull back, holding her close for a long, slow, blood-warming kiss.

When he finally released her she was flushed and breathless. She saw the lazy, sexy gleam in his eyes and knew that she wasn't the only one who had been affected by the embrace.

"Thanks, I needed that," he said. "I had a hell of an afternoon."

"What happened?"

"Mitchell, Sullivan, and your father all arrived unannounced in my office two hours ago, just as I was thinking of leaving early for the day. It was nothing short of an ambush."

She wrinkled her nose. "Now what?"

He did not answer immediately. Instead he went to stand in front of her newest creation, an unfinished portrait of her mother and her grandmother and herself. The three figures were arranged around Eclipse Arch. They looked out at the viewer with steady gazes, each woman bringing the perspective of her particular phase of life to the scene, each silently acknowledging her links to the other two.

Gabe studied the picture.

"Damn, you're good," he said at last. "You really are good."

"Thanks, but you're avoiding the subject."

"I'm a CEO. I've got a natural aptitude for avoiding unpleasant subjects."

She did not like the sound of this. "What did they want, Gabe?"

"They presented a new business proposition."

"Uh-oh."

"Yeah, that was sort of my response, too."

"Gabe?"

"They want to do a merger."

She stared at him. It took her a few seconds to get her tongue untied. "A merger? You mean of Madison Commercial and Harte Investments?"

"Yeah."

"Oh, my."

"An equal exchange of stock between the companies. Family members only would be allowed to possess shares in the new corporation. The board of directors would consist of an equal number of Hartes and Madisons. I would be the CEO."

"Oh, my."

"In many ways, there is a lot to be said for the deal," Gabe continued, sounding as if he was reading from an investor's prospectus. "It would double the assets of the company overnight. It would allow us to extend the range and scope of our activities. It would give us the opportunity to provide extended management and consulting services to our clients."

"Oh, my." She felt the laughter bubble up inside and hastily clapped a hand over her mouth.

"It is also of course, my worst nightmare."

"I can understand that." She gave up the attempt to swallow her laughter. "The very thought of having to ride herd on a board of directors and a group of stockholders composed entirely of Hartes and Madisons would be enough to strike terror into the heart of any prudent, cautious, sensible CEO."

"You can say that again."

"But you're a Madison. I'll bet you didn't even swallow hard or blink. So, what are we going to call this new company?"

"The suggestion was made that the new firm should be known as Harte-Madison. Your father's idea, I believe. Some sentimental claptrap about re-creating the original company founded by Mitch and Sullivan. I, however, took strong exception."

"So what is it going to be?"

He turned away from the portrait and came toward her, giving her the patented Madison grin, the really sexy one that showed his excellent teeth and made her pulse beat faster.

"Madison-Harte, of course," he said.

"Of course. I like it. It's got a ring to it."

"It does, doesn't it?"

He wrapped his arms around her and pulled her close. His mouth came down on hers in a kiss that demonstrated once again that nothing came between a Madison and his passion.